John Willcock

Sir Thomas Urquhart of Cromartie, knight

John Willcock

Sir Thomas Urquhart of Cromartie, knight

ISBN/EAN: 9783742858900

Manufactured in Europe, USA, Canada, Australia, Japa

Cover: Foto ©Raphael Reischuk / pixelio.de

Manufactured and distributed by brebook publishing software
(www.brebook.com)

John Willcock

Sir Thomas Urquhart of Cromartie, knight

SIR THOMAS URQUHART.

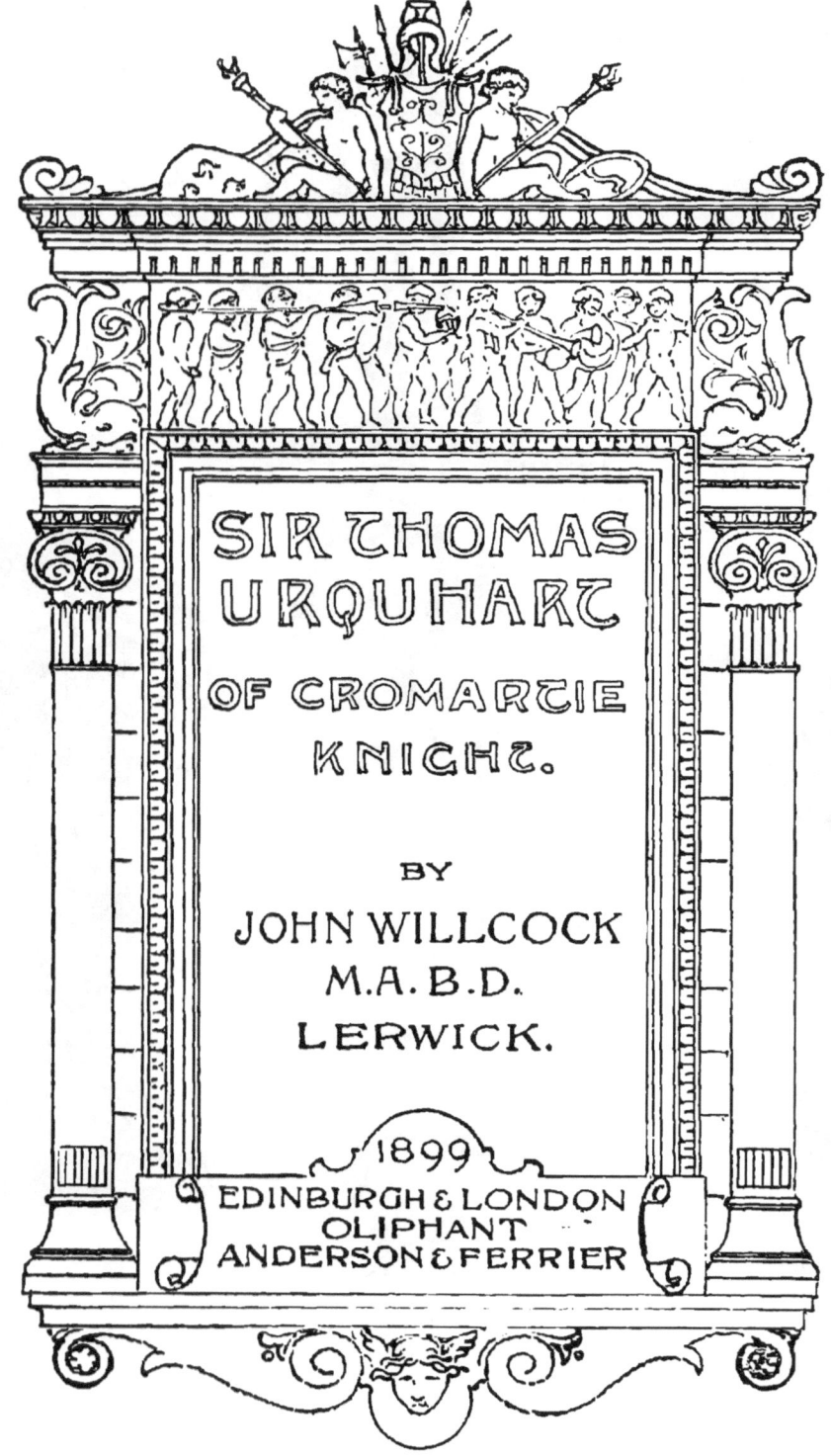

SIR THOMAS URQUHART

OF CROMARTIE KNIGHT.

BY

JOHN WILLCOCK
M.A. B.D.
LERWICK.

1899

EDINBURGH & LONDON
OLIPHANT
ANDERSON & FERRIER

SIGNATURE OF SIR THOMAS URQUHART,
SLIGHTLY ENLARGED.

PREFACE

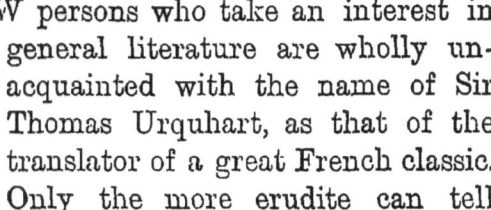

EW persons who take an interest in general literature are wholly unacquainted with the name of Sir Thomas Urquhart, as that of the translator of a great French classic. Only the more erudite can tell how the name of another literary man, Pierre Antoine Motteux, comes to be associated with his in connexion with the translation in question, and are aware that the Scottish knight is the author of original compositions in such diverse departments as poetry, trigonometry, genealogy, and biography, and that he played a prominent part in the public life of his time.

It has been my object to bring together in the following volume all the materials which are available for giving a vivid picture of the personality of Sir Thomas Urquhart, and of the circumstances in which his life was passed, as I think it would be a pity if his romantic, fantastical figure were to pass into oblivion. The materials for his life are fairly abundant, though they have to be sought for in many out-of-the-way corners. The slight but fairly accurate sketch prefixed to his *Works* in the

Maitland Club edition, and the carefully written articles in Dr Irving's *Scottish Writers*, and the *Dictionary of National Biography*, contain the only previous attempts which have been made to give his history. The limits within which the authors of these notices had to work, have, however, prevented their giving more than a bare outline of his career. I have attempted, with what success it is for my readers to say, to clothe the skeleton with sinews and flesh, and to impart to the figure some measure of animation.

As I have had to do my work at a great distance from public libraries, I have been obliged to enlist the services of friends, more fortunately situated, in the task of looking up multitudinous references and allusions, which bore upon the history of the person in whom I was interested, or of the time in which he lived. Miss Kemp, James Walter, Esq., and Alexander Middlemass, Esq., Edinburgh, have been extremely serviceable to me in this way.

A variety of details of historical and biographical interest has been furnished me by Dr Milne, King-Edward; Garden A. Duff, Esq., Hatton Castle, Turriff; Capt. Douglas Wimberley, Inverness; J. L. Anderson, Esq., Edinburgh; and P. J. Anderson, Esq., of Aberdeen University Library.

Professors Crum Brown, Saintsbury, Butcher, and Eggeling of my own *Alma Mater* have been very willing to give the information I have sought from them; and through Professor Grierson of Aberdeen I have had the loan of many books containing material of value for my purpose.

Sheriff Mackenzie, Wick, and Sheriff Shennan, Lerwick, have aided me in questions of literary taste and of legal information ; and from W. F. Smith, Esq., Fellow of St John's College, Cambridge, I have received valuable help in writing the chapter on the translation of Rabelais. From the latter's scholarly volumes upon the great Frenchman I have borrowed some notes, which appear with his initials attached to them. To Professor Ferguson of Glasgow I am indebted for the photograph of Urquhart's handwriting.

In the work of correcting proofs—a somewhat laborious task in the present case—I have had kindly assistance from Dr Milne, above mentioned, and also from A. J. Tedder, Esq., London, Rev. T. Mathewson, Rev. D. Houston, M.A., and J. M. Goudie, Esq., Lerwick.

If I have omitted the name of any helper, or if by frivolous comment I have done wrong to the shade of Sir Thomas, I would adopt the language of Mr Collins in *Pride and Prejudice.* "We are all liable to err," he says. "I have certainly meant well through the whole affair ; . . . and if my manner has been at all reprehensible, I here beg leave to apologize."

JOHN WILLCOCK.

United Pres. Manse, Lerwick,
    Shetland.

CONTENTS

ILLUSTRATIONS

SIR THOMAS URQUHART

CHAPTER I

The Urquharts and their Predecessors in Cromartie—Sir
Thomas Urquhart, senior—Birth of our Author—School
and University Days—Pecuniary and other Troubles at
Home—The Castle of Cromartie—Our Author's Studious
Bent—Foreign Travel—The Englishman Abroad—The
Scot Abroad.

THE right of Sir Thomas Urquhart of
Cromartie to be included in the
list of famous Scots will scarcely
be granted by many of his fellow-
countrymen without some inquiry
into the grounds upon which it
is based. He himself, undoubtedly, would not
have been backward in asserting his claim to such
honourable distinction, though he would have
entered a protest against the presence of some of
those in whose company he would find himself.
In the ecclesiastical and political controversies of
the first half of the seventeenth century, he was,
as an Episcopalian and a Cavalier, connected with

the losing side, and, consequently, it is not to be
expected that posterity should be so impartial as
to cherish his name along with those of the victors
in the conflict.   It is to his literary, and not to
his martial achievements, that he owes his fame.
His translation of Rabelais is probably the most
brilliant feat of the kind ever accomplished, and
casts all his own original writings into the shade.
The fantastical character of his own compositions,
indeed, both in regard to their subject-matter and
the diction in which they are clothed, forbids their
ever having a large circle of readers.   An author
whose phraseology is like a combination of that
used by Ancient Pistol with that of Sir Thomas
Browne may have enthusiastic admirers, but they
are almost certain to be few in number.   Yet his
works contain much interesting matter, and to
them we are indebted for many details of the life
of their author.

Though it is hard to believe Sir Thomas
Urquhart's assertion that the connexion of the
Urquharts with the north-west of Scotland dates as
far back as the year B.C. 554, when an ancestor of his
named Beltistos crossed over from Ireland, and built
a castle near Inverness, the family was of considerable antiquity, and for many generations was one of
the most distinguished in that part of the country.
Nisbet, the great authority on heraldry, says that
" they enjoyed not only the honourable office of
hereditary Sheriff-Principal of the Shire of Cromartie; but the far greater part, if not the whole of
the said shire did belong to them, either in property

or superiority, and they possessed a considerable estate besides in the Shire of Aberdeen."[1] The admiralty of the seas from Caithness to Inverness also belonged to them.

The Urquharts were not, however, the earliest to bear rule in the part of Scotland with which their name is connected. Cromartie was originally the Crwmbawchty (or Crumbathy) of which Macbeth was reputed thane, before he became king. Wyntown in his *Cronykil* relates Macbeth's dream that he was first Thane of Cromartie, then Thane of Moray, and then King of Scotland.[2] After the first and second titles had been conferred upon him, he took steps to secure the third. Probably the mote-hill of Cromartie was the site

---

[1] *System of Heraldry*, ii. 274.

[2] Wyntown's narrative is as follows (quoted in Sir William Fraser's *Earls of Cromartie*) :—

> "A nycht he thowcht in hys dreming,
> Dat syttand he wes besyd þe Kyng
> At a Sete in hwnting ; swà
> Intil his Leisch bad Grewhundys twà.
> He thowcht, quhile he wes swà syttand,
> He sawe thre wemen by gangand ;
> And þai wemen þan thowcht he
> Thre werd Systrys màst lyk to be.
> De fyrst he hard say gangand by,
> 'Lo yhondyr þe Thayne of Crwmbawchty.'
> De toyir woman sayd agayne,
> 'Of Morave yhondyre I se þe Thayne.'
> De thryd þan sayd, 'I se þe Kyng.'
> All þis he herd in hys dreming,"
>
> Wyntown's *Cronykil*, i. 225.

Wyntown's date is about A.D. 1395. Macbeth was killed at Lumphanan by Macduff, 5th December A.D. 1056.

of his official residence as thane of the district when he was at the beginning of his ambitious career.

In the thirteenth century the family of Mouat (then *de Monte Alto*) were in possession,[1] but early in the following century the estate had accrued to King Robert the Bruce, probably because the Mouats had submitted to the English king, Edward I. King Robert granted Cromartie to Sir Hugh Ross, eldest son of William, Earl of Ross, in 1315, and by him it was afterwards, in the reign of King David Bruce (1329–70), given to an Adam of Urquhart (" de Vrquhartt "),[2] with whose descendants it remained for many generations. In 1357 he got from the Crown the hereditary sheriffdom of Cromartie, and eight years later the same Hugh Ross gave him the estate of Fisherie, in King-Edward, Aberdeenshire. This Adam is the first of the family to emerge from the darkness of antiquity into the light of history, and probably his name, as the founder of the Urquhart fortunes, suggested the still more famous progenitor to whom our Sir Thomas traced back his pedigree link by link, as our readers will afterwards hear.

[1] A charter of lands in Cromartie granted by William de Monte Alto, between 1252 and 1272, is still in existence. The granter of the charter, having been owner of Cromartie, was claimed by Sir Thomas Urquhart as one of his Urquhart ancestors, but with no better authority than the earlier ancestors who figure in our author's *Pedigree*. See *Earls of Cromartie*, by Sir William Fraser.

[2] It would seem from this that Urquhart was originally a place-name, probably Gaelic. There were two parishes of Urquhart in the old province of Moray—one with a priory near Elgin, and the other with a castle in what is now Inverness-shire.

Our author's father, also a Thomas, and the first of his line who was a Protestant in religion, was born in 1585. He succeeded to the property in 1603, and in 1617 was knighted by James VI. in Edinburgh. As he was left an orphan at an early age, he was brought up under the care of his grand-uncle, John Urquhart of Craigfintray, who has been commonly called from this circumstance " the Tutor of Cromartie." [1] His great-grand-nephew, our Sir Thomas, has celebrated his praise in very high terms. " He was," he says, " over all Britain renowned for his deep reach of natural wit, and great dexterity in acquiring of many lands and great possessions, with all men's applause." [2]

From all accounts, it seems that the " Tutor " was

[1] "Tutor" here simply means "legal guardian"—for boys until fourteen years of age, and for girls until twelve. After these ages and before that of twenty-one such wards are in the charge of "Curators." Owing to our author's having the same Christian name as his father, the mistake is often made of asserting that John Urquhart was *his* tutor.

[2] *Works*, p. 172. In a MS. volume of unpublished poems by Sir Thomas, which is described on p. 116, there is the following :—
"Upon the tutor of Cromarty, my great-grandfather's younger brother, and my father's tutor :

" The present tyme, the preterit, nor futur
T' ourselves, our fathers, nor posteritie,
Do now, have yet, nor will produce a tutor,
For's Pupils weil of more dexteritie,
   For he left free th' estate he had in charge :
   And by meer industrie did's own enlarge " (iii. 7).

We are sorry to quote a poem of Sir Thomas's at this early stage, before the atmosphere has been created which is needed for perceiving and appreciating its true value. The judicious reader will, however, return to it with interest when that process has been completed.

faithful in the discharge of all the duties belonging to his office,[1] though he did not succeed in imparting to his pupil the secret of acquiring landed property, either with or without applause.

Sir Thomas Urquhart, senior, received his estates, we are informed, "without any burthen of debt, how little soever, or provision of brother, sister, or any other of his kindred or allyance wherewith to affect it."[2] He married Christian, the fourth daughter of Alexander, fourth Lord Elphinstone (1552–1638), and received with her a dowry of nine thousand merks Scots (*i.e.* £500 Sterling). The date of our author's birth is given by Maitland as 1605, but it is now certain that this is an error, and that the true date is 1611.[3] Sir Thomas was the eldest of the family, and he tells us that he was born five years after the marriage of his parents. He also informs us that his mother's father, Lord Elphinstone, held the office of High Treasurer in Scotland at the time of the marriage. As that nobleman was High Treasurer only from just before 19th April, 1599, till 22nd September, 1601, it would not have been unreasonable to fix the date of the marriage as probably some time in 1600, if we had no other information on the subject. But it so happens that the marriage-

---

[1] John Urquhart, "the Tutor of Cromartie," died in 1631, at the age of eighty-four, and was buried in the old church of King-Edward, Aberdeenshire, where there is a marble monument to his memory.

[2] *Works*, p. 340.

[3] Another erroneous date is in the edition of the *Tracts* of 1774, where 1613 is given as the year of our author's birth.

contract is in existence,[1] and is dated the 9th of July, 1606, and consequently Sir Thomas's birth would fall in the year 1611. Our author must therefore have been in error in describing his grandfather as being High Treasurer at the time of his daughter's marriage. He had, indeed, occupied this office some years before. Sir Thomas should have said "had been," instead of "was," but his lordly disposition of mind would probably make him contemptuous of such trifles.

In 1611, James VI. was drawing near to the end of the first period of his reign, during which he had been under the influence of the traditions of the days of Elizabeth and Burghley, and had not yet

---

[1] This is now amongst the Gardenston papers, having been formerly in the possession of Mr Dunbar Dunbar. An account of its contents is given in *Antiquarian Notes*, by C. Fraser Mackintosh, p. 195. An independent corroboration of the above date of the marriage is given by a document now in the Register House in Edinburgh (*Aberdeen Sasines*), in which Sir Thomas Urquhart, senior, gives sasine of the barony of Fisherie to Lady Christian Elphinstone. The "precept," or clause in the marriage-contract, which directs the notary to give sasine of the estate settled on the bride, is also dated the 9th of July, 1606, and in it she is described as being *in sua purâ virginitate*. Probably the marriage took place either on that day or very soon afterwards. The bridegroom was just of age, while Lady Christian was under sixteen, the date of her birth being 19th December, 1590 (*The Lords Elphinstone*, Fraser, i. 167).

The issue of this marriage were at least the following sons and daughters :—(1) THOMAS ; (2) Alexander ; (3) George ; (4) John ; (5) [name unknown] ; (6) Henry ; and (7) Jane, *m.* Sir Alexander Abercromby of Birkenbog ; (8) Helen, *m.* Sir James Gordon of Lesmoir ; (9) Annas, *m.* Alexander Strachan of Glenkindie ; (10) Margaret, *m.* John Irving of Brucklay ; (11) [name unknown], *m.* —— Campbell of Calder.

passed into his own keeping, and the hands of profligate favourites. Bacon was still in the shade of distrust, from which, however, he was soon to emerge : he was now, indeed, Solicitor-General, but his ambition was not satisfied by this post. The heir-apparent to the throne was Prince Henry, who died in the following year. Charles, his brother, was now eleven years of age. Shakespeare brought out this year his play of *The Winter's Tale*, and Ben Jonson his *Catiline*. Sir Walter Raleigh was a prisoner in the Tower, and was busily engaged in writing his *History of the World*, which he completed in the following year, though it was not published until 1614. The Authorised Version of the English Bible appeared this year. Milton was now a child of scarcely three years old, and Cromwell a boy of twelve.

The birthplace of our author is unknown; for though the castle of Cromartie was the official residence of the sheriffs, Sir Thomas Urquhart, senior, is known to have had several other manor-houses, one of which was Fisherie,[1] in the parish of King-Edward, Aberdeenshire, in which he resided from time to time. It is probable that the future translator of Rabelais laid the foundation of the erudition by which in after years he was distinguished, in Banff,[2] which then possessed a grammar-

---

[1] Fisherie is about six miles from Banff.

[2] It is quite possible, however, that, in the parish school of King-Edward, our author could have got the rudiments of a classical education. In 1649 (15th Nov.), Mr James Petrie, who was schoolmaster there, applied for the school of Banff, and, as a test of his powers, "was ordeined to teache the sext satyr of Persius to-

school, rather than in the more northern town which is associated with his name.

Sir Thomas was only eleven years old when, in 1622, he entered the University of Aberdeen,[1] but there is no reason to believe that the average age of the "men" of his year would be in excess of his own. Donne was the same age as Urquhart when he entered Oxford. The famous Crichton went up to St Andrews at the age of ten, though up to that time he had not given evidence of any extraordinary precocity. A generation before, Montaigne had already completed his collegiate course when he attained his thirteenth year. It seems strange to us that boys of such tender age should have been found able to pass through a university curriculum ; and we are forced to conclude either that the boys of those days were intellectually superior to those with whom we are familiar, or that the studies which occupied them were less deep and severe than those which are now pursued in seats of learning. The latter is probably the true explanation of the matter. University education in Scot-

morrow in the school of Banf be nyne hours in presence of the bailyies and others in the toune who wer scholars." He passed through the test successfully, and was appointed to the office (*Annals of Banff*, ii. 30, New Spalding Club).

[1] The entry of his name as a student on the roll is in the following terms : "In Academiam regiam Aberdonensem recepti sunt adolescentes quorum nomina sequuntur, præceptore Alexandro Lunano, Anno 1622.

. . . . .

Thomas Urquhardus de Cromartie.

. . .

Fasti Aberdonenses, 1854.

land had been remodelled, and adapted to the requirements of the time and of a Protestant society in the previous generation, and in this work Andrew Melville had a very notable part. In 1583 a new constitution had been drawn up for the University of Aberdeen, and the arrangements prescribed by it may have existed there when our author was a student. The Principal, according to this constitution, was Professor of Theology, as well as incumbent of the parish of Old Machar, and was responsible for the government and discipline of the college.[1] Under him were four Regents, one of whom was Sub-Principal, and to them was assigned the duty of training students in various departments of learning. Thus physiology, geography, astrology, history, and Hebrew were assigned to the Sub-Principal. Another Regent explained " the principles of reasoning from the best Greek and Latin authors, with practice in writing and speaking"; while a third lectured upon Greek, and read the more elementary Latin and Greek authors. The fourth Regent taught arithmetic and geometry, and, along with them, a portion of Aristotle's *Organon*, *Ethics, and Politics*, and Cicero's *De Officiis*. This attempt to assign special departments to the various regents respectively, was a marked improvement upon the older system, under which they were each responsible for teaching all the subjects included in the curriculum.

The students paid fees, which varied in amount

[1] *King's College: Officers and Graduates*, by P. J. Anderson, M.A., pp. 347, 348.

according to their social standing. On entering the
university they were required to take an oath of
loyalty to the Reformed religion. None were
allowed to carry arms, or to converse in any other
tongue than Greek or Latin. Perhaps, however,
this latter rule was merely an attempt to restrain
the measureless tide of human speech. And in
order that nothing might interfere with the progress
of the students, the *Nova Fundatio*, or new constitution of Aberdeen University, abolished all holidays
(" omnes consuetas olim a studiis vacationes aboleri
penitus ").[1]

Sir Thomas Urquhart's name does not appear in

[1] An "eminent Yorkshire educationist" introduced the same rule
into the establishment under his charge. It is probable, however,
that in Mr Squeers's case the arrangement was the result of independent research into methods of education, rather than a hint
borrowed from Andrew Melville. "No holidays—none of those
ill-judged comings home twice a year that unsettle children's
minds so!" (*Nicholas Nickleby*, chap. iv.).

It is only fair to say that there are doubts as to how far the
arrangements under the *Nova Fundatio*, as above described, were
in force in Sir Thomas Urquhart's student days. If the older
system were still in operation, the Alexander Lunan, who is mentioned as his preceptor, would virtually have taught our author
all the subjects contained in the curriculum through which he
passed. As there is no proof that Alexander Lunan was another
Admirable Crichton, the fact of his doing so would strengthen
what we have said above as to the comparative slightness of the
erudition imparted in a university education in those days. Sir
Thomas Urquhart speaks of having "learned the elements of
his philosophy" in the University of Aberdeen under William
Seaton (*Works*, p. 263). It has been suggested that it is an error
for John Seaton, and that it indicates that our author, like many
other students of King's College, took a session or two at Marischal
College (see Anderson's *Fasti Acad. Marisc.* ii. 34, 588).

the list of graduates in 1626, so that there are no means of determining from the records of King's College how many years he spent there. For the city in which he had received his education he ever afterwards had a high regard. Thus he says of it: " For honesty, good fashions, and learning, Aberdeen surpasseth as far all other cities and towns in Scotland, as London doth for greatness, wealth, and magnificence, the smallest hamlet or village in England." [1]

He gives unmeasured praise to some of those eminent men who were associated with the fame of Aberdeen University in what has been called its " Augustan age "—the first four or five decades of the seventeenth century. Thus, according to him, William Lesley, D.D., [2] was " one of the most profound and universal scholars then living "—like Socrates in having published no works, but, unfortunately, unlike that philosopher in not having among his disciples a Plato and an Aristotle to receive their master's knowledge and transmit it to future generations. [3] Of his successor in the principalship, Dr William Guild, he says: " He deserveth by himself to be remembered, both for that he hath committed to the press many good books, tending to the edification of the soul, and bettering of the minde ; and that of all the divines that have lived in Scotland these hundred yeers, he hath been

---

[1] *Works*, p. 395.

[2] Dr Lesley was successively Humanist, Regent, Sub-Principal, and Principal of King's College. In 1639 he was deprived of his office by the Covenanting party.

[3] *Works*, p. 262.

the most charitable, and who bestowed most of his own to publike uses." [1]   At the time when he wrote these estimates of the sages at whose feet he had sat as a student, some of his old friends were under a cloud, and he had to be careful not to compromise them by his praise.   And so he says of "Master William [?] Seaton," who had been his tutor, "[he was] a very able preacher truly, and good scholar, and [one] whom I would extoll yet higher, but that being under the consistorian lash, some critick Presbyters may do him injury, by pretending his dislike of them, for being praised by him who idolizeth not their authority." [2]

At the time of the marriage of Sir Thomas Urquhart, senior, Lord Elphinstone, who was fully acquainted with the prosperous condition of his son-in-law's affairs, made him pledge himself to manage his property so that it might descend to his heir as he had himself received it.   Unfortunately this pledge was not fulfilled.   Through mismanagement and neglect his affairs got into disorder, and the later years of his life were troubled by pecuniary difficulties. [3]   His son says of him:

---

[1] *Works*, p. 263.   The editor of the *Book of Bon Accord* gives a lower estimate of Dr Guild's character : he says that his works are of no literary merit, and that he got fame by his wealth and ostentatious liberality.   He was minister of King-Edward before he went to Aberdeen ; and his widow, Catharine Rolland, founded a bursary at the university for young men belonging to that parish.

[2] *Ibid.* p. 263 ; see p. 11, note.

[3] Lord Elphinstone died 14th January, 1638.   During the four preceding years his son-in-law had "made ducks and drakes" of his ancestral possessions.   His portrait, which is still preserved at Carberry Tower, is engraved in Sir William Fraser's work, *The*

" Of all men living [he was] the justest, equallest, and most honest in his dealings, [and] his humour was, rather than to break his word, to lose all he had, and stand to his most undeliberate promises, what ever they might cost; which too strict adherence to the austerest principles of veracity, proved oftentimes dammageable to him in his negotiations with many cunning sharks, who knew with what profitable odds they could scrue themselves in upon the windings of so good a nature. . . . By the unfaithfulnes, on the one side, of some of his menial servants, in filching from him much of his personal estate, and falsehood of several chamberlains and bayliffs to whom he had intrusted the managing of his rents, in the unconscionable discharge of their receits, by giving up one account thrice, and of such accounts many: and, on the other part, by the frequency of disadvantagious bargains, which the slieness of the subtil merchant did involve him in, his loss came unawares upon him, and irresistibly, like an armed man; too great trust to the one, and facility in behalf of the other, occasioning so grievous a misfortune, which nevertheless did not proceed from want of knowledge or abilitie in natural parts, for in the business of other men he would have given a very sound advice, and was surpassing dextrous in arbitrements, upon any

Lords Elphinstone. It gives one the impression of a grave, melancholy man. He had fourteen sons and five daughters. It is to be hoped that none of his sons and no other of his sons-in-law had the faculty for getting into difficulties which Sir Thomas Urquhart, senior, displayed.

reference submitted to him, but that hee thought it did derogate from the nobility of his house and reputation of his person, to look to petty things in matter of his own affairs." [1]

One of the ways in which the elder Sir Thomas succeeded in impoverishing himself and his family was in becoming bail for people who absconded ; so, at least, we would infer from an entry in the Court-book of the Burgh of Banff, under date of 21st April, 1629, in which we find that " Sir Thomas Urquhart of Cromarty, having become caution for the appearance of Alexander Forbes, merchant in Balvenye, alleged forestaller, and the said Alexander not having appeared, Sir Thomas is decerned to pay £40 Scots (£3, 6s. 8d. Sterling)." [2]

In 1637 we find that he was obliged to appeal to his sovereign against the urgency of his creditors, and a Letter of Protection was issued in his favour. It ran as follows : " Letter of Protection granted by King Charles the First, under his great seal, to Sir Thomas Urquhart of Cromarty, from all dilligence at the instance of his creditors, for the space of one year, thereby giving him a *persona standi in judicio*, notwithstanding he may be at the horn, and taking

---

[1] *Works*, p. 336.

[2] The offence of *forestalling* consisted in buying merchandise, victuals, etc., before they appeared in a fair or market-place for sale, or in taking steps to raise the prices of such things, or in dissuading anyone coming to market from carrying his goods thither. The amount of fine for a first offence was, as above, £40 Scots (or £3, 6s. 8d. Sterling) ; for a second offence, 100 merks (or £5, 11s. 1d. Sterling) ; while for a third offence it was forfeiture of movable goods.

him under his royal protection during the time. Dated at St James's, 20th March, 1637."[1]   A somewhat humorous situation is suggested by this document.   The creditors might "put him to the horn," *i.e.*, according to the usual legal form, order him in the king's name to pay his debts on penalty of being outlawed as a traitor, while the king himself authorised him to take no notice of the proceedings.

In the same year we have intimation of the elder Sir Thomas's pecuniary misfortunes being aggravated by domestic strife, for we find him instructing a high legal functionary to raise an action against his sons, Thomas and Alexander, for their unfilial conduct.   The charge was that of " putting violent hands on the persone of the said Sir Thomas Urquhart of Cromartie, Knycht, their father, taking him captive and prissoner, and detening him in sure firmance within ane upper chalmer, callit the Inner Dortour, within his place of Cromertie, *tanquam in privato carcere*, fra the Mononday to the Fryday in the efter none therefter, committit in the moneth of December last, 1636." The case came up for trial before the Court of Justiciary on the 19th of July, and was postponed for a week, when it was abandoned.   The Lords of Council had appointed a commission to settle all differences between the father and sons, and on receiving their report the Court dismissed the case.[2]   We have no particulars as to the causes of

---

[1] M'Farlane's *Genealogical Collections*, ii. 283.   MS. Advocates' Library.

Records of the Court of Justiciary.

disagreement which led to such an unhappy state of affairs, but we are not likely to be far wrong in assuming that the sons wished to prevent their father's taking some legal step which they considered would be detrimental to his and their interests. The affectionate terms in which our author describes his father's character ten years after his death, in the words above quoted, make us sure that he sincerely regretted any wrong towards him of which he may have been guilty at this time.

The old castle of Cromartie has now long disappeared, the stones of which it was built having been used for the erection of a modern house in 1772, after the estate had passed, by purchase, from the family of Urquhart to Mr George Ross. It was a building of considerable antiquity. In 1470 a royal grant was made by James III. to William Urquhart of the Motehill, or Mount of Cromartie, with permission to erect on this a tower or fortalice. Advantage was taken of this permission to fortify the family mansion, and it was converted into a castle of considerable strength.[1] Sir Thomas says of it: " The stance thereof is stately, and the house it selfe of a notable good fabrick and contrivance."[2] An interesting description

---

[1] It was built in the old turreted style, and defended on the south by a moat and high wall. When it was taken down, in the surrounding ground were found human skeletons, and urns containing human remains, both enclosed in graves made of flags (*Old Stat. Account*).

[2] *Works*, p. 312. " The situation appears in every view most delightful " (Pococke's *Tour*, 1760).

2

of the building as it was just before its demolition is given by Hugh Miller. "Directly behind the site of the old town," he says, " the ground rises abruptly from the level to the height of nearly a hundred feet, after which it forms a kind of table-land of considerable extent, and then sweeps gently to the top of the hill. A deep ravine, with a little stream running through it, intersects the rising ground at nearly right angles with the front which it presents to the houses ; and on the eastern angle, towering over the ravine on the one side, and the edge of the bank on the other, stood the old castle of Cromarty. It was a massy, time-worn building, rising in some places to the height of six storeys, battlemented at the top, and roofed with grey stone. One immense turret jutted out from the corner, which occupied the extreme point of the angle, and looking down from an altitude of at least one hundred and sixty feet on the little stream, and the struggling row of trees which sprung up at its edge, commanded both sides of the declivity and the town below." Of the interior we are told by the same writer, on the authority of an old woman who, as a child, had lived in the castle, that "two threshers could have plied their flails within the huge chimney of the kitchen ; and that, in the great hall, an immense, dark chamber, lined with oak, a party of a hundred men had exercised at the pike."[1]

The elder Sir Thomas had also a winter residence in Banff.[2] In the Court-book of the Burgh of Banff

[1] *Scenes and Legends of the North of Scotland*, pp. 78, 80.
[2] This was a fortalice-tower, with gardens, orchards, dovecots,

we have the following entry: "1630, July 21st, Sir
Thomas Urquhart of Cromartie gave in ane Act of
the Session of Banff, geiveing licence to him to erect
ane desk and loft in the kirk of Banff (seeing he is
both a parochiner and resident within the said toun)
for his accomodatione.   The brethren gave their
approbatione with express provision that neither
the edifice nor lichtes of the said kirk suld be
deteriorat."[1]

Beyond the bare fact of his having been a
student in the University of Aberdeen, we have no
information concerning the manner in which the
earlier years of our author's life were passed, or the

etc., in the south part of Banff, which afterwards came into the
possession of the Earl of Airlie.   The bounds are thus described:
"The common vennel at the north, the loch called the Saltlochs
at the east, the lands called Little Guishauch at the south, and the
road to Overak at the west."   Shortly before its demolition it
was the headquarters of the Duke of Cumberland's army on
its passage to Culloden.   Besides this house and the castle of
Cromartie, the Urquharts occasionally occupied their mansion-
house of Fisherie.   This stood a few yards to the south-west of
the present farmhouse of Mains of Fisherie.   It was taken down
some sixty years ago.   Some old trees still stand near the site of
the house and garden.

[1] *Annals of Banff* (New Spalding Club), ii. 28.   The old
church in which Sir Thomas had a "desk" or pew, and a "loft"
or small gallery, is now in ruins.   Only the south transept is
standing.   In the parish church of King-Edward, Aberdeenshire,
the handsome silver communion cups bear an inscription to the
effect that they were a joint present from Dr William Guild, the
then incumbent of the parish, Sir Thomas Urquhart, and his
uncle John Urquhart of Craigfintray.   That the Sir Thomas
Urquhart here named is not our author but his father, is evident
from the date of the incumbency of his fellow-donor, Dr Guild,
who was minister of King-Edward from 1608 to 1631.   The cups
bear date of 1619.

circumstances in which he acquired the miscellaneous erudition which his writings display. The only remark he makes about the education he received is to the effect that his father laid out but a very insignificant portion of his income upon this item of family expenses. Yet, however little the expenditure may have been, Urquhart evidently profited fully by the education which he had received, and attained to something more than a gentlemanly acquaintance with some of the abstruser departments of learning.

The special bent of his mind in early years, and his love for study rather than sport, are shown in the following reminiscence of his youth, which he narrates with his characteristic diffuseness. "There happening," he says, "a gentleman of very good worth to stay awhile at my house, who, one day amongst many other, was pleased, in the deadst time of all the winter, with a gun upon his shoulder, to search for a shot of some wild-fowl; and after he had waded through many waters, taken excessive pains in quest of his game, and by means thereof had killed some five or six moor fowls and partridges, which he brought along with him to my house, he was by some other gentlemen, who chanced to alight at my gate, as he entered in, very much commended for his love to sport; and, as the fashion of most of our countrymen is, not to praise one without dispraising another, I was highly blamed for not giving my self in that kind to the same exercise, having before my eys so commendable a pattern to imitate; I answered, though the gentleman deserved praise for the evident proof he had given that day of his inclination to thrift and laboriousness, that nevertheless I was not to blame, seeing whilst he was busied about that sport, I was imployed in a diversion of another nature, such as optical secrets, mysteries of natural philosophie, reasons for the variety of colours, the finding out of the longitude, the squaring of a circle, and wayes to accomplish all trigonometrical calculations by sines, without tangents, with the same compendiousness of computation,—which, in the estimation of learned men, would be accounted worth six hundred thousand partridges, and as many moor-fowles."

There can be little doubt that Sir Thomas had the best of the argument. But he was not satisfied with this: for nothing less would content him than vanquishing his opponent on his own ground, as well as with the weapons of logic. With the same lordliness of temper which had led him to recapitulate the dignified subjects which had occupied his studious mind—the squaring of the circle being but one of them—he chose the breaking-in of a horse as a set-off against his friend's achievements of the day before. The success of the scientific student and the discomfiture of the mere sportsman are told in the conclusion of the story. "In the mean while," he says, " that worthy gentleman, being wet and weary after travel, was not able to eat of what he had so much toyled for, whilst my braine recreations so sharpened my appetite, that I supped to very good purpose. That night past, the next morning I gave six pence to a footman of mine, to try his fortune with the gun, during the time I should disport my self in the breaking of a young horse; and it so fell out, that by [the time] I had given my selfe a good heat by riding, the boy returned with a dozen of wild fouls, half moor foule, half partridge, whereat being exceeding well pleased, I alighted, gave him my horse to care for, and forthwith entred in to see my gentlemen, the most especiall whereof was unable to rise out of his bed, by reason of the Gout and Sciatick, wherewith he was seized for his former daye's toyle."[1]

In the early years of his manhood, before our author felt himself qualified to take part in public life, he spent some time in foreign travel. The kind of figure cut by a young *English* gentleman of that period upon the Continent we know from the testimony of Portia, for it can scarcely be that much change had taken place in the interval of a generation, between her time and the end of the first quarter of the seventeenth century. He was generally unversed in the languages of the countries he visited, and, from his lack of Latin, French, or Italian, was apt to fail in understanding the natives, or in making himself understood by them. He might be handsome in figure, but conversation with him was reduced to the level of a dumb-show. His dress was often very odd, and his manners eccentric, as though he had bought his doublet in Italy, his round hose in France, his bonnet in Germany, and his behaviour—everywhere. A strong contrast to him in the matter of language was the young

[1] *Works*, p. 381.

Scotchman of the period, if Sir Thomas Urquhart
is to be taken as at all an average specimen of his
nation, and if his account of himself can be relied
upon.   He says of himself that when he travelled
through France, Spain, and Italy, he spoke the
languages to such perfection that he might easily
have passed himself off as a native of any one of
these countries.   Some advised him to do so, but
his patriotic feelings were too strong to allow him
to follow such a course: "he plainly told them
(without making bones thereof), that truly he thought
he had as much honour by his own country, which
did contrevalue the riches and fertility of those
nations, by the valour, learning, and honesty,
wherein it did parallel, if not surpass them." [1]

It is somewhat difficult for the mind to grasp
the idea of a Scotchman in those days, when so
many of the things which we now associate with
the nationality were not in existence—when his
Church was Episcopalian in constitution, the Shorter
Catechism not yet written by Englishmen for his
use, Burns unborn, and distilled spirits not exten-
sively used as a beverage.   We could scarcely even
know him by his costume.   For no self-respecting
representative of that country would assume the
Highland garb which so many Englishmen believe to
be generally worn north of the Tweed, if we are to
credit the authoritative statement of Macaulay to
the effect that "before the Union it was considered
by nine Scotchmen out of ten as the dress of a
thief." [2]   The characteristics by which "a Scot

[1] *Works*, p. 272.   [2] *History of England*, chap. xiii.

abroad" in those days was recognised, were, from
some accounts, not shrewdness in making bargains,
economical habits, indomitable perseverance, and
unsleeping caution, but the pride and high-spirited-
ness which made him keen in detecting and swift
in avenging slights that might be cast upon the
country from which he came. So deep was the
impression made by these peculiarities upon foreign
nations, that they became proverbial. "He is a
Scot, he has pepper in his nose!"[1] said they, somewhat familiarly, yet with a touch of fear, when they
noticed the flashing eye, and the hand instinctively
seeking the sword-hilt. "High-spirited as a Scot!"[2]
they exclaimed with admiration, when among themselves some soul was moved to unwonted courage.
Such, at least, is the impression produced upon the
mind by some of those novels in which Scott and
his imitators trace the wanderings of their fellow-
countrymen through European lands in those
earlier times. That there is some foundation of
truth for the lofty superstructure is rendered
credible by the case of Sir Thomas Urquhart.
"My heart,"[3] he says, "gave me the courage for
adventuring in a forrain climat, thrice to enter

---

[1] "*Scotus est, piper in naso*," Mediæval proverb.

[2] "*Fier comme un Ecossais*," French proverb.

[3] It may be as well to warn our readers at this point that Sir
Thomas Urquhart's vanity, or what would be called vanity in any
other man, was unbounded. So calm and unconscious is it, that
it often seems to betray a disordered mind. Those who seek in
his estimates of himself for illustrations of the grace of humility
will seek in vain. They may, however, find other things, which,
if not so edifying, are far more amusing.

the lists against men of three severall nations, to vindicate my native country [1] from the calumnies wherewith they had aspersed it ; wherein it pleased God so to conduct my fortune, that, after I had disarmed them, they in such sort acknowledged their error, and the obligation they did owe me for sparing their lives, which justly by the law of arms I might have taken, that, in lieu of three enemies that formerly they were, I acquired three constant friends, both to my selfe and my compatriots, whereof by severall gallant testimonies they gave evident proofe, to the improvement of my country's credit in many occasions." [2]

The fair critic, whose estimate of the young Englishman has been referred to, gives her opinion also of his Scottish rival ; but, strangely enough, she observes in him qualities of a kind opposite to those displayed by Sir Thomas Urquhart. She was struck by his neighbourly charity, " for he borrowed a box of the ear of the Englishman, and swore he would pay him back again when he was able." [3] Can it be that the words put into her mouth are merely the ribald wit of an envious

---

[1] The reader who has sufficient curiosity and leisure may compare with the above the account which his contemporary, Lord Herbert of Cherbury (1581–1648), gives of his duels in his *Autobiography.* That nobleman was a kind of Sir Thomas Urquhart in water-colour, and his single combats are surrounded with a proportionately milder glow of romance.   Indeed, they seem to have been generally undertaken in order to compel impudent young men to give back pieces of riband to charming young ladies from whom they had snatched them.

[2] *Works*, p. 311.

[3] *Merchant of Venice*, Act I. Scene ii.

Southron, or are we to understand that the spirit which triumphed over so many inferiors was yet wise enough to discern when it stood in the presence of a mightier than itself?

How a young man on his travels should occupy his time, had been laid down in a little volume which had been published just before Urquhart set out to see the world abroad. In this he might read a list of the things which should engage his attention, drawn up in sonorous language by no less a personage than a late Lord Chancellor of England—a man who was ready to give advice to all his fellow-creatures in all conceivable circumstances. "The things," says Lord Bacon, "to be seen and observed are: the courts of princes, especially when they give audience to ambassadors; the courts of justice, while they sit and hear causes; and so of consistories ecclesiastic; the churches and monasteries, with the monuments which are therein extant; the walls and fortifications of cities and towns, and so the havens and harbours; antiquities and ruins; libraries, colleges, disputations and lectures, where any are; shipping and navies; house and gardens of state and pleasure near great cities; armories, arsenals, magazines, exchanges, burses, warehouses; exercises of horsemanship, fencing, training of soldiers, and the like; comedies, such whereunto the better sort of persons do resort; treasuries of jewels and robes, cabinets and rarities; and, to conclude, whatsoever is memorable in the places where they go. . . . As for triumphs, masks, feasts, weddings, funerals, capital executions, and such shows, men need not be put in mind of them ; yet they are not to be neglected."[1]

To what extent Urquhart followed a plan of this kind it is impossible to say ; for, though his writings are so discursive that we might expect to find in them allusions to anything remarkable he had seen or heard, he has very little to say about his foreign experiences. Dr Johnson spoke with contempt of an English peer, who had extended his travels as far as Egypt, but who had brought back only one small contribution to the general stock of human information—the fact that he had seen " a large serpent in one of the pyramids of Egypt." Urquhart was not quite so poverty-stricken as this ; for he seems to have observed examples of mental infirmity, illustrations of which he might doubtless have found nearer home.

" I saw at Madrid," he says, " a bald-pated fellow who beleeved he was Julius Cæsar, and therefore went constantly on the streets with a laurel crown on his head ; and another at Toledo, who would not adventure to goe abroad unlesse it were in a coach, chariot, or sedane, for fear the heavens should fall down upon him. I likewise saw one in Saragosa, who, imagining himself to be the lawfull King of Aragon, went no where without a scepter in his hand ; and another in the kingdome of Granada, who beleeved he was the valiant Cid that conquered the Mores. At Messina, in Sicilie, I also saw a man that conceived himself to be the great Alexander of Macedone, and that in a ten years space he

[1] *Essays, Civil and Moral*, xviii.

should be master of all the territories which he
subdued; but the best is, that the better to
resemble him he always held his neck awry,
which naturally was streight and upright enough;
and another at Venice, who imagined he was
Soveraign of the whole Adriatick Sea, and sole
owner of all the ships that came from the Levante.
Of men that fancied themselves to be women, beasts,
trees, stones, pitchers, glasse, angels, and of women
whose strained imaginations have falne upon the
like extravagancies, even in the midst of fire and
the extremest pains fortune could inflict upon them,
there is such variety of examples, amongst which
I have seen some at Rome, Naples, Florence, Genua,
Paris, and other eminent cities, that to multiply
any moe [more] words therein, were to load your
ears with old wives' tales, and the trivial tattle of
idly imployed and shallow braind humorists." [1]

He also tells, though not in the same connexion,
of his having been witness of the honour and
admiration lavished upon one of his fellow-countrymen, Dr Seaton, by the *élite* of Parisian society.
" I have seen him," he says, " circled about at
the Louvre with a ring of French lords and
gentlemen, who hearkned to his discourse with
so great attention, that none of them, so long as
he was pleased to speak, would offer to interrupt
him, to the end that the pearles falling from his
mouth might be the more orderly congested in the
several treasures of their judgements." [2]

Part of his time abroad was devoted to the

[1] *Works*, p. 364.   [2] *Ibid.* p. 256.

fascinating occupation of book-hunting, and he had great pleasure in the spoils he had won. When they were set in order on shelves in the library of the castle of Cromartie, he looked on them with the joy which only book-collectors know. " They were," he says, " like to a compleat nosegay of flowers, which, in my travels, I had gathered out of the gardens of above sixteen several kingdoms." [1]

[1] *Works*, p. 402.

CHAPTER II

HILE Urquhart was engaged in
foreign travel, the ecclesiast-
ical and political controversies
in Scotland came to such a
height, that it was evident
that matters could only be settled by an appeal
to the sword, and, accordingly, he returned home
to assist the party to which his family adhered.
He, doubtless, like Milton, considered it disgraceful
that, while his fellow-countrymen were fighting at
home for liberty, he should be travelling abroad for
amusement and intellectual culture. His father,
who had been the first of the Urquharts to give
up Roman Catholicism for Protestantism, took the
unpopular side in the conflict that agitated the
Church of Scotland. He was a staunch Episcopalian, and refused to accept the National Covenant,
when those who had voluntarily and enthusiastic-

ally entered into it attempted to coerce others into following their example, and so turned it into an instrument of tyranny.

The determined efforts of Charles I. and his advisers to make the Church of Scotland in all respects like the Church of England, were fiercely opposed, and, for a time, the party which was resolved to make them as dissimilar as possible prevailed. Episcopacy, liturgy, ancient ecclesiastical customs and rites, and all that savoured of Prelacy or Popery, were swept away by the rising flood. Yet, without committing oneself to the doctrine of passive obedience, it may be doubted whether the course of policy followed by the Covenanters was either wise or scriptural. For, notwithstanding the vehement protestations of loyalty expressed in the National Covenant, armed resistance to the royal authority was not obscurely hinted at in it. "We," said the subscribers, "promise and swear by the great name of the Lord our God to continue in the profession and obedience of the said religion : and that we shall defend the same, and resist all those contrary errors and corruptions, according to our vocation, and to the utmost of that power which God hath put into our hands, all the days of our life." It is quite possible, it may be hoped, for one to be in sympathy with a certain political party, and yet to regret that the Church should identify itself with that party ; and it certainly was not in the end a good thing for the cause of religion that it should have been so closely allied as it was with party politics in the seventeenth century. "My kingdom is not of this world," said Christ; "if My kingdom were of this world, then would My servants fight." "Put up again thy sword into his place," He said to St Peter, "for all they that take the sword, shall perish with the sword." It is difficult to see how these clear and emphatic utterances can be made to harmonise with the resolution not only to use force in the correction of ecclesiastical abuses and religious errors, but also to coerce those who were not prepared to follow the same course of policy.[1]

The Covenanting party were successful beyond their hopes. The influence of the Marquis of Argyle secured the allegiance to the cause of the Highlanders in the west of Scotland; while, in Inverness and the region north of the Moray Firth, the movement was enthusiastically welcomed. Only one district in Scotland held aloof—that of which Aberdeen was the centre. The community there had probably but little sympathy with the innovations which Laud was bent upon bringing in, but they had still less with the Covenant. They were attached to the modified form of Episcopacy which had now existed in Scotland since the

---

[1] The utter chaos which resulted from the fusion of religion and politics may be estimated from the fact that, in the October of 1650, there were in the narrow bounds of Scotland four different armies, at enmity with each other, and each prepared to maintain with the sword a different cause, namely, the Scottish (Presbyterian) army under General Lesley, for King and Covenant combined; the English (Independent) army, under Cromwell, which was against both; the Highland army, under General Middleton, which was for the King without the Covenant; and the Westland, or ultra-Covenanting army, which was for the Covenant without the King.

Reformation (with the exception of the years between 1592 and 1610), in which the bishops were little more than permanent moderators of Presbyteries, and were subject to the General Assembly, and in which the ritual was of a very simple character.

As a University and Cathedral city, and the residence of a large number of wealthy landed proprietors, Aberdeen occupied a position of great importance in Scotland, and was by no means under the command of the capital. The heads of the Covenanting party very speedily found it necessary to take steps for bringing this corner of the kingdom into subjection to themselves. They could scarcely hope to succeed in overcoming the powerful forces at the command of the English Government, if they were to allow this enemy to remain undisturbed in their rear.

Accordingly, at a very early stage in the proceedings, they attempted to gain over to their side the great territorial magnate of the district, the Marquis of Huntly, who, from his rank and wealth and hereditary loyalty to the throne, was likely to be the leader of the King's party in the North. Had they succeeded, they would virtually have had the whole country at their back, for the community of Aberdeen, and the few neighbouring lairds, who, like Sir Thomas Urquhart, refused to accept the Covenant, would not have dared to resist the national policy by force of arms. In the negotiations between the Covenanting leaders and the Marquis of Huntly, we have an illustration of the very muddy roads along which religion is dragged,

3

when it forms an alliance with a political party.
It is certainly with somewhat of a shock that one
who is under the impression that all the Covenanters were saints of a very spiritually-minded
type, learns of the grim option which they offered
to their possible opponent.   Colonel Robert Munro,
who had seen service in Germany, was appointed
to wait upon the Marquis at Strathbogie, and to
acquaint him with the resolutions to which the
Covenanters had come.   "The sum of his commission to Huntly was," we are told, "that the
noblemen Covenanters were desirous that he should
join with them in the common cause; that, if he
would do so, and take the Covenant, they would
give him the first place, and make him leader of
their forces; and, further, they would make his
state and his fortunes greater than ever they were;
and, moreover, they should pay off and discharge
all his debts, which they knew to be about one
hundred thousand pounds sterling; that their
forces and associates were a hundred to one
[in comparison] with the king; and, therefore, it
was to no purpose to him to take up arms against
them, for if he refused this offer and declared
against them, they should find means to disable
him for to help the king; and, moreover, they
knew how to undo him, and bade him to expect
that they will ruinate his family and estates."
The hands were, perhaps, the hands of Christian,
the voice was certainly the voice of Mr Worldly
Wiseman !
The reply of the Marquis was admirable for the

spirit of generosity and chivalry which it breathed. "To this proposition," we are told, "Huntly gave a short and resolute repartee, that his family had risen and stood by the kings of Scotland; and for his part, if the event proved the ruin of this king, he was resolved to lay his life, honours, and estate under the rubbish of the king's ruins."[1]

Though Sir Thomas Urquhart, senior, was a staunch Episcopalian and a devoted Royalist, the circumstances in which he was placed forbade his aiding the ecclesiastical and political causes which were dear to him with more than good wishes. He was surrounded by neighbours of the opposite party,[2] and isolated from those with whom he would gladly have co-operated. Consequently, it remained for his eldest son, our author, who apparently was residing at that time at Balquholly Castle, in Aberdeenshire, where the adherents of the Royalist cause were numerous, to play a more heroic part.

Between the date of the signing of the Covenant and that of the meeting of the General Assembly in Glasgow in 1638, The Tables, for such was the name by which the executive government estab-

[1] Gordon's *Scots Affairs*, i. 49, 50. James Gordon (? 1615–1686) was minister of Rothiemay in Banffshire. His *History of Scots Affairs from 1637 to 1641* is one of the principal authorities for this period. It has no pretensions to style, but is correct and impartial. It was first published in 1841 by the Spalding Club.

[2] Early in the year 1638 some account was given to King Charles of the chief persons in the north of Scotland whom he might regard as faithful to his cause. "In Rosse," it was said, "Sir Thomas Urqhward, Sheriff of Cromerty, with his following, but they [are] environed with Covenanters, ther neighbours" (*ibid.* i. 61).

lished by the revolutionary party was designated, decided to subdue the city of Aberdeen and the neighbouring country, and to compel the people there to accept the Covenant. Before resorting to force, however, an attempt was made to persuade. A committee of three eminent clergymen, Henderson, Dickson, and Cant, with the Earl of Montrose as president, was sent north to deal with the somewhat unimpressible Aberdonians. The hospitable corporation of the northern city invited the visitors to a banquet of wine, but their invitation was scornfully declined. The deputation " would drink with none till first the Covenant was subscribed." Such incivility was new in the history of the city, and a very satisfactory rebuke was given to it by the materials for the proposed banquet being distributed among the poor. It can be easily imagined that after this unsatisfactory beginning the sermons delivered by the clerical deputation fell upon unsympathetic ears, and made but few converts. " The commissioners had one powerful ally in the town, in the person of Earl Marischal, the son of the founder of the College, who had died in 1623; and, when they were refused licence to preach in the city churches, they adjourned to his residence at the north end of what is now Marischal Street. The mansion consisted of several buildings with galleries surrounding a courtyard, and from these galleries the three Covenanting ministers held forth from eight o'clock in the morning till four in the afternoon, trying to convince the people of the truth of the

Covenant. The children of granite, however, proved absolutely impervious to the 'apostles,' whom they scornfully pelted with mud." [1]

A paper-war, which attracted considerable notice, sprang up between the commissioners and six of the Aberdeen clergy—popularly designated in contemporary literature as " the Aberdeen Doctors." [2] In this warfare the representatives of the Covenanting party came off rather badly. " The position taken by the Doctors," says John Hill Burton, " is the unassailable one of the dry sarcastic negative. Whatever the Covenant might be—good or bad—and whatever right its approvers had to bind themselves to it, how were they entitled to force it on those who desired it not ? And when their adversaries became eloquent on its conformity to Scripture and the privileges of the Christian Church, the Doctors ever went back to the same negative position—even if it were so, which we do not admit, yet why force it upon us ? " [3]

Early in the following year, 1639, The Tables resolved to suppress the northern Malignants, as they were called, before preparing to enter on a campaign against their enemy in the south, and

[1] *A History of the University of Aberdeen*, 1495–1895, by J. M. Bulloch, p. 110.

[2] These courageous worthies were the bishop's son, Dr John Forbes, Professor of Divinity in King's College ; Dr Robert Baron, Professor of Divinity, and minister in Aberdeen ; Dr Alexander Scrogie, minister of Old Aberdeen ; Dr William Leslie, Principal of King's College ; and Drs James Sibbald and Alexander Ross, both ministers in Aberdeen.

[3] *History of Scotland*, vi. 235.

thus save themselves from the dangers involved in having an enemy in their rear.   The Earl of Montrose went north at the head of a considerable body of troops, and took possession of Aberdeen. The opponents of the Covenant fled from the city, and Huntly, the leader of the Royalists, felt unable to offer effective resistance.   In spite of a safe-conduct granted him by Montrose on his coming in to a conference, he was taken prisoner to Edinburgh and lodged in the Castle.

This kidnapping of the Royalist chief caused great irritation : and upon a rumour of the fleet's coming to the Firth of Forth, and of the Royal army's approach to the Scottish border, the northern Royalists, of whom our Sir Thomas Urquhart was one, resolved to take arms on the King's side.   The first mention of our author in history is in connexion with this rising ; and the annalist Spalding relates two exciting incidents that occurred in one week, in both of which he took part.

The first, which happened on Friday, the 10th of May, was an attempt made by him and some of the other Royalist lairds or " barons," as they are called,[1] to take the castle of Towie-Barclay,[2] in

---

[1] See note on p. 123.

[2] Towie-Barclay is the name of an estate in the south-east corner of Turriff parish, Aberdeenshire, near Auchterless Station, and four and a half miles south-east of Turriff.   The castle is supposed to have been built in 1593.   It remained pretty perfect till 1792, was re-roofed in 1874, and retains a fine baronial hall with vaulted ceiling.   From at least the beginning of the fourteenth century till 1733, the estate belonged to the Barclays, one of whose line was the celebrated Russian general, Prince Michael Barclay de

Aberdeenshire. It seems that the lairds of Delgatie
and Towie-Barclay had plundered the house of
Balquholly,[1] which was occupied by our author, and
carried off a large supply of "muskets, guns, and
carabines." Sir Thomas was not a man to submit
quietly to such an outrage as this; and, doubtless,
to his desire for vengeance was added a strong wish
to get possession of the firearms, now that there
was a good cause to be defended and brave men to
use the weapons. They had intended to surprise
the castle, but when they came to it they found
the gates shut, and the place strongly guarded.
Lord Fraser and the eldest son of Lord Forbes
had already known that an attempt was to be
made to recover the weapons, and had manned

Tolly (1759–1818). In 1792 it was sold to the governors of
Gordon's Hospital, Aberdeen, for £21,000. Towie is a corruption
of Tolly. See Billing's *Baronial Antiquities*, vol. iv.

[1] Balquholly, now Hatton Castle: a square, castellated mansion
of 1814, with finely wooded grounds, in Turriff parish, three and a
quarter miles south-east of Turriff. It comprises a considerable
fragment of the ancient baronial castle of Balquholly (Gael. *bailc-
coillc*, "town in the wood"), the seat of the Mowats from the
thirteenth century till 1729, when the estate was sold to Alexander
Duff, Esq. Sir Thomas Urquhart must either have rented the
house from the Mowats, or have obtained leave to keep arms
there. The cellars in which the arms were probably kept are
exactly as they were in 1638, except that the old loop-holes are
partly filled up. The name of the mansion was changed to Hatton
Lodge in 1745, and to Hatton Castle in 1814, when the modern part
was built—Hatton being the name of the property in Auchterless,
which previously belonged to the Duff family. The present proprietor is Garden Alexander Duff, Esq., who succeeded to the
estates in 1866. There is behind Hatton Castle a small croft
called Cromartie (see Ordnance Map), probably from our author's
occupancy of Balquholly or connexion with it.

the castle so effectually that the idea of storming
it was out of the question. A few shots were
exchanged, and then the attacking party rode away.
The only casualty was the death of a David Prott,
who was a servant of the laird of Gight,[1] one of
Urquhart's friends. "This," the historian remarks,
"was the first time that blood was drawn here
since the beginning of the Covenant." [2]

Four days after, a more serious encounter took
place between the two forces. The Covenanters of
the north had decided to assemble in force, and
fixed upon Turriff, in Aberdeenshire, as their headquarters. The Royalists drew to a head at Strathbogie, some eleven miles off, and resolved to disperse
their opponents. The Covenanting party was
about twelve hundred strong, and the Royalists
about eight hundred, but the latter had four brass
cannon, which very materially strengthened them
as an attacking force. They were under the
leadership of skilful officers, among whom Arthur
Forbes of Blacktown [in King-Edward] is specially mentioned. Sir Thomas himself informs us
that, "having obtained, though with a great deal
of pain, a fifteen hundreth [hundred] subscrip-
tions to a bond conceived and drawn up in
opposition of the vulgar [popular] Covenant, he
selected from amongst them so many as he
thought fittest for holding hand to [taking in

---

[1] An ancestor of Lord Byron.

[2] Spalding's *Memorials*, i. 185. Until within living memory
the exact site of Prott's [or Pratt's] grave was pointed out; but it
is now quite obliterated by being ploughed over repeatedly.

hand] the dissolving of their committees and un-
lawful meetings."[1]

About ten o'clock on the night of Monday, the
13th of May, they started for Turriff, marching in
a "very quiet and sober manner," and by day-
break managed to steal upon the village by an
unguarded path. The sound of trumpets and of
drums aroused the unsuspecting Covenanters to
the fact that they had been fairly surprised.
"Some were sleeping, others drinking, and smoak-
ing tobacco, others walking up and down." A
few volleys of musketry, and a few shots discharged
from the cannon, served to disperse them, and the
village was taken possession of by the attacking
force. It was but a slight skirmish,[2] in which
three men were killed, two of the Covenanters,
and one of the Royalists; but it was the first
of the battles in the great Civil War, which
raged for so many years, and deluged with blood

[1] MS. *Epigrams :* The Animadversion.

[2] "Ther fell only two gentlemen upon the Covenanters syde ;
one Mr James Stacker, a servant to the Lord Mucholles ; and
one Alexander Forbesse, servante to Forbesse of Tolqhwone : upon
the Gordons syde, one common foote souldiour killed, (by the
unskilfullnesse of his owne comerades fyring ther musketts, as was
thoughte), whom the Gordons caused bufye solemnly, that day,
out of ane idle vante, in the buriall place of Walter Barcley of
Towey, within the church of Turreffe ; not without great terror to
the minister of the place, Mr Thomas Michell, who all the whyle,
with his sonne, disgwysd in a womans habite, had gott upp and
was lurkinge above the syling of the churche, whilst the soul-
diours wer discharging volleyes of shotte within the churche, and
peircing the syling with ther bulletts in severall places" (Gordon's
Scots Affairs, ii. 258). The reader will keep in mind that
Gordon was the family name of the Marquis of Huntly.

so many fruitful plains in each of the three kingdoms.   On this account "the Trot of Turriff," as
it was called, should not be forgotten.

After this victory, the Royalists being masters of
the village, the common soldiers, who were hungry
after their night's march, plundered the houses of
those they thought were Covenanters, and supplied
themselves with meat and drink.   The greatest loss
fell upon the minister, Mr Mitchell, who, however,
received very liberal compensation from Parliament
in the following year.   They next gathered as many
of the inhabitants of Turriff together as they could
find, and made them accept and subscribe the King's
Covenant.[1]   This device for securing adherents was,
however, ineffectual, for, a few weeks later, those

---

[1] This was originally the King's Confession, and was drawn up
in 1580 by John Craig, minister of Holyrood House, and subscribed
by James VI. and his household on 28th January, 1580–81.   It is
printed at length in Row's *Historic of the Kirk of Scotland.*   It
reaffirms the Confession of Faith of 1560, but contains also a
solemn renunciation in great detail of the errors of Popery.   It
was approved by the General Assembly in April, 1581.   A
"General Band [Bond] for Maintenance of the true Religion" was
added in 1588.   The National Covenant of 1637 was an amplification of the previous Confessions, containing in addition an
abjuration of Episcopal Church-government, as the King's Confession did of Popery.   In September, 1638, Charles I. issued a
proclamation for the Scottish people to subscribe this King's Confession and General Band, but the Covenanters regarded this as a
subtle plot to divide them, and destroy the National Covenant,
and, therefore, protested against the proclamation.   The Confession
and Band so subscribed, for it was subscribed by some, got the
name of the "King's Covenant."   It did not, of course, contain the
abjuration of Episcopal Church-government.   Those who adhered to
it were called Malignants ; while the name Covenanters was applied
to those who subscribed the National Covenant.

who had sworn to the King's Covenant, on a declaration that they had acted under compulsion, were solemnly absolved by their minister from all obligation to keep it.

The Royalist leaders now began to think of further projects, as the number of their followers increased after the victory at Turriff. They lost no time in marching upon Aberdeen, and in quartering themselves upon its inhabitants, especially upon those who were known to belong to the Covenanting party. In a few days, however, they found their position untenable. A considerable number of their Highland forces disbanded, and marched away to their homes, plundering as they went—" a thing," the historian remarks, " verye usuall with them." The others retreated from Aberdeen, when the Covenanting army under the Earl Marischal entered the city, on the 23rd of May, 1639.

A small number of prominent Royalists,[1] of whom our Sir Thomas was one, now resolved to leave Scotland, where the cause to which they were devoted was at such a low ebb. A ship, belonging to one Andrew Findlay, had been kept in readiness for an emergency like this, and on it they embarked hastily, and sailed away to England, to offer their services to Charles I. " Urquhart," says Dr Irving, " who professes to have launched

---

[1] Among those who made their escape from Aberdeen along with Urquhart were Adam Bellenden, the bishop of the diocese ; Alexander Innes, minister of Rothiemay ; Alexander Scrogie, a Regent of King's College ; together with the bishop's son, nephew, and servant (Spalding's *Memorials*).

forth in the view of six hundred of his enemies, was, within two days, landed at Berwick, where he found the Marquis of Hamilton, and delivered to him a letter from the leaders of the northern Royalists. He had likewise undertaken to be the bearer of despatches to the King, containing the signatures of the same chieftains; and, having proceeded to the royal quarters, he obtained an audience of His Majesty, and explained to him their past exertions and future plans for his service. He appears to have been satisfied with his own reception, and the written answer 'gave great contentment to all the gentlemen of the north that stood for the king.'"[1]

In one of our author's tracts, published in 1652, we have a pedigree of the family of Urquhart. Under his own name he states that "he was knighted by King Charles, in Whitehall Gallery, in the yeer 1641, the 7 of April." In the same year he first made his appearance as an author in the publication of his three books of *Epigrams, Moral and Divine*, of which a fuller notice will be found in a later chapter. Let us now for a little leave Sir Thomas, happy in his sovereign's favour, his head encircled with the ivy-wreath that clothes the brows of learned poets, and his eye fixed upon a prominent crag of Mount Parnassus as henceforth specially his own, and turn to his father, whose golden dreams have long since fled away, and left him but the dreariest and shabbiest prose.

[1] *Lives of the Scottish Writers*, vol. i.; Urquhart's MS. *Epigrams: The Animadversion.*

For thirty-six years the elder Sir Thomas had been in possession of the ample estates of the house of Urquhart, and during nearly the whole of this time the country had been at peace, so that he had no one but himself to blame for the impoverished condition in which they were when his son received them. The latter described the state of matters in the following terms: "All he bequeathed unto me, his eldest Son, in matter of worldly means, was twelve or thirteen thousand pounds sterling of debt, five brethren all men, and two sisters almost mariageable, to provide for, and lesse to defray all this burden with by six hundred pounds sterling a year, although [*i.e.* even if] the warres had not prejudiced me in a farthing, then [than] what for the maintaining of himself alone in a peaceable age he inherited for nothing." [1]

So exasperated was the old man by the importunity of his creditors, that at last, we are told, the sound of one of their voices was in his ears as "the hissing of a basilisk." The great Civil War itself, which brought calamity and grief to so many homes, was almost welcomed by him for the relief it brought him from the "hornings" and "apprisings," and other legal processes, which threatened him in times of peace. "The disorderly troubles of the land," says his son of him, "being then far advanced, though otherways he disliked them, were a kind of refreshment to him, and intermitting relaxation from a more stinging disquietnesse. For that our intestin troubles and dis-

[1] *Works*, p. 340.

tempers, by silencing the laws for a while, gave some repose to those that longed for a breathing time, and by hudling up the terms of Whitsuntide and Martimass, which in Scotland are the destinated times for payment of debts, promiscuously with the other seasons of the year, were as an oxymel julip wherewith to indormiat them in a bitter sweet security." [1]

The most importunate of all the creditors, or, as Urquhart describes them, "the usurious cormorants," who harassed the unhappy proprietor of Cromartie, was a certain Robert Lesley of Findrassie. He held a mortgage upon the estate, and though he was indebted to its owner for many acts of kindness, he had been the first to foreclose upon the property, and had persuaded other creditors to join with him in taking this step. The annoyance and mortification caused by these proceedings hastened Sir Thomas's death. Two days before that event, animated by regret for the wrong he had done his heir by the impoverishment of the family property, he assembled his younger children, and bound them, "under pain of his everlasting curse and execration," to do all in their power to help their elder brother. The terms of this extraordinary bond, his son tells us, were these: "to assist, concur with, follow, and serve me, to the utmost of their power, industry, and means, and to spare neither charge nor travel, though it should cost them all they had, to release me from the undeserved bondage of the domineering creditor, and

[1] *Works*, p. 346.

extricate my lands from the impestrements wherein
they were involved ; yea, to bestow nothing of their
owne upon no other use, till that should be done :
and all this under their own handwriting, secured
with the clause of registration to make the oppro-
brie the more notorious in case of failing, as the
paper itself, which I have *in retentis*, together with
another signed to the same sense, by my mother,
and also my brothers and sisters, Dunbugar [Dun-
lugas][1] only excepted, will more evidently testifie." [2]
Sir Thomas Urquhart, the elder, died in April [?],
1642, after a long and lingering illness.[3]

Our author now returned home to enter on possession of his estates, and to attempt to reduce to
something like order the chaos in which the family
affairs were.   He resolved to commit the management of his ·property to trustees, who, after paying
his mother's jointure, were to devote the whole of
the rest of the rents to the reduction of debt.   He
himself went to live on the Continent, in the hope

[1] Dunlugas is in the parish of Alvah, close by the river Deveron,
on the east side.

[2] *Works*, p. 341.

[3] "He was alive last Whitsuntide ! said the coachman. . . .
Whitsuntide !—alas ! cried Trim. . . . What is Whitsuntide,
Jonathan, or Shrovetide, or any tide or time past, to this ! "
(*Tristram Shandy*, vol. v. chap. vii.).

Our author states (*Works*, p. 341) that "his father's death
occurred in August in the year 1642, some four yeares after the
hatching of the Covenant."   He is, however, very careless in details
of fact, and is in error concerning this date.   Sir Thomas Urquhart,
senior, is termed "*umqll*" (*i.e.* "*the late*") in the Burgess Roll of
Banff, on 14th June, 1642 (*Annals of Banff*, ii. 418).   Perhaps
the date was April instead of August.   The Covenant was signed
1st March, 1638.

that in a few years he would be able to return home and enjoy his inheritance unencumbered by debt. These proceedings, with the disappointing results that followed them, are related in a passage of his *Logopandecteision*, which is worth quoting. "Immediately after my father's decease," he says, "for my better expedition in the discharge of those burthens, having repaired homewards, I did sequestrate the whole rent (my mother's joynture excepted) to that use only, and, as I had done many times before, betook myself to my hazards abroad, that by vertue of the industry and diligence of those whom, by the advise and deliberation of my nearest friends, I was induced to intrust with my affairs, the debt might be the sooner defrayed, and the ancient house releeved out of the thraldome it was so unluckily faln into. But it fell out so far otherwayes, that after some few years residence abroad, without any considerable expence from home, when I thought, because of my having mortified and set apart all the rent to no other end then [than] the cutting off and defalking of my father's debt, that accordingly a great part of my father's debt had been discharged, I was so far disappointed of my expectation therin, that whilst, conform to the confidence reposed in him whom I had intrusted with my affairs, I hoped to have been exonered and relieved of many creditors, the debt was only past over and transferred from one in favours of another, or rather of many in the favours of one, who, though he formerly had gained much at my father's hands, was notwithstanding at the time of his decease none of his creditors, nor at any time mine ; my Egyptian bondage by such means remaining still the same, under task masters different only in name, and the rents neverthelesse taken up to the full, to my no small detriment and prejudice of the house standing in my person. The aime of some of those I concredited [committed] my weightiest adoes [affairs] unto, being, as is most conspicuously apparent, that I should never reap the fruition nor enjoyment of any portion, parcell, or pendicle of the estate of my predecessors, unlesse by my fortune and endeavours in forrain countries, I should be able to acquire as much as might suffice to buy it, as we say, out of the ground. And verily," he concludes, "though not in relation to these ignoble and unworthy by-ends, it was my purpose and resolution to have done so, which assuredly, had not the turbulent divisions of the time been such as to have crossed and thwarted the atchievements of more faisible projects, I would have accomplished two or three severall ways ere now." [1]

One is inclined to wonder what the two or three lucrative undertakings were, which this Highland gentleman had in view when he spoke in this way of the practicability of making enough money to purchase back his estates. "What song the syrens sang," says Sir Thomas Browne, "or what name Achilles assumed when he hid himself among women, though puzzling questions are not beyond all conjecture." But even as wise a man as Sir

[1] *Works*, pp. 346, 347.

4

Thomas Browne might well pause before venturing on a conjecture in connection with this matter.

In one of the official records of the time,[1] there is an entry which shows that Urquhart was resident in London in 1644. On the 9th May of that year he is assessed for a forced loan at £1000; and, on the 16th of the same month, there is an order for him to be brought up in custody to pay his assessment; while, on the 21st, it is noted that his assessment is "respited till he shall speak with the Scottish committee and take further orders, he engaging to appear whenever required." He no doubt proved to the committee that he had no property in London, but was only a sojourner there, and was accordingly virtually discharged. His place of residence in London at this time was Clare Street,[2] then newly erected upon St Clement's

[1] *Calendar of Proceedings of Committee for Advances of Moneys-Taxes*, i. 381.

[2] The neighbourhood is now a cluster of narrow, dirty streets and passages, lined chiefly with butchers' and grocers' shops, which overflow into the adjacent streets, and are supplemented by fishmongers' and miscellaneous stalls and barrows—a crowded, noisy, and unsavoury place on Saturday nights. In 1640, Charles I. granted his licence to Thomas York, his executors, etc., to erect as many buildings as they thought proper upon St Clement's Inn Fields, the inheritance of the Earl of Clare. He issued another licence in 1642, permitting Gervase Holles, Esq., to make several streets of the width of thirty, thirty-four, and forty feet. These streets still retain the names and titles of their founders—Clare Street, Denzil Street, and Holles Street. Clare Street is somewhat rich in interesting associations. There is a letter of Steele's to his wife, dated from the Bull Head Tavern in this street, 24th August, 1710. It seems likely that he was hiding there. Mrs Bracegirdle, a celebrated actress of that time, "was in the habit of going into that neighbourhood, and giving money

Inn Fields, on the east side of Drury Lane, and called after John Holles,[1] second Earl of Clare, whose town-house was near by.

Sir Thomas Urquhart now resolved to take the management of his own affairs, and, if possible, so to conduct matters as to secure subsistence for himself, as well as satisfaction for his father's creditors; and, in the year 1645, he went to live in the ancestral home at Cromartie. His rental still amounted to £1000 Sterling a year, which represents about £7000 in our time, but a debt of twelve or thirteen years' income was a very serious burden upon such an estate.

There can be little doubt that the entanglement in which the financial affairs of the house of Urquhart were involved became none the less confused and confusing when the gallant knight applied himself to unravel it. That was scarcely a task for which he was fitted. Much more appropriate would it have been for him to draw the sword, like Alexander, and cut the Gordian knot. Perhaps his failure, as in another well-known case,[2] is partly to

to the poor basket-women, insomuch that she could not pass without having thankful acclamations from people of all degrees." It was to Clare Street and Clare Market that Jack Sheppard went, after his escape from Newgate: he there bought a butcher's frock and woollen apron, which he was wearing when captured at Finchley. Here was Johnson's Hotel, celebrated for upwards of seventy years for its *à la mode* beef. Isaac Bickerstaffe, too, lived in this street.

[1] John Holles, created Baron Houghton of Houghton, in the county of Nottingham, in 1616, and Earl of Clare in 1624.

[2] "If I had known that young man [Uriah Heep]," said Mr Micawber, "at the period when my difficulties came to a crisis, all

be attributed to his not having had a legal adviser,
familiar with the intricacies of the law, and able to
prevent his creditors getting more than their pound of
flesh, if not to save even that from them.   Charles I.
once said that he knew as much law as a gentleman
ought to know.   Sir Thomas Urquhart seems to have
had a somewhat similar acquaintance with the same
subject, and this, like that of the person mentioned
in the foot-note on the preceding page, was probably
acquired "as a defendant on civil process."   There can
be no doubt that he "made an effort" more than once.
In vain did he have recourse to " pecunial charms,
and holy water out of Plutus' cellar."[1]   The charms
were indeed potent, but they were not applied long
enough ; the holy water was composed of the right
ingredients, but there was too little of it in the
cellars at Cromartie.   He could not, with all his
struggles, succeed in curing what the Limousin
scholar in Rabelais calls " the penury of pecune in
the marsupie " [i.e. the want of money in the purse]
—that complaint which is so mortifying to the pride
of any gentleman, but which is specially exasperat-
ing to a Highland gentleman.   His cares and distresses, or, as he calls them, his " solicitudinary and
luctiferous discouragements," were enough " to appall
the most undaunted spirits, and kill a very Paphla-
gonian partridge, that is said to have two hearts."[2]

I can say is, that I believe my creditors would have been better
managed than they were " (*David Copperfield*, chap. xvii.).

[1] *Works*, p. 347.

[2] *Ibid.* p. 346.   For the authority on which this interesting
ornithological statement is made the reader will overhaul his Pliny
(*H. N.* xi. chap. 3).

Probably Sir Thomas Urquhart was harshly dealt with by his father's creditors, though, of course, it is possible that in the story as told by them they would appear in a more favourable light. They had to do with a man who was unpractical and fantastical in the highest degree, and morbidly sensitive in all matters that seemed to lower his dignity or to cast a slur upon his honour. His brains seethed with plans for the improvement of agriculture, trade, and education, but none of these did the importunity of his creditors permit him to carry into effect. " Truly I may say," he complains, " that above ten thousand severall times I have by these flagitators been interrupted for money, which never came to my use, directly or indirectly one way or other, at home or abroad, any one time whereof I was busied about speculations of greater consequence then [than] all that they were worth in the world; from which, had I not been violently pluck'd away by their importunity, I would have emitted to publick view above five hundred several treatises on inventions never hitherto thought upon by any." [1]   Before his imagination there floated the dream of what he might have been, and his mind alternated between passionate remonstrances against his unfortunate circumstances and delusive hopes and anticipations.

The editor of the Maitland Club edition of Urquhart's works truly remarks that there is a melancholy earnestness, almost approaching insanity, in his wild speculations on what he might

[1] *Works*, p. 326.

have done for himself and his country but for the
weight of worldly incumbrances. "Even so," he
says, "may it be said of myself, that when I was
most seriously imbusied about the raising of my
own and countrie's reputation to the supremest
reach of my endeavours, then did my father's
creditors, like so many millstones hanging at my
heels, pull down the vigour of my fancie, and
violently hold that under, what [which] other wayes
would have ascended above the sublimest regions of
vulgar conception." [1]

So convinced was he that the schemes and inventions with which his thoughts were occupied
were of immense value, that he declared that he
ought to have the benefit of that Act of James III.
(36th statute of his fifth Parliament) which pro-
vides that the debtor's movable goods be first
"valued and discussed before his lands be apprised."
He claimed this as a right from the State; "and
if," he says, "conform to the aforesaid Act, this be
granted, I doe promise shortly to display before the
world, ware of greater value then [than] ever from
the East Indias was brought in ships to Europe." [2]
But unfortunately the Philistines were too strong
for him.

To these pecuniary difficulties were added annoy-
ances and wrongs, which the meekest of mankind,
among whom Sir Thomas is not to be reckoned,
would have found it hard to bear.

Mention has already been made of Robert Lesley
of Findrassie, the most relentless of all the creditors,

[1] *Works*, p. 328.   [2] *Ibid.* p. 325.

who, according to Sir Thomas Urquhart's account
of matters, made life bitter for him, and defeated his
many schemes for the benefit of the human race.
The injurious proceedings of this man form a subject which our author can never leave for any
length of time, and to which it is necessary for his
biographer to revert occasionally.   His unfortunate
debtor found a certain grim satisfaction, as well as
an opportunity for gratifying his taste for genealogical research, in tracing Robert's descent from a
celebrated murderer—that Norman Lesley whose
hands were dipped in the blood of Cardinal Beaton.
It is certain, however, that there was no real
foundation for this opinion.[1]

Unless Robert Lesley is a much-maligned man,
his conduct towards the son of his patron was both
rapacious and ungrateful.   On one occasion at least
he acted in a very high-handed manner.   " With
all the horse and foot he was able to command,"
says Sir Thomas, " he came in a hostile manner to
take possession of a farm of mine called Ardoch ;
unto which . . . he had no more just title then
[than] to the town of Jericho mentioned in the
Scriptures ; and at the offer of such an indignity to
our house, some of the hot-spirited gentlemen of
our name would even then have taken him, with his
three sons, bound them hand and foot, and thrown

---

[1] Norman Lesley, Master of Rothes, eldest son of George, fifth
Earl of Rothes, died without issue in 1554.   This disposes of Sir
Thomas Urquhart's statement.   The Lesleys of Findrassie them-
selves claimed to be descended from Robert, the fourth son of Earl
George.   See *Scotch Peerage Law*, by J. Riddell, p. 190.

them within the flood-mark, into a place called the Yares of Udol, there to expect the coming of the sea in a full tide, to carry him along to be seized in a soil of a greater depth, and abler to restrain the insatiableness of his immense desires, then [than] any of my lands within the shire of Cromartie." Sir Thomas, according to his own account, hindered the perpetration of this violence, and gave his enemy and those who accompanied him " a pass and safe-conduct to their own houses."[1]

Yet so far was the caitiff creditor from being touched by this proof of magnanimity on the part of his debtor, that he applied himself with renewed vigour to the concoction of schemes for his total destruction.   So at least Sir Thomas would have us believe.   On one occasion Lesley tried to inveigle him to Inverness, with the intention of having him arrested at the suit of an accomplice—James Sutherland, " Tutor of Duffus "—and kept in durance until he had satisfied all his enemy's demands. On another occasion Lesley managed to get a troop of horse quartered upon the tenants of Cromartie, till, says our author, " I should transact for a sum, of money to be paid to his son-in-law : which verily was the greater part of his portion."[2]   In addition to this, a garrison was stationed for nearly a year in the castle of Cromartie, where they conducted themselves in a way calculated to wound and humiliate the proud spirit of its proprietor.   Among other wrongs and losses inflicted upon him was the sequestration of his library, which he had

[1] *Works*, p. 379.   [2] *Ibid.* p. 380.

collected with such pains. Sir Thomas says that
he sought eagerly to be allowed to purchase back
the precious volumes, but was hindered by the
spitefulness and indifference of those to whom he
made application, and was ultimately able to secure
only a few of them, which had been stolen from
the collection and dispersed through the country.[1]

In an amusing passage in the *Logopandecteision*,
our author gives us a specimen of the peculiarities
of speech which distinguished his arch-enemy,
Lesley of Findrassie. As we read it we seem to
hear the very tones in which he enunciated or
defended his "felonious little plans." "Several
gentlemen of good account," he says, "and others of
his familiar acquaintance, having many times very
seriously expostulated with him why he did so im-
placably demean himself towards me, and with such
irreconciliability of rancor, that nothing could seem
to please him that was consistent with my weal,
his answers most readily were these: 'I have (see
ye ?) many daughters (see ye ?) to provide portions
for, (see ye ?), and that (see ye now ?) cannot be done,
(see ye ?) without money; the interest (see ye ?) of
what I lent, (see ye ?), had it been termely [regu-
larly] payed, (see ye ?), would have afforded me (see
ye now ?) several stocks for new interests; I have

[1] One of these volumes containing the signature of our author is
still in existence. It is a copy of Arthur Johnston's Latin poems,
printed at Aberdeen by Raban, 1632, and is in the possession of
the Rev. J. B. Craven, Kirkwall. It is a very fragile volume.
The signature in this volume, and two others, attached to legal
documents, are all that are known to be extant. We give a
fac-simile of one of the latter on p. iv.

(see ye ?) apprized [1] lands (see ye ?) for these summes (see ye ?) borrowed from me, (see ye now ?), and (see ye ?) the legal [time] being expired, (see ye now ?), is it not just (see ye ?) and equitable (see ye ?) that I have possession (see ye ?) of these my lands, (see ye ?), according to my undoubted right, (see ye now ?) ? ' With these over-words of ' see ye '

---

[1] "*Apprizing*" is a legal process to which Sir Thomas several times refers with great horror, and it may be as well to explain to our readers what it was, for fortunately it is now a thing of the past. It was for long the only method of attaching a debtor's heritable property. By the Act, 1469, c. 36, when payment of a debt could not be obtained out of the debtor's movables (including rent), "the King's letters might be obtained, under which a debtor's land might be sold by the Sheriff to the amount of his debts, and the creditor paid out of the proceeds. If within six months no purchaser could be found, a portion of the land equal to the debt was to be apprised by thirteen men chosen by the Sheriff, and the portion apprised by them was to be made over to the creditor." The debtor could redeem within seven years. This procedure at first took place in the head burgh of the shire, where the jury probably knew enough to make a fair valuation of the land. But after a time the proceedings often took place in Edinburgh, where the jury had no special knowledge, and might be packed by the creditor. So that large estates were sometimes carried off in payment of trifling debts. The appriser at once entered into possession, and was not obliged to account for the rents (until 1621, c. 6). It was thus a powerful engine of oppression. If A. wished B.'s land, and B. owned land and nothing else, it was possible for A., if he could only get B. as his debtor even in a small sum, so to work matters that for the debt he might apprise all B.'s land. Being then in right of B.'s rents, he had B. completely in his power, and B. had no resources for gathering together the amount of the debt which he must pay in order to redeem his lands within the seven years allowed. The law was much relaxed by the Act, 1621, c. 6, but the above will enable us to understand how an unscrupulous creditor might get an easy-going, thriftless man into his clutches, and impoverish him and his family.

and 'see ye now,' as if they had been no less
material then [than] the Psalmist's *Selah*, and
Higgaion Selah, did he usually nauseate the ears of
his hearers when his tongue was in the career of
uttering anything concerning me; who alwayes
thought that he had very good reason to make use
of such like expressions, 'do you see' and 'do you
see now,' because there being but little candour in
his meaning, whatever he did or spoke was under
some colour." [1]

It must have been very hard for the proud-
hearted chieftain to see his farms devastated, his
tenants maltreated, his library thrown to the winds,
a garrison placed in his house, and troops of horse
quartered upon his lands without any allowance,
in addition to all the misery and impoverishment
which his father's wastefulness and neglect had
brought down upon his head.

In 1647 an event occurred which seriously

[1] *Works*, p. 382. The evident meaning of the last sentence is
that Lesley's ways were so dark that it was highly necessary for
him often to ask, "See ye?" Yet one cannot help feeling that
this relentless creditor may not have been solely animated by
malignant hatred of his debtor. Even in the above speech there
seem to be claims which cannot be lightly brushed aside. One is
again reminded of Mr Micawber, and of the sudden and unex-
pected glimpse of a better nature in his most truculent creditor,
which was vouchsafed him when he got his discharge in bank-
ruptcy. "Even the revengeful bootmaker," we are told, "declared in open court that he bore him [Mr M.] no malice, but that
when money was owing to him he liked to be paid. He said he
thought it was human nature" (*David Copperfield*, chap. xii.).
An eminent American philosopher has said that there is a great
deal of human nature in man. There seems at any rate to have
been a great deal in Mr Lesley of Findrassie.

affected the interests of our author, and placed him in a still more humiliating position. Sir Robert Farquhar [1] of Mounie had "apprised" the estate and sheriffship of Cromartie, and was now confirmed in the possession of them. He proceeded to sell his rights to (Sir) John Urquhart of Craigfintray, the great - grandson of the Tutor of Cromartie. Immediately upon this (Sir) John purchased a commission from Charles I. to become hereditary Sheriff of Cromartie. In this way the ancestral domains and jurisdiction of which Sir Thomas Urquhart was so proud virtually passed out of his hands. It was not, however, till after the Restoration apparently that the new proprietor entered into possession. He evidently allowed his claims to lie dormant until the death of his cousin, Sir Thomas, and then put them in force. Even if our author had no other troubles to contend with, the knowledge that this Damoclean sword was suspended above his head would have been enough to destroy his peace.

No doubt Sir Thomas sometimes thought that he was the most unlucky chieftain the Urquhart race had yet known,—that such a multitude of misfortunes had never come upon one who bore his name since that day when, on a sunny plain in Achaia, wild armed men first raised Esormon "aloft on the buckler-throne, and with clanging armour and hearts" hailed him as "fortunate and well-

---

[1] In one of his queer *Epigrams*, after comparing the insatiable demands of his creditors to those of the grave and of the sea, he closes with the following alliterative litany :

"Free me from Farcher, Fraser, Fendrasie."

beloved." [1]   Sir Theodore Martin, indeed, says that Urquhart's statements with regard to his misfortunes should not be construed to the letter, any more than should the announcements of his wonderful inventions and designs.   They were both, he considers, in a great degree pet objects on which he had permitted his imagination to rest, till they had been transfigured into a magnitude to which the reality probably bore but a faint resemblance.[2]   There is, however, ample evidence in what we have already quoted, to show that certain of the grievances he complained of were by no means imaginary.   It is beyond dispute that he suffered heavily in his property in consequence of his adherence to the Royalist cause.   In 1663 his brother, Sir Alexander, presented a petition asking compensation for the losses suffered in the time of his father and brother.   The Commissioners appointed to examine into these claims reported that, before 1650, the damage inflicted upon the Urquhart property amounted to £20,303 Scots, and during 1651–52 to £39,203 Scots—in all £59,506 Scots, which is almost £5000 Sterling.[3]

The relations of Sir Thomas Urquhart with the ministers of the churches of which he was patron were unfortunately of a painful character.   The grounds of misunderstanding and dispute were numerous.   In addition to political and ecclesi-

---

[1] "His subjects and familiars surnamed him [Esormon] οὐρο-χάρτος, that is [to] say, 'fortunate and well-beloved'" (*Works*, p. 156).

[2] Rabelais, p. xv.

[3] *Acts of the Parliament of Scotland*, vol. vii. 479, *a*, *b*.

astical differences of opinion between the ministers
of the three parishes [1] (of which Sir Thomas was the
sole heritor) and himself, there were disputes about
augmentation of stipends,[2] which they thought in-
adequate but with which he had no fault to find,
the abolition of his heritable right to the patronage
of these churches, the legal proceedings taken by the
incumbents to compel him to agree to arrangements
decided upon by the Presbytery with regard to
stipends and the upkeep of buildings, and there were
also personal quarrels with the ministers themselves.
In the following passage he tells his side of the story,
and gives us a vivid, though not an edifying glimpse
of the parochial politics of that far-off time and
remote corner of Scotland.   It is to be noticed

[1] The parish of Cromartie consists of the north-east portion of
the peninsula called the Black Isle, terminating eastward in the
precipice called the Southern Sutor, and stretches for about four
miles along the shore of the Moray Firth on the east, and about
six along that of the Firth of Cromartie on the north and west.
To the west of the parish of Cromartie were situated the joint
parishes of Kirkmichael and Cullicudden, on the southern shore of
the Cromartie Firth.   In Sir Thomas Urquhart's time these were
separate parishes, but they were united in 1662, and a new church
was built at Resolis, in Kirkmichael, near the border of Cullicudden.
The newly-constituted parish bore and still bears the name of Resolis.

[2] In his *Logopandecteision* he speaks of the "stipauctionarie
tide" which began to overflow the land.   He thought "with
sufficient bulwarks of good argument to have stayed the inundation
thereof from two of his churches"; but, he says, "I was violently
driven like a feather before a whirlewind, notwithstanding all my
defences, to the sanctuary of an inforced patience" (*Works*, p. 352).
He does not, however, appear to have stayed long in this sanctuary,
or else the shelter it afforded was but imperfect.   His "*stipauctionarie*" (*i.e.* stipend-increasing) reminds us of Mr Micawber's
calling his salary his "*stipendiary emoluments.*"

that Sir Thomas writes of himself in the third
person. "I think," says the supposed anonymous
writer of him, "there be hardly any in Scotland
that proportionably hath suffered more prejudice by
the Kirk then [than] himself; his own ministers
(to wit, those that preach in the churches whereof
himself is patron, Master Gilbert Anderson, Master
Robert Williamson, and Master Charles Pape by
name, serving the cures of Cromartie, Kirkmichel,
and Cullicudden), having done what lay in them
for the furtherance of their owne covetous ends, to
his utter undoing : for the first of those three, for
no other cause but that the said Sir Thomas would
not authorize the standing of a certain pew (in that
country called a desk), in the church of Cromarty,
put in without his consent by a professed enemy to
his House, who had plotted the ruine thereof, and
one that had no land in the parish, did so rail
against him and his family in the pulpit at several
times, both before his face and in his absence, and
with such opprobrious termes, more like a scolding
tripe-seller's wife then [than] good minister, squirt-
ing the poyson of detraction and abominable fals-
hood (unfit for the chaire of verity) in the eares
of his tenandry, who were the onely auditors, did
most ingrately and despightfully so calumniate
and revile their master, his own patron and benefactor, that the scandalous and reproachful words
striving which of them should first discharge against
him its steel-pointed dart, did oftentimes, like
clusters of hemlock or wormewood dipt in vinegar,
stick in his throat ; he being almost ready to choak

with the aconital bitterness and venom thereof, till the razor of extream passion, by cutting them into articulate sounds, and very rage it self, in the highest degree, by procuring a vomit, had made him spue them out of his mouth into rude, indigested lumps, like so many toads and vipers that had burst their gall.[1]

" As for the other two, notwithstanding that they had been borne, and their fathers before them, vassals to his house, and the predecessor of one of them had shelter in that land, by reason of slaughter committed by him, when there was no refuge for him anywhere else in Scotland; and that the other had never been admitted to any church had it not been for the favour of his foresaid patron, who, contrary to the will of his owne friends and great reluctancy of the ministry it self, was both the nominater and chuser of him to that function; and that before his admission he did faithfully protest he should all the days of his life remain contented with that competency of portion the late incumbent in that charge did enjoy before him; they nevertheless behaved themselves so peevishly and unthankfully towards their forenamed patron and master, that, by vertue of an unjust decree, both procured and purchased from a promiscuous knot of men like themselves,[2] they used all their utmost endeavours, in absence of their above recited patron, to whom and

---

[1] The attention of the reader is specially directed to the marvellous felicity and vigour of the above description. Sir Thomas himself has never written anything better in its way.

[2] We fear that this is meant as a description of a presbytery.

unto whose house they had been so much beholding, to outlaw him,[1] and declare him rebel, by open
proclamation at the market-cross of the head town of
his owne shire, in case he did not condescend [con-
sent] to the grant of that augmentation of stipend
which they demanded, conforme to the tenour of
the above-mentioned decree ; the injustice whereof
will appeare when examined by any rational judge.

" Now the best is, when by some moderate gentlemen it was expostulated, why against their master,
patron, and benefactor, they should have dealt with
such severity and rigour, contrary to all reason and
equity ; their answer was, They were inforced and
necessitated so to do by the synodal and presbyterial
conventions of the Kirk, under paine of deprivation,
and expulsion from their benefices : I will not say,
κακοῦ κόρακος κακὸν ᾠόν [an evil egg of an evil
crow], but may safely think that a well-sanctified
mother will not have a so ill-instructed brat, and
that *injuria humana* cannot be the lawfull daughter
of a *jure divino* parent." [2]

Sir Thomas Urquhart is not to be taken as
infallible in the opinions which he formed and
expressed concerning the quality of the sermons
which were delivered from the Presbyterian pulpits
of his time.   But there can be no doubt that
he hits upon one great fault by which many of
them were marred—that of being rather political
harangues than exhortations to godliness after the
Pauline fashion.   Indeed, he goes so far as to say

---

[1] The reference is to the process of " horning " described on p. 16.
[2] *Works*, p. 280–282.

5

that, as a rule, the preachers of his time seldom
gave such exhortations, as they were "enjoyed by
their ecclesiastical authority [authorities ?] to preach
to the times,[1] that is, to rail against malignants and
sectaries, or those whom they suppose to be their
enemies."[2]   Preaching "to the times" Sir Thomas
found meant in his neighbourhood preaching against
him; and one may be allowed, it is to be hoped,
without unduly wounding the feelings of those who
admire the Covenanters, to think sympathetically
of his sufferings.   Sydney Smith once spoke of a
form of capital punishment in which the victim
was to be "preached to death by wild curates."   If
the above description of Mr Gilbert Anderson's
sermons be true, he certainly was eminently qualified
to officiate as one of the executioners in carrying
out such a death sentence.[3]

[1] That Sir Thomas Urquhart is not exaggerating matters in
speaking of such injunctions being given by ecclesiastical authorities, is proved by the following well-known passage in the memoir
prefixed to the *Works* of Archbishop Leighton :—"It was a
Question asked at [of] the Brethren, both in the classical and pro-
vincial Meetings of Ministers, twice in the Year, If they preached
the Duties of the Times?   And when it was found that *Mr
Leighton* did not, he was quarrelled [*sic*] for this Omission, but
said, *If all the Brethren have preached to the* Times, *may not one
poor Brother be suffered to preach on* Eternity ?"

[2] *Works,* p. 280.

[3] The notice given us by Sir Thomas of Mr Anderson's preaching
makes us desirous of knowing more about him ; but, unfortunately,
only a very few facts concerning him are known.   He was born in
1597 ; he graduated at Aberdeen in 1618 ; was settled at Cawdor,
near Nairn, some time before 30th October, 1627 ; was transferred
to Cromartie between 5th October, 1641, and 11th January, 1642 ;
died in November, 1655, and was succeeded in the benefice by his
son Hugh (Scott's *Fasti*).

But though Sir Thomas Urquhart was a Royalist
in politics, and an Episcopalian in religion, he was
certainly no bigot in his devotion to the King or
the Church.   In a passage in *The Jewel*, he plainly
declares his belief " that there is no government,
whether ecclesiastical or civil, upon earth that is
jure divino, if that divine right be taken in a sense
secluding all other forms of government, save it
alone, from the privilege of that title." [1]   Indeed,
he treats such an idea as merely a pious fraud,
by which despotism is established and maintained
at a very cheap rate over tender consciences by
threatening them with the vengeance of Heaven in
case of disobedience.   Such a man was not likely to
be a blind partisan of any cause.   Differences in
religious beliefs and practices he attributed to
differences of temperament among individuals, and
to climatic and national peculiarities ; and in no
obscure terms he hints that he was of the opinion
of Tamerlane, " who believed that God was best
pleased with diversity of religions, variety of worship, dissentaneousness of faith, and multiformity
of devotion." [2]   However powerfully such opinions
may appeal to a certain class of minds, it is hard to
conceive of their being associated with deep religious
feeling ; and accordingly we can scarcely be wrong
in concluding that one of the reasons why Sir
Thomas Urquhart held aloof from the Covenanting
movement was that he was at the antipodes to
the majority of his fellow-countrymen in the matter
of religious belief.   A certain measure of aversion,

[1] *Works*, p. 276.   [2] *Ibid.* p. 261.

suspicion, and horror is still manifested by many
towards those whose creed is supposed to be of too
limited and negative a character ; and we can easily
believe that in the middle of the seventeenth
century this attitude was taken up even more
openly and emphatically.   On a later occasion,
when, as we shall relate, Sir Thomas Urquhart
applied to the Commission of the General Assembly
to pardon his having taken part in the capture of
Inverness, his case was referred to the minister of
that town, Mr John Annand, " that he might confer
with him [Sir Thomas] concerning some dangerous
opinions, which, as is informed, he hes sometimes
vented. " [1]   In the view of the Commission of
Assembly the guilt of cherishing " dangerous
opinions " was as great as that of rekindling the
flames of civil war, if, indeed, it did not surpass it.

[1] See p. 83.

CHAPTER III

SHORTLY after the news of the execution
of Charles I. reached Scotland, a rising
on the part of some of the leading
Cavaliers in the north took place, with
the view of restoring the Royal Family.
The most prominent person in this attempt was
Thomas Mackenzie of Pluscardine, a younger brother
of George, the second Earl of Seaforth, who for nearly
ten years past had managed the affairs of the family,
and was looked up to, both on account of his ability
and also on account of the great territorial influence
he represented. He had seen a good deal of service
abroad, and was at one time governor of Stralsund.[1]
Along with him, and only second to him, was our
Sir Thomas Urquhart, to whom even civil war was
scarcely more fraught with anxiety and danger
than was the life he had been forced to lead for

[1] *Antiquarian Notes*, by C. Fraser-Mackintosh, p. 156.

some time past. Together with them were associated eight other Royalists of good standing,—among whom Colonel Hugh Fraser of Belladrum and John Munro of Lemlair had a certain preeminence,— and these ten formed a kind of revolutionary committee for the control of the movement they had set on foot, and the government of the district that might become subject to them.

Montrose had determined, on hearing of the execution of the King, to renew the war in Scotland, but Pluscardine and his associates did not wait for his arrival. Charles was beheaded on Tuesday, the 30th of January, 1649, and, by the 22nd of the next month, the Scottish gentlemen in the north had already taken the field, and captured Inverness. Four days after, on Monday, 26th February, a meeting of the Committee of War was held in that town, the minutes of which are still in existence,[1] and contain the name of our author next in order to that of Pluscardine himself.

The Committee passed certain enactments, by which they took into their own hands the customs and excise of the six northern counties—Inverness, Sutherland, Cromartie, Caithness, Nairn, and Elgin. An inventory of all the ammunition of the garrison was ordered to be taken. It was also decided that Sir Thomas's house at Cromartie should be put in a state of defence, and that the work should be

[1] *Antiquarian Notes*, pp. 155-158; *History of the Clan Mackenzie*, by Alex. Mackenzie.

carried out by the tenants of Sir James Fraser, a
bitter Parliamentarian, and opponent of the Stuarts
in the north, and by those of our knight's old
enemy, Lesley of Findrassie.[1] It is easy for un-
regenerate human nature to understand the pleasure
with which the members of the Committee of War
would give this last order. By another enactment, the
Committee declare that they consider it expedient
for their safety that the works and forts of Inverness be demolished and levelled with the ground,
and they ordain that each person appointed to this
work should complete his proportion of it before
eight days have passed, " under pain of being
quartered upon and until the said task be performed."

On the 2nd of March, Mackenzie of Pluscardine, Sir Thomas Urquhart, and their associates,
were proclaimed as rebels and traitors by the
Estates of Parliament,[2]—as " wicked and malignant
persouns intending so far as in thame lyes, for

---

[1] The enactment in question runs as follows :—"It being
thought expedient by the said Committee that the house of
Cromartie be put in a posture of defence, and that for the doing
thereof it is requisite some faill [turf] be cast and led, the said
Committee ordains all Sir James Fraser's tenants within the
parochins [parishes] of Cromartie and Cullicudden, together with
those of the Laird of Findrassie, within the parochin of Rosemarkie,
to afford from six hours in the morning to six hours at night, one
horse out of every oxengait [= about 18 Scotch acres] daily
for the space of four days to lead the same faill to the house of
Cromartie." Of this enemy, Sir James Fraser, our author remarked at a later time with regrettable bitterness, that he knew
only one good thing about him, and that was that he was dead.

[2] *Acts of the Parliament of Scotland*, vi. 392.

their own base ends to lay the foundation of a new bloodie and unnaturall warre within the bowells of this their native country," etc. etc.

On the 1st of March the Commissioners of the General Assembly had written to Pluscardine and his associates expressing their wonder and grief at such a rising in the interests of "the Popish, Prelaticall and Malignant party," and threatening the penalty of excommunication within ten days if they would not "desist from and repent of that horrid insurrection." [1] The reply to this letter came in due time, and was signed by the principal leader in the insurrection, and by some other members of the Clan Mackenzie, and is, it must be confessed, a distinctly prevaricating and hypo-critical document. For one sentence at least in it our author was responsible, though he neither signs the letter nor is named in it. His pedantic phraseology reveals his hand in the construction of the reply to the Commissioners' remonstrances and threats.

The letter is addressed " to the Honourable and Right Reverend," and begins as follows :—" Wee have lately received yours of the first of Merch, 1649, for the which and your wisdomes Christian care of ws, and your fatherly admonition to ws, we humbly and heartily rander yow all possible thanks." This lamb-like tone is maintained with admirable gravity all through the epistle, and is combined with a canting phraseology which was meant to be impressive, but which must have

[1] *General Assembly Commission Records*, 1648–49, p. 220.

entertained any members of the Commission of the General Assembly who originally possessed and still retained a sense of humour. "And quheras [whereas]," so it goes on, "your wisdomes taks it a matter of no lesse wonder then [than] greife that we, being vnder the oath of God and tye of our Nationall Covenant, would make insurrection and take armes against the Lords people, certainly, if it were so, we acknowledge your wisdomes had reason to wonder and to be grieved. And it is no lesse winder and griefe to ws, being wnder the said oath and tye of Covenant, furthering the same with all our power and meanes, and at all occasions desireing nothing els then [than] the enjoying of the liberty of the subject, and proprietie of our goods, intended and promised in and by our Covenant." No one who has read any of Sir Thomas Urquhart's original works can doubt that the next sentence was either composed or revised by him. The two phrases which we have taken the liberty of putting into italics could scarcely have occurred to any other member of the Committee of War. "Yet we find, that evill willers and envyous vnder-miners, *in a singular and prœtextuous way* aiming at our ruine, doe spend *the quintessence of their witts* to find out means whereby, under specious pretences of the publick [good?] to extermine ws with povertie, and by inventing fresh occasions to make ws odious, and bring ws vpon fresh stages [*sic*] vnder the base name of Malignancy." It is unnecessary to quote the whole of the letter, but a couple of sentences, which describe what the insurgents had done at Inverness, deserve notice. "But the whole countrey of all degrees, being sensible of the oppression and insolency of the vnnecessary and vnprofitable garison of Innernes to Church or State, did heartily and vnanimously contribute to the demolishing thereof, which being done, all disbanded peaceablie, and the people retired peaceablie to their owne homes, without offence to any nighbour of any degree or condition. . . . And now, when the said garison is dismantled, we shall be found not only disposed to live peaceablie, bot also ready to obey all publick ordours for the good of the Kingdome." The writers ask that "the taxes and impositions," which pressed with special severity on the class to which they belonged, should be remitted, and liberty given them to lead that religious, peaceful life, to which both by nature and by deliberate choice, they seem to say, they were strongly inclined. The sting of the letter is in its closing words. If these "evill willers" succeed in persuading the Commissioners of Assembly to go on with the sentence of excommunication, as fully deserved, they (the writers) formally appeal against such a decision from the Commission to the next General Assembly.[1]

The ecclesiastical court to which the above letter was sent *may* have contained a goodly sprinkling of fanatics, but it is certain that in it there were but few, if any, imbeciles ; so that the communication from the Committee of War did not succeed in imposing upon those to whom its contents were

[1] *General Assembly Commission Records*, 1648–49, pp. 249, 250.

read. They did not condescend to answer it, but at once issued a pamphlet, entitled *A Declaration and Warning to all Members of this Kirk*, "to recover, if possible, the disturbers of the peace of God's people out of the snare of Sathan, and to prevent others from falling therein." The document displays very genuine indignation and dismay at the possibility of the negotiations which were being carried on for restoring Charles II. as a "covenanted king" to the throne of his ancestors, being defeated, and of his coming back as an arbitrary ruler and oppressor of the Church. Those who have any doubt about the deterioration of both religion and politics when they are fused together, should read this and other State Papers of the period, and their eyes would be opened. The calm assumption by the writers that political opponents are the enemies of God, the claim to knowledge of the Divine purposes and counsels, the free use of the most sacred words of Scripture, the dark fanaticism which inspires so many of the utterances, and the intense passion which makes so many of them sound like mere raving—all combine to make these documents very painful reading. A circular letter of warning and exhortation was sent to Presbyteries, attempts were made to persuade individuals to disconnect themselves from the insurrectionary movement, and a message of encouragement was sent to Lieutenant-General David Lesley to strengthen his hands in the work of putting it down by fire and sword.[1]

[1] *General Assembly Commission Records*, 1648–49, pp. 252–262.

The insurgents, after demolishing the fortifications of Inverness, retired before the troops sent
to suppress them, and took refuge among the
mountains of Ross-shire.   Lesley advanced to Fortrose and garrisoned the castle there, and then
proceeded to endeavour to make terms with the
leaders of the insurrection.   The only one who
would listen to no accommodation was Mackenzie
of Pluscardine.   Immediately on Lesley's return
south, he descended from the mountains, and attacked and took the castle of Chanonry.   Our Sir
Thomas Urquhart was now safely out of the conflict; but our readers may wish to know what
became of the insurrectionary movement which he
had such a large share in setting on foot, and from
which he found it prudent to retire at an early stage.

Mackenzie's force was brought up to eight or
nine hundred men by the accession of his nephew,
Lord Reay, with three hundred followers.   Soon
afterwards he was joined by General Middleton and
Lord Ogilvie, and advanced into Badenoch, with the
view of raising the people in that and the neighbouring districts.   In what is called the Wardlaw
MS. a very vivid picture is given of the behaviour
of the Highlanders from the Reay country, when
they poured into Inverness on the morning of
Sunday, the 2nd of May, 1649.   "They crossed
the bridge of Ness," says the Royalist minister of
Kirkhill, "on the Lord's Day in time of divine
service, and alarmed the people of Inverness, im-
peding God's worship in the town.   For instead of
bells to ring in to service I saw and heard no other

than the noise of pipes, drums, pots, pans, kettles, and spits in the streets to provide them victuals in every house. And in their quarters the rude rascality would eat no meat at their tables until the landlord laid down a shilling Scots upon each trencher,[1] calling this '*airgiod cagainn*' (chewing-money), which every soldier got, so insolent were they."

The campaign was a very brief one. The Royalists, joined by the Marquis of Huntly, attacked and took the castle of Ruthven, but, soon after, being hardly pressed by Lesley, they turned southwards and took up their quarters in Balvenie Castle. General Middleton and Mackenzie were despatched to treat with Lesley, but before they reached their destination, the troops from Fortrose, after a rapid march, surprised the Royalist forces at Balvenie. A fierce engagement took place, in which both sides suffered severely.[2] Eighty of the

---

[1] Strangely enough, in Hope's *Anastasius*, a Tatar messenger travelling through Asia Minor to Constantinople is described as acting in the same insolent manner. "He would not," says Anastasius, "even after the daintiest meal in the world, forego the douceur he expected for what he used to call the wear and tear of his teeth" (ii. 320).

[2] An account of the battle is given in a letter addressed by the victorious generals, Ker, Halket, and Strachan, to the Moderator of the Commission of Assembly, dated 9th May, 1649. In it they say : "We were in Innernes vpon Sunday at night, when we received intelligence that the enemie were come from Torespay to Balvine, presently to discusse ws (*sic*). We could not hear from the Livetennent-Generall [Lesley], and the enemy was making himselfe strong in many severall quarters in [the] countrie. We conceived it better to suppresse nor [than] to be suppressed. We in our weak maner beged the Lords direction, that His blissing might wait His owne and our labours, and, with great freedome

insurgents fell in defence of the castle. The Highlanders were dismissed to their homes on swearing
never again to take up arms against the Parliament;
while their leaders were sent as prisoners to Edinburgh, where most of them were set free soon
after, on payment of fines, and on giving security
that they would keep the peace. By sharp and
vigorous action the remain˙ ⸴ sparks of insurrection
in the north were stamped out, and fresh bodies of
troops were stationed in the principal strongholds
of that part of the country. Thus ended a rising
which would probably have had a very different
result, if it had been postponed until the arrival of
Montrose.

The same writer [1] who gave an account of the
riotous and insolent demeanour of the Highland
soldiers in Inverness, furnishes us with a companion-

concluded to march with all expedition to Torispay, intelligence
having come certaine that they were lyeing in Balveine at a wood,
where we engaged with them ; and there the Lord delivered them
vnto our hands. We were not abone six score fighting horsemen
and tuelfe muskiteires. We had some more, but they were
wearied. We have at this tyme about 800 prisoners, betuixt
3 or 4 scoir killed, and tuo or thrie hundred fled. My Lord
Rae and all the officers are, according to the capitulatioun,
prisoners ; the rest are to be conveyed to their countrey, after we
receive order from the publick ; and therefore we shall expect such
further directions from you as you shall thinke fit, for securing
and obliging, by oath, such as shall returne to their countrey "
(*General Assembly Commission Records*, 1648–49, p. 263). There is a
genuine Cromwellian ring about the phrases "beged the Lord's
direction," and "the Lord delivered them vnto our hands," which
we cannot help admiring ; and there is a beauty of its own in the
phrase "with great freedome" in the connection in which it
stands.

[1] Wardlaw MS.

picture—that of them on their way back to their homes after their defeat at Balvenie. It is as follows :—" Next twenty horse, and three companies of foot, were ordered to convey the captives back over the Spey, and through Moray to Inverness, where I saw them pass through ; and those men who, in their former march, would hardly eat their meat without money, are now begging food, and, like dogs, lap the water which was brought them in tubs and other vessels in the open streets. Thence they were conducted over the bridge of Ness, and dismissed everyone armless and harmless to his own house. This is a matter of fact which I saw and heard."

The profound feelings of anxiety which this abortive attempt at insurrection had excited in the minds of the ecclesiastical rulers of Scotland are very clearly indicated by the exuberance of joy with which the tidings of the victory at Balvenie were received by the Commission of Assembly.[1] They instantly decided to appoint a solemn Day of Thanksgiving, on the 25th of May, for " the Lord's mercifull defeat of the enemies of the peace of this land."[2] They tacked on a postscript to the above-

[1] The Commission of the General Assembly is each year nominated by that body, and is responsible to it, and is empowered to dispose of all items of business remitted to it, and to act in the interests of the Church during the months between the meeting of the Assembly which nominated them, and that to which they report their proceedings. They are authorised to meet on certain specific days, and oftener, when and where they think fit. The next General Assembly may reverse their sentences, if they have exceeded their powers, or have acted in any way which is considered prejudicial to the interests of the Church.

[2] *General Assembly Records*, 1648-49, p. 264.

mentioned *Declaration and Warning*, containing a statement of the causes of the Thanksgiving, and ordered both to be read from all the pulpits in Scotland. Letters of congratulation were despatched to the victorious officers, and to others who had been faithful in the recent crisis, and full particulars of what had taken place were sent to the Commissioners of Scotland at the Hague, who were engaged in the negotiations with "the young man, Charles Stuart." In the last-mentioned document there is a flicker of grim humour, as the writers send intelligence of the destruction of the hopes which news of the rebellion might have excited in the minds of Charles and his friends. The last sentence in the letter can scarcely have been written or read without a smile. "We have appointed," they say, "the twenty-fift day of Maij for a solemn thanksgiving for this and other late mercies, wherewith we thought good to acquaint yow, that yow manage this to the best advantage of the work in your hands, according as yow shall thinke fitt." [1] It was once said of a good man that he would have been better if he had had a little more of the devil in him ; and one is inclined to think more highly of these good men for the touch of malice, which relieves the sombre character of their communication.[2]

[1] *General Assembly Records*, 1648–49, p. 270. The instructions given to the Commissioners suggest the process known to us in modern times as "rubbing it in" (the phrase is a technical one).

[2] In March of the following year, 1650, occurred the descent of Montrose on the north of Scotland, which ended so disastrously for him. After spending a few weeks in the Orkneys, where he collected a few recruits, he landed in Caithness, and proceeded

The threatened bolt of excommunication was not launched, but our author found it necessary to apply to the Commission of General Assembly in order to make his peace with the ecclesiastical power. Accordingly, on the 22nd of June, 1650, he appeared in Edinburgh before this body, and presented his " supplicatioun " for pardon for the guilt of taking part in the Northern insurrection, and of assaulting and razing the walls of Inverness.

The Commission met, doubtless, in that " little roome of [off] the East Church " of St Giles, which Baillie describes as having been " verie handsomelie dressed for our Assemblies in all time coming,"[1] and from which, three years later, the English officers, under Cromwell's order, ejected the members of the General Assembly. The Commission on that day, when our author appeared before them, consisted of twenty-four members—the most distinguished divines and politicians in Scotland of the Covenanting party. The moderator, or chairman, was Robert Douglas,[2] " a great State preacher,"

into Sutherland, where he suffered a crushing defeat at the hands of Strachan and Halket, the generals who had successfully suppressed the insurrection in the north in the previous year. Montrose was taken prisoner, and was executed in Edinburgh, on Tuesday, 21st May, 1650.

[1] Baillie's *Letters* (Edinburgh, 1841), ii. 84.

[2] Robert Douglas (1594–1674) had been chaplain to a brigade of Scottish auxiliaries, sent with the connivance of Charles I. to the aid of Gustavus Adolphus, in the Thirty Years' War. He was minister of the second charge of the High Church, Edinburgh, and then of the Tolbooth Church, and was five times Moderator of the General Assembly (1642, 1645, 1647, 1649, and 1651). Wodrow says, "He was a great man for both great wit, and grace,

6

who had been chaplain to the Scots troops in the service of Gustavus Adolphus, and had won the esteem of that monarch, and who in little more than six months' time would officiate at the coronation of Charles II., for whom Sir Thomas Urquhart had prematurely drawn the sword. Beside him was Samuel Rutherford, the Principal of St Andrews, whose fervid piety has found no lack of admirers in every generation since his time. Robert Baillie, the writer of the *Letters* which contain so many vivid pictures of events in that stirring period; David Dickson, Professor of Divinity in Glasgow, whose name we have heard as one of the deputation to persuade the people of Aberdeen to take the Covenant ; and James Guthrie, who died as a martyr, the year after the Restoration, were present there that day. The contrast between these grave, dignified, saintly Covenanting leaders, and the brilliant Cavalier, Sir Thomas Urquhart, is one which, by its picturesqueness, strongly impresses the imagination.

The Commission, after hearing the petitioner's statements, did not, apparently; treat the matter as of very serious moment. The dangerous crisis was over, and they could afford to be merciful. They seem to have condoned the political offence, but referred Sir Thomas to Mr John Annand, minister of Inverness, one of their number, " that he might

and more than ordinary boldness and authority and awful majesty appearing in his very carriage and countenance." Burnet affirms that he had " much wisdom and thoughtfulness, but was very silent and of vast pride " (*Dictionary of Nat. Biog.* xv. 347).

confer with him concerning some dangerous opinions which, as was informed, he had sometimes vented." If these could be explained away, and no further complicity in disloyal schemes were brought home to him, Mr Annand was empowered, acting at all times under the advice of the Presbytery of Inverness, to receive his public " satisfaction " in the church of that city. How the matter ended we do not know. But there is very little doubt that Sir Thomas's nebulous heterodoxy proved no bar to his being freed from ecclesiastical censure, and that, in due course, according to the custom of that time, he stood, as a penitent, before the congregation of the Parish Church, in that city the walls of which he had assisted to assault and over-throw.

A fortnight after Sir Thomas Urquhart's appearance before the Commission of the General Assembly, Charles II. landed in Scotland, and was accepted, though at first not without deep mis-givings, as " covenanted King." The party to which our author belonged was for a time excluded from all share in public life : and even the army, which was to defend the sovereign against the English sectaries, was carefully sifted, to remove those whose presence might bring a curse upon it. So that, though the land resounded with war and the rumour of war, Sir Thomas remained in an enforced quietude in his castle at Cromartie. The effect of the battle of Dunbar (3rd September) was to depress the faction which had excluded the Royalist partisans from the army, and kept the King himself in something very like bondage. Charles II., indeed, is said to have given thanks to God for the victory of Cromwell over the Covenanting forces at this battle, and the only difficulty in the way of believing this statement lies in the fact that he so seldom gave thanks for anything.

The Royalist party now began to rally about their sovereign. Charles II. was crowned at Scone on the 1st January, 1651, and in due time an army, which included many of the so-called Malignants, was ready for trying conclusions once again with the terrible English General. And now for the third time our author took up arms on behalf of the Stuarts. After some months of endless marchings and counter-marchings, in which Cromwell evidently endeavoured to provoke his enemies into a repetition of the blunder by which they had lost the battle of Dunbar, the Scottish forces found an opportunity of marching into England.

The latter, under David Lesley, had taken up a strong position on the height of the Tor Wood, between Stirling and Falkirk, from which they refused to be drawn out to battle; and Cromwell resolved to take up his post on the other side of the Royalist army. Accordingly, he crossed the Forth at Queensferry, and, after defeating an attempt to intercept him at Inverkeithing, reached and occupied Perth. The way to England was now open, and the Scottish army swiftly and silently entered upon it, resolved to stake everything upon a great battle.

Sir Thomas Urquhart left his castle of Cromartie, and took part in this expedition, though apparently he held no position of command in the army, and was very much out of sympathy with many of those who journeyed with him. Indeed, his unfortunate prejudices against the Presbyterian and Covenanting party come out in the statement he makes, that many of those who started out to smite "the Midianites and Philistines," when it came to the push, managed to make their way home, "being loth to hazard their precious persons, lest they should seem to trust to the arm of flesh."[1] The mass of those, however, who formed the Scottish army were of very different mettle, and the battle in which they staked and lost everything was one of the fiercest in the whole of the great Civil War.

The course of their journey southward was through Biggar and Carlisle, and then through Lancashire. To their disappointment, they received no great accession of Royalists, nor of any others who were inclined to join them in the attempt to overthrow the Commonwealth. "They marched," says the historian, "under rigorous discipline, weary and uncheered, south through Lancashire; had to dispute . . . the Bridge of Warrington with Lambert and Harrison, who attended them with horse - troops on the left; Cromwell with the main army steadily advancing behind. They carried the Bridge at Warrington; they summoned various Towns, but none yielded;

[1] *Works,* p. 279.

proclaimed their King, with all force of lungs and heraldry, but none cried, God bless him. Summoning Shrewsbury, with the usual negative response, they quitted the London road; bent southward towards Worcester, a City of slight Garrison and loyal Mayor; there to entrench themselves, and repose a little." [1] Yet but slight opportunity for this was given them. The course taken by Cromwell was through York, Nottingham, Coventry, and Stratford-on-Avon, and when he arrived at Worcester with his army from Scotland, and with the county militias, who had risen at his summons, his forces numbered over thirty thousand men as against the enemy's sixteen thousand.

Meantime Sir Thomas Urquhart had taken up his quarters in Worcester, in the house of a Mr Spilsbury, " a very honest sort of man, who had an exceeding good woman to his wife." His luggage, which was stored in an attic, consisted, besides " scarlet cloaks, buff suits, and arms of all sorts," of seven large " portmantles," three of which were filled with unpublished works in manuscript, and other valuable documents—the amount of which he gives us in quires and quinternions, but which need not be repeated here. " Peace hath her victories no less renowned than war," sang Milton in his sonnet to the Lord General Cromwell; and perhaps Sir Thomas Urquhart hoped, after achieving victory in war, to win a second set of laurels by means of the contents of the three " portmantles."

[1] Carlyle's *Oliver Cromwell*, iii. 148.

On the evening of the 3rd September, the anniversary of the battle of Dunbar, and afterwards to be the date of Cromwell's own death, the battle of Worcester was fought, and the Royalist cause utterly shattered. "The fighting of the Scots," says Carlyle, "was fierce and desperate. ' My Lord General did exceedingly hazard himself, riding up and down in the midst of the fire; riding, himself in person, to the Enemy's foot to offer them quarter, whereto they returned no answer but shot.' The small Scotch Army, begirdled with overpowering force, and cut off from help or reasonable hope, storms forth in fiery pulses, horse and foot; charges now on this side of the River, now on that;—can on no side prevail. Cromwell recoils a little, but only to rally and return irresistible. The small Scotch Army is, on every side, driven in again. Its fiery pulsings are but the struggles of death : agonies as of a lion coiled in the folds of a boa. ' As stiff a contest,' says Cromwell, ' for four or five hours as ever I have seen.' " [1]

The conquered lost six thousand men, and all their baggage and artillery; and Charles only with difficulty, and after many romantic adventures, succeeded in escaping to the Continent when the fight was over. Ten thousand prisoners, including eleven of the Scottish nobility, were taken. The sufferings of many of these brave men were severe in the extreme. Some perished from want of food and from gaol diseases, and large numbers of the survivors were shipped for the plantations, and sold as slaves.

[1] Carlyle's *Oliver Cromwell*, iii. 154.

Sir Thomas Urquhart, and, apparently, more than
one of his brothers, were among the prisoners, but
appeared to have fared better than many of their
companions in arms.   The greatest of the misfortunes that fell upon him was, in his estimation, the
sad fate that overtook his precious manuscripts.
The whole story, related in his own inimitable
style, may be read in Chapter vi.   It is enough to
say here that a party of marauders broke into his
quarters in search of valuables, that they forced
open the "portmantles" and turned their contents
out upon the floor, and afterwards carried off the
papers to use them for wrapping up articles of
plunder, and for lighting their pipes.   Fortunately
some bundles of these papers were afterwards picked
up in the streets and brought back to him, and in
due time found their way to the printer's.

After the battle of Worcester, Sir Thomas
Urquhart and some of the other Scottish gentlemen
who had been taken prisoners there were confined
in the Tower of London.   He seems to have
speedily gained the favour of his captors, and to
have been treated with remarkable leniency.   Indeed,
he speaks in terms of affectionate respect of various
officers of the Parliamentary army from whom he
had received kindness, and acknowledges courtesies
extended towards him by the Lord General himself.
Thus he places on record his indebtedness to a
"most generous gentleman, Captain Gladmon," for
speaking in his favour to the Protector.   And of
another, whom he calls the Marshal-General, in
whose charge he had been placed, he has set down

the praise in the following elaborate sentence:—
" The kindly usage of the Marshal - General,
Captain Alsop, whilst I was in his custody, I am
bound in duty so to acknowledge, that I may
without dissimulation avouch, for courtesies conferred on such as were within the verge of his
authority, and fidelity to those by whom he was
intrusted with their tuition [oversight of them] in
that restraint, that never any could by his faithful-
ness to the one and loving carriage to the other
bespeak himself more a gentleman, nor in the
discharge of that military place acquit himself
with a more universally-deserved applause and
commendation." [1]

The severity of his imprisonment was soon abated ;
and he was removed from the Tower to Windsor
Castle,[2] and not long after, by the orders of Cromwell, was paroled *de die in diem*.[3] The comparative
liberty he now enjoyed enabled him to repair the
loss of his manuscripts after the battle of Worcester,
and he set himself to make the best of the frag-
ments he had recovered, and to prepare them for
publication, as well as to compose new material.
A paragraph in the Epilogue of one of his works,
in which he describes his warm appreciation of
the measure of freedom he now enjoyed, is worth
quoting. " That I, whilst a prisoner," he says,
" was able to digest and write this Treatise, is an
effect meerly proceeding from the courtesie of my
Lord General Cromwel, by whose recommendation
to the Councel of State my parole being taken for

[1] *Works*, p. 408.   [2] *Cal. State Papers, Dom.*   [3] *Ibid.*

my true imprisonment, I was by their favour enlarged to the extent of the lincs of London's communication; for had I continued as before, coopt up within walls, or yet been attended still by a guard, as for a while I was, should the house of my confinement have never been so pleasant, or my keepers a very paragon of discretion, and that the conversation of the best wits in the world, with affluence of all manner of books, should have been allowed me for the diversion of my minde, yet such an antipathie I have to any kinde of restraint wherein myself is not entrusted, that notwithstanding these advantages, which to some spirits would make a jayl seem more delicious then [than] freedom without them, it could not in that eclipse of liberty lie in my power to frame myself to the couching of one sillable, or contriving of a fancie worthy the labour of putting pen to paper, no more then [than] a nightingale can warble it in a cage, or linet in a dungeon." [1]

Another friend whom Sir Thomas Urquhart found in the time of need was the celebrated Roger Williams, the apostle of civil and religious liberty, and the founder of the settlement of Providence, Rhode Island, and missionary to the Indians. In the Epilogue to the *Logopandecteision* he thus acknowledges his obligations to him : " [I cannot] forget my thankfulness to that reverend preacher Mr Roger Williams of Providence, in New England, for the manifold favours wherein I stood obliged to him above a whole month before

[1] *Works*, p. 408.

either of us had so much as seen other, and that by his frequent and earnest solicitation in my behalf of the most especial members both of the Parliament and Councel of State; in doing whereof he appeared so truely generous, that when it was told him how I, having got notice of his so undeserved respect towards me, was desirous to embrace some sudden opportunity whereby to testifie the affection I did owe him, he purposely delayed the occasion of meeting with me till he had, as he said, performed some acceptable office worthy of my acquaintance; in all which, both before and after we had conversed with one another, and by those many worthy books set forth by him, to the advancement of piety and good order, with some whereof he was pleased to present me, he did prove himself a man of such discretion and inimitably-sanctified parts, that an Archangel from heaven could not have shown more goodness with less ostentation." [1]

[1] *Works,* p. 419. Roger Williams (c. 1600–c. 1684) was himself a remarkable man. He was a native of Wales, was educated at Oxford, and entered into holy orders; but his aversion to the government and discipline of the Church of England led him to seek for greater freedom in America. He was a strenuous asserter of religious toleration at a time when it was little understood and less practised anywhere. His liberty of thinking and speaking led to his being banished from Massachusetts; and, thereupon, he purchased a tract of land from the Indians, and founded a settlement, which he named Providence. At the time when he generously interceded in favour of Sir Thomas Urquhart, he was residing in London as the agent of the new settlement, of which he was afterwards chosen president. He was on intimate terms with Cromwell, Milton, and other leading Puritans, and consequently would be in a position to render great service to his friend Urquhart.

The years 1652 and 1653 form a period of astonishing literary activity on the part of our author, for no fewer than five separate works were then published by him, two of which were of very considerable bulk. The motive that had led him to bring out his two former works—the *Epigrams* and *The Trissotetras*—had been a desire to benefit mankind and to advance the glory of his native land. But now he had to consider his own interests, and to exert himself to promote them. Accordingly, his present aim was to convince his captors of his extraordinary merits and gifts, and of the incomparable glory of that family which he had the honour of representing.

In 1652 he issued his **ΠΑΝΤΟΧΡΟΝΟ- ΧΑΝΟΝ**; *or, a Peculiar Promptuary of Time*, of which a detailed description is given in Chapter v. The object of this treatise is to show the Protector and the English Parliament that the family of the Urquharts could be traced back, link by link, to the red earth out of which Adam was made, and to suggest how lamentable it would be, if the ruling power extinguished a race which had successfully resisted the scythe of Time, and was capable of rendering great services to the State.

This small treatise was closely followed by a more important production, upon which Sir Thomas's fame as an author largely rests—his **ΕΚΣΚΥΒΑ- ΛΑΥΡΟΝ**; *or, The Discovery of a most Exquisite Jewel*. The title of this work is intended to be an abbreviation of a Greek phrase—"*Gold from a dunghill*"—and contains an allusion to the fact that the first half of it was, in its manuscript form, one of the bundles of paper which the soldiers treated with such disrespect after the battle of Worcester, and which, indeed, was found next day in a kennel of one of the streets of that city. This book, a fuller account of which we give later on, consists of an introduction to a work on a Universal Language, to which is added a rhapsodical panegyric on the Scottish nation, and an account of his fellow-countrymen who had been famous as scholars or soldiers during the previous fifty years.

In the course of the early part of 1652 Urquhart had in some way excited the suspicions of the Government, and in the month of May his papers were seized by the authorities. Nothing treasonable, however, was found among them, and probably the harmless character of his pursuits, which was thus brought to light, made a favourable impression upon the Council of State. For, a few weeks later, he was allowed, in answer to a petition which he presented to the Council, and which was referred to Cromwell, to return to Scotland to arrange his private affairs, and to be absent for five months.[1] The only condition imposed upon him was that during this time he should do nothing to the prejudice of the Commonwealth.

Sir Thomas Urquhart's creditors had been told

---

[1] The leave granted was for five months from the 14th of July, 1652. Before the expiration of this time, Sir Thomas asked for liberty to stay for six weeks longer in Scotland, and this was granted (*Acts of Parliament*, vol. vi. pt. 2, p. 748*b*).

that he had been killed at the battle of Worcester, and, as he says in his own characteristic way, "for gladness of the tidings [they] had madified [moistened] their nolls to some purpose with the liquor of the grape,"[1] and had possessed themselves of all his property.   When they were assured by letters from himself that he was still alive, they claimed payment for debts which had been long discharged, under the impression that the receipts had perished along with other papers after the battle.   They even plotted, we are assured, to arrest our author in London, after he had been liberated upon parole.   By the thoughtful discretion of a Captain Goodwin, of Colonel Pride's regiment, the receipts in question had been saved out of the spoil of Worcester, and Sir Thomas Urquhart was able to display them to the unjust creditors.   "And when," he says, "they saw that those their acquittances . . . were produced before them, they then, looking as if their noses had been ableeding, could not any longer for shame retard my cancelling of the aforesaid bonds."[2]

In the midst of so many complaints of the iniquity of creditors, it is gratifying to find Sir Thomas acknowledging that there was one of that class who treated him with forbearance and even with kindness.   His thankfulness at discovering this green oasis in the arid desert in which so much of his life had been passed, is expressed in his own characteristic way.   "But may," he says, " William Robertson of Kindeasse, or rather *Kindnesse* (for so

[1] *Works*, p. 377.   [2] *Ibid.* p. 378.

they call this worthy man), for his going contrary to that stream of wickedness which carryeth headlong his fellow-creditors to the black sea of unchristian-like dealing, enjoy a long life in this world, attended with health, wealth, a hopeful posterity, and all the happiness conducible to eternal salvation ; and may his children after him, as heires both of his vertues and means, derive [transmit] his lands and riches to their sons, to continue successively in that line from generation to generation, so long as there is a hill in Scotland, or that the sea doth ebbe and flow. This hearty wish of mine, as chief of my kinred [kindred], I bequeath to all that do and are to carry the name of Urquhart, and adjure them, by the respect they owe to the stock whence they are descended, for my father's love and mine to this man, to do all manner of good offices to each one that bears the name of Robertson."[1]

His old enemy, Lesley of Findrassie, endeavoured in vain to persuade the officers of the English garrison, then stationed in Urquhart's house at Cromartie, to arrest him as a prisoner of war, and keep him in confinement "till he [Lesley] were contented in all his demands."[2] An attempt was also made to apprehend him at Elgin ; but he escaped all these machinations, and, after travelling in safety through many of the principal towns of Scotland, returned to London within the specified time, and gave himself up to the Council of State.

[1] *Works*, p. 384.   [2] *Ibid.* p. 380.

In the course of the year 1653 Sir Thomas
Urquhart published the last of his original works
—his *Logopandecteision,* and the translation of the
first two books of Rabelais, in connection with
which his name is best known.   The object of the
former of these was to suggest a wonderful scheme
for a universal language, with the idea of being
restored by the Government to the full possession
of his liberty, and of being reinstated in the position
of power and wealth, which he maintained was his
by hereditary right, in order to carry out the
scheme.   His hopes and anticipations of success in
this appeal to the English Government were not
daunted by the fact that to do what he required
would need several legislative changes, a reversal of
proceedings in Scottish courts of law, and a substantial grant from the Treasury.   This, after all,
he considered, was a very small price to pay for the
benefits he would thereby confer upon the world.
That the appeal was not successful needs scarcely
be told.   Probably in no country in the world,
and at no period in history, could any be found
more likely to turn a deaf ear to such requests,
than such men as Cromwell, Fleetwood, and
Overton.   Men like these were too practical, and
of too hard a nature, to be impressed by any such
visionary schemes as those which their prisoner
delighted in constructing.

A veil of obscurity hangs over the closing years
of our author's life.   His last appearance before
the public was in the issuing of the books above
mentioned.   The only further record of him is in the

continuation of the Pedigree of the Urquharts, which is contained in the Edinburgh edition of his Tracts. In this we read that "he was confined for several years in the Tower of London; from whence he made his escape, and went beyond seas, where he died suddenly in a fit of excessive laughter, on being informed by his servant that the King was restored."[1] If this account of matters be true, it would seem that Sir Thomas had forfeited some of those privileges which he had won so soon after he had become a State prisoner. It is quite possible that this was in consequence of having joined in some Royalist plot against the Commonwealth and for the restoration of Charles II.

In the preface to the second book of Rabelais, Sir Thomas promises very speedily to translate the three remaining books of that author, so that the whole "Pentateuch of Rabelais," as he calls it, might be in the hands of English readers. But this design was never completed. The translation of the third book was found among his papers, and was published in 1693 by Pierre Antoine Motteux, but it is probable that the editor himself had some share in the work as issued to the public.

Sir Theodore Martin considers that there is a strong presumption against the truth of the above account of Sir Thomas's death, in his entire silence during the long period which elapsed between the publication of his last work and 1660, the date of the Restoration of Charles II. "Men," he says, "so deeply smitten with the *cacoëthes scribendi* as Urquhart was, do not thus readily cast the pen

[1] P. 37.

aside ; nor was the lack of a publisher likely to have stood in the way of his literary career.   His writings, if for no other cause but the number of his friends, must always have been a safe specu- lation for a printer, at a time when printing was cheap and readers numerous.   But the imperfect state of his translation of Rabelais is perhaps the best evidence of the inaccuracy of the current belief. . . . Motteux says that Urquhart's version 'was too kindly received not to encourage him to English the three remaining books, or at least the third, the fourth and fifth being in a manner distinct, as being Pantagruel's voyage.   Accordingly he trans- lated the third book, and would have finished the whole, had not death prevented him.'   This bears hard against the supposition of that event having occurred upwards of six years after the two first books had been given to the world.   It is probable that he died much sooner, a victim in all likelihood to that fiery restlessness of spirit,

> 'Which o'er-informs its tenement of clay,
> And frets the pigmy body to decay.'"[1]

This conjecture is, however, improbable.   A petition from our author's brother, Sir Alexander Urquhart, is still in existence, in which he asks for a new commission of hereditary Sheriffship of Cromartie to be made out for him, on the ground of his being the eldest surviving son of the Sir Thomas Urquhart who died in 1642.[2]   Though this document is undated, it is assigned by the editor of the volume of State Papers in which it is

[1] *Rabelais*, p. xiv.   [2] *Cal. State Papers, Domestic*, 1660–61, p. 237.

to be found, to August of 1660.   If this date be trustworthy, we may be almost sure that the traditional statement as to the year of our author's death is correct.

The cause of his giving up his literary labours, and of omitting to carry through the work of translation on which he had entered, is, of course, unknown to us.   His health, physical or mental, may have become seriously impaired, or his spirits may have been too much depressed by the misfortunes that crowded upon him, to allow him to engage in literary work.   Indeed, the alleged cause of death from violent agitation of feeling caused by hearing of the Restoration of Charles II., argues in itself a previous condition of great physical weakness.

There seems at first a certain grotesqueness in such a fatal exuberance of joy in connexion with such an event as Charles II. regaining the crown which his father had lost, and of which in another generation all of his blood were to be deprived. But we have to keep in mind that Sir Thomas was not alone in his folly, if folly it were ; for a great wave of exultation swept over the three kingdoms at that time.   Our author had, like many of his fellow-Royalists, staked and lost everything he possessed in the defence of the House of Stuart, and one can have little difficulty in understanding how the announcement of the triumph of the cause, which was so dear to him, should have agitated him profoundly.[1]

---

[1] In the preface to a new translation of Rabelais by W. F. Smith, Esq., Fellow of St John's College, Cambridge, some doubt is cast upon the above narrative of Sir Thomas's death.   Mr Smith

Sir Alexander Urquhart failed to recover possession of either the barony or the Sheriffship of
Cromartie, and a year after the supposed date of

remarks, "This looks something like an imitation of Rabelais in
his account of the death of Philemon." The reference is to the
following passages in Rabelais, who alludes to the story no fewer
than three times. In Book i. 10, we read: "Just so the heart
with excessive joy is inwardly dilated, and suffereth a manifest
resolution of the vital spirits, which may go so farre on, that it
may thereby be deprived of its nourishment, and by consequence
of life itself, by this Pericharie or extremity of gladnesse, as Galen
saith . . . and as it hath come to passe in former times . . . to
Philemon and others, who died with joy." In chap. xx. some
more particulars are given of the case: "As Philemon, who, for
seeing an asse eate those figs, which were provided for his own
dinner, died with force of laughing." But in Book iv. 17, we are
told the whole story: "[Neither ought you to wonder at] the
death of Philomenes, whose servant, having got him some new
figs for the first course of his dinner, whilst he went to fetch wine,
a straggling . . . ass got into the house, and, seeing the figs on
the table, without further invitation, soberly fell to. Philomenes
coming into the room, and nicely observing with what gravity the
ass eat its dinner, said to his man, who was come back, 'Since
thou hast set figs here for this reverend guest of ours to eat,
methinks it is but reason thou also give him some of this wine to
drink.' He had no sooner said this, but he was so excessively
pleased, and fell into so exorbitant a fit of laughter, that the use
of his spleen took that of his breath utterly away, and he immedi-
ately died." The story is taken from Lucian ($\mu\alpha\kappa\rho\sigma\beta\acute{\iota}o\iota$, c. 25)
or from Valerius Maximus (ix. 12), in which in the Paris folio
edition (1517) the name is given as Philomenes. There is undoubtedly a resemblance between the account of Philemon's death
and that of our author, but we think it can only be accidental.
The editor of the Edinburgh edition of the Tracts is, as I have
said, our only authority for the story of Urquhart's death ; but
there is no adequate reason for doubting it. He seems to have
been well versed in the history of the Urquhart family, which he
brings up to date, and must have derived his information from
some members of it. It would be strange if in little more than a
century after our author's death, an utterly mythical account of it
should have sprung up and found a place among the details of

his petition, he is said to have ratified his cousin's rights,[1] and in 1663 he formally " disponed " the estate (*i.e.* his title to it) to Sir John.[2]   The new

family history.   According to Lowndes's *Bibliographer's Manual*, the editor of the volume was David Herd, the well-known antiquary.   If this statement be correct, we have all the more reason to rely upon the supplementary information the volume contains, as Herd's acquaintance with Scottish history and biography was very extensive and accurate.   In one of the *Noctes Ambrosianæ* (*Blackwood's Magazine*, September, 1832), a highly extravagant version is given of Urquhart's death.   It is intended to be humorous, but is merely flat and silly.   Only those can smile at it who have been trained up to believe that the *Noctes* contain exquisite humour, and who have, therefore, been accustomed to welcome passages from it as mirth-inspiring.   The statement made in this mention of Urquhart, that his death was caused by excessive alcoholic celebration of the happy event of the Restoration, is utterly baseless and offensive ; and it is a pity that in Allibone's *Dictionary* and in the *Dictionary of National Biography* this article in *Blackwood's Magazine* should be referred to as one of the sources of information concerning Urquhart.   The author of it had not access to any other account of Sir Thomas's death than that given in the above-mentioned edition of the Tracts.

[1] *Acts of Parliament*, vii. 70.

[2] *Inverness Sasines*.   The date when Sir Alexander Urquhart received knighthood seems to be approximately fixed by the fact that in a grant under the Privy Seal of 5th March, 1661, he is called Alexander, and in a notice of him of the 29th of the same month and year he appears as Sir Alexander (*Acts of Parliament*, vii. 93). From the fact that in this year the succession to the estates and hereditary Sheriffship of Cromartie were entered upon by his cousin Sir John Urquhart of Craigfintray, it was taken for granted by the editor of the Tracts (Edinburgh, 1774) that Sir Alexander had died. This error is repeated by Hugh Miller, and by most of those who have made any reference to him.   He was still alive in 1667, for during that year he sold his salmon fishings in Over-rak and the King's Water to John Gordon (see also *Acts of Parliament*, vii. 537). He is spoken of as *quondam* in a charter of certain lands which had belonged to him, 19th June, 1668.   His cousin, Sir John Urquhart, received knighthood about the same time ; at least he appears in Parliament as Sir John, 1st January, 1661 (*Acts of Parliament*, vii. 4).

possessors were, however, as unfortunate as their immediate predecessors, for in no very long time they were overwhelmed by distresses like those which had burdened and embittered the lives of our author and his father.   In 1682 the celebrated Sir George Mackenzie, whose name, like that of Queen Mary of England, is usually associated with an unenviable epithet, as that of a cruel persecutor,[1] "apprized" the estate from Sir John's[2] son, Jonathan.[3]

[1] "There was the Bluidy Advocate Mackenyie, who, for his worldly wit and wisdom, had been to the rest as a god" ("Wandering Willie's Tale" *Redgauntlet*, chap. xi.).

[2] There is said to have been some tragedy in connection with the death of this Sir John Urquhart. According to Wodrow, as quoted by Hugh Miller, after having posed as an ultra-Presbyterian, he became the friend and counsellor of the Earl of Middleton, Charles II.'s Commissioner for Scotland, under whom Presbyterianism was overturned and Episcopacy set up in its place (1661). Tradition says that "about eleven years after the passing of the Act, he fell into a deep melancholy, and destroyed himself with his own sword in one of the apartments of the old castle. The sword, it is said, was flung into a neighbouring draw-well by one of the domestics, and the stain left by his blood on the walls and floor of the apartment was distinctly visible at the time the building was pulled down" (*Scenes and Legends of the North of Scotland*, p. 111). Tradition is wrong, however, in saying eleven years after 1661; for on August 7th, 1677, Sir John, along with others, received a commission "for putting the laws against conventicles and other disorders into execution" (*Wodrow*, ii. p. 366).

[3] On the death of Jonathan's son, Colonel James Urquhart, in 1741, the shadowy honour of the headship of the family passed to the Urquharts of Meldrum, who were descended from the Tutor of Cromartie by a third marriage with Elizabeth Seton, only daughter of Alexander Seton of Meldrum, and ultimately heiress of that estate.   The last male representative of this line was Major Beauchamp Colclough Urquhart, who closed a promising career by a heroic death at the battle of Atbara, in the Sudan, on 8th April, 1898.   His sister, Isabel Annie, is wife of Garden Alexander Duff, Esq., Hatton Castle, Turriff.

No one who knows what this means [1] will be surprised to hear that it soon afterwards passed into his possession. On his elevation to the peerage (1685) as Viscount Tarbat, first Earl of Cromartie, he put his third-born son, Sir Kenneth, into possession of the estate, with the view of establishing a branch of his family to be known as the Mackenzies of Cromartie. This plan was doomed to be defeated, for Sir Kenneth's son George had no family, and sold the estate to Captain William Urquhart of Meldrum in 1741.[2] The lands were again sold to Patrick, Lord Elibank,[3] in 1763, and by him to George Ross of Pitkerrie, nine years afterwards. Mr Ross had amassed a large fortune in England as an army agent,[4] and part of this he expended in the purchase of the estate, and in the extensive improvements which he effected in it. One wishes he had not thought it desirable to pull down the picturesque old castle, which had stood on the mote-hill of Cromartie for three hundred years, and which had sheltered so many generations of the

[1] See p. 58.

[2] Pococke, in his *Tour through Scotland* (1761), says of the castle of Cromartie : "It has fallen into the hands of one Mr Urquhart, who had commanded a Spanish Gally, and died a Convert to Popery ; which slip his son, now eighteen years old, has in some degree recovered, by conforming to the Church of England" (p. 176 ; *Scottish History Society*).

[3] In the old Statistical Account of Cromartie, and in the preface to the Maitland Club edition of Urquhart's Works, the estate is said to have passed into the hands of Sir William Pulteney.

[4] Mr Ross is mentioned in the *Letters* of Junius (see those of 29th November and 12th December, 1769). He was succeeded by his nephew, from whom the present proprietor of Cromartie, Major Walter Charteris Ross, is descended.

Urquhart family.   Let us now, however, return to our author.

In telling the story of Sir Thomas Urquhart's life, some of his most striking peculiarities have been displayed and illustrated, so that no one who has read the foregoing pages is altogether dependent upon what may now be said for forming an estimate of his character.   His vanity is perhaps the most striking trait in it; but only a very hard-hearted moralist would call it a vice in his case, for it is as artless as it is boundless, and is combined with so much kindness of heart and generosity of feeling, that we are more entertained by it than indignant at it.   No one who looks into his works can doubt the intensity of his patriotism.   Indeed, his passionate longing after personal fame is in all cases combined with the wish to confer additional glory upon the land of his birth.   His devotion to the Royalist cause [1] is of the purest and most heroic type, and the general tone of his character, as revealed to us in his books, is elevated and noble. At the same time there is an element of the grotesque in it, so that in his disinterested and chivalrous disposition he reminds us of Don Quixote,[2]

[1] Our Sir Thomas's memory should be cherished by defenders of the name and fame of Mary Queen of Scots, for he goes so far as to say that "ignorance, together with hypocrisie, usury, oppression, and iniquity, took root in these parts [Scotland], when uprightness, plain-dealing, and charity, with Astrœa, took their flight with Queen Mary of Scotland into England."   Probably few of her admirers would be so daring as to assert this, though many of them doubtless would be glad to hear the assertion made.

[2] We take the liberty of extracting these few sentences from the letter of a friend, who has taken great interest in the execution of this work :—"Sir Thomas would have been an original character in

while in his frequent allusions to struggles with pecuniary difficulties, as well as in his use of magniloquent language, he distinctly recalls Wilkins Micawber. A lively fancy, a strain of genuine erudition beneath his pedantry, and some sparks of insanity, are other elements in his fantastical character. Only a mind like his own could trace the maze of its windings and turnings, and fathom the depths of its eccentricity. In his thoughts "truth is constantly becoming interfused with fiction, possibility with certainty, and the hyperbolical extravagance of his style only keeps even pace with the prolific shootings of his imagination." [1]

It is perhaps expected that one should, in a measure, apologize for the eccentricities of Urquhart's character and literary style, by explaining that he was a humourist. But, unfortunately, humour is a quality in which Urquhart was lacking, unless we understand by the word mere fantastical quaintness of thought and speech. In one passage of his works he speaks with contempt of "shallow-brained humourists," [2] and we should wrong his ghost by putting him among those whom he abhorred. Not a single trace of that subtle, graceful play of fancy and of feeling which enters into our conception of humour is to be found in his works. [3] His readers may smile as they

almost any surroundings—a kind of literary Quixote, with what may be called a 'parenthetical' genius, branching off at every comma into the fresh images furnished by a teeming imagination. He was more than a translator of Rabelais—he seems to have been a kind of Rabelais himself."

[1] Sir Theodore Martin, *Rabelais*, p. xix.   [2] See p. 28.

[3] A different opinion is expressed in the preface to W. Harrison Ainsworth's capital novel of *Crichton*. "Sir Thomas," he says,

turn over his pages, but he is always in deadly earnest. The quality of wit he occasionally manifests in the form of keen sarcasm, when he gives full vent to his feelings of scorn and contempt; as when, for example, he describes those who went out to fight, "but did not hazard their precious persons, lest they should seem to trust to the arm of flesh." [1]

He can never give a simple statement of matters of fact. Thus in his account of the Admirable Crichton, instead of saying that the rector of the university addressed a few complimentary sentences to Crichton, and that the latter replied in the same vein, he says: "In complements after this manner, *ultro citroque habitis*, tossed to and again, retorted, contrerisposted, backreverted, and now and then graced with a quip or a clinch for the better relish of the ear, being unwilling in this kind of straining curtesie to yeeld to other, they spent a full half-hour and more." [2] Everything must be dressed up "with divers quaint and pertinent similes" before it is fit to be introduced to the reader's notice. To quote again from the most accomplished literary critic who has written upon him: "History, philosophy, science, literature are ransacked for illustrations of the commonest subject. His fancy is ever on the alert, and you are constantly surprised by some incongruous image, begotten in its wanton dalliance

"'is a joyous spirit—a right Pantagruelist; and if he occasionally

'Projicit ampullas et sesquipedalia verba,'

he has an exuberance of wit and playfulness of fancy that amply redeem his tendency to fanfaronade." Our readers have abundance of material before them for coming to a decision upon this question.

[1] See p. 85.   [2] *Works*, p. 226.

with knowledge the most heterogeneous. He has always an eye to effect. His own learning must be brought into play, rhetorical tropes must flourish through his periods, 'suggesting to our minds two several things at once,' and, of course, as diverse as possible, that 'the spirits of such as are studious in learning may be filled with a most wonderful delight.'"[1] His style reacts upon and controls his thoughts, and often carries him, as Ariosto's Hippogriff carried Astolfo, up into the skies, whither those are unable to follow him who are mounted on humbler animals, or have no other means than those with which they were born for plodding along the dusty roads of earth.

If we can trust the two engraved portraits of Sir Thomas Urquhart which have come down to us, he was a man of handsome presence, and accustomed to deck himself in all the splendour of costume to which so many of his brother-cavaliers were addicted. George Glover, the famous engraver, drew both the portraits of him which are extant. One of these appears as a frontispiece to the *Epigrams* and to the *Trissotetras*. It is a small whole-length, and represents Sir Thomas in rich dress,[2] holding out his hand to receive from some

[1] Sir Theodore Martin, *Rabelais*, p. xx.

[2] In Granger's *Biographical Dictionary* (1779), this portrait is described erroneously, as Sir Thomas Urquhart is said in it to be dressed in armour. Probably the description was given from memory. In the second volume of Bohn's edition of *Rabelais*, the frontispiece is a half-length portrait of the translator, evidently reproduced from the above. The effect, however, is highly disagreeable, and the likeness must have produced an unfavourable opinion of our author in the minds of most of those who have looked upon it.

allegorical personage a laurel wreath "for Armes and Artes."[1]   On a table beside him are his hat and embroidered cloak.   In the vacant spaces on each side of the upper part of the figure are his name and titles: "Sr Thomas Urchard, Knight, of Bray and Udol, etc., Baron of Ficherie and Clohorby, etc., Laird Baron of Cromartie and Heritable Sheriff thereof, etc."   The portrait is described as taken from the life, and engraved in 1641 ;[2] and beneath it is a couplet by W. S., as follows:

"Of him whose shape this Picture hath design'd,
Vertue and learning represent the Mind."

Who W. S. was we do not know.   The date forbids our identifying him with the Bard of Avon.   He was probably one of those mysterious personages, who were always at hand to write epistles of commendation to works by Sir Thomas, and to testify on their "book-oath" to his gifts and graces.

The second engraved portrait is of great rarity, and only one impression of it is known to be in

[1] In this engraving, which is our frontispiece, the Greek inscription runs thus: τοῖς σε πέμψασιν καὶ προστάξασιν εὐχαριστῶ, and means, "*I thank those who sent you and gave the order.*" These words are, of course, addressed to the messenger who has been commissioned by the Muses to convey the wreath to Sir Thomas. Above the wreath itself is an obscure phrase—Μουσαρυ[μ] στόλος— which is evidently a mixture of Latin and Greek, *musarum στόλος* (=ἀπόστολος ?), "*messenger of the muses.*" It may, however, be that στόλος is to be taken as "*equipment*" or "*decoration,*" as referring to the wreath. The courage with which Greek and Latin forms are mixed up, and an old word despatched on its way with a new meaning, of which this brief phrase gives evidence, is highly characteristic of Cromartian Greek. For further illustration of the peculiarities of this local variety of Hellenic speech, see p. 149.

[2] Sir Thomas, therefore, claims by anticipation the titles of Baron and Sheriff, which were afterwards to be his.

The Poet surrounded by the Muses.

existence. It was probably meant to be a frontispiece to the unpublished volume of Epigrams
described on p. 116, the title of which was to have
been *Apollo and the Muses*, but which never found
its way into print. In this engraving Sir Thomas
is depicted as seated with great complacency upon
Mount Parnassus, in the midst of the Muses, seven
of whom are pressing upon his attention wreaths of
laurel of which he is worthy, " for Judgment, Learning, witt, Invention, sweetness, stile." At his feet
is the sacred fountain of Castalia or Hippocrene,
into the waters of which the other two Muses are
sportively dipping "sprinklers" or asperges. One
of them seems inclined to give Sir Thomas a
sprinkling, but refrains, either because it was
unnecessary or for fear of spoiling his nice clothes.
In the background, the winged horse Pegasus is
flying sufficiently low down to allow a woman to
pluck a couple of feathers from his wings.[1] These

[1] This use of the quills is referred to in the following passage in
Sir Thomas Urquhart's *Epigrams* (MS.):—

"The Invocation to Clio.

Book 2.

Wench wholly martial, to whose inspiration
The Colophonian Pöet ow'd his skill:
Let my verse merit no Lesse estimation,
Then [than] if the point of a Pegasid quill,
    Dip'd in the sacred fontain Caballine,
    Character'd the Impression of each Line."

The "Colophonian Pöet" is—"not to put too fine a point upon it"
—Homer, who, according to some, was born at Colophos, in Asia
Minor. The phrase "Pegasid quill" in this passage strengthens
our opinion that this second portrait of Sir Thomas, which we give
here, was intended to be a frontispiece to a second volume of
poems. The similarity of diction between this "Invocation" and
the speeches of Ancient Pistol is very great.

are no doubt intended to provide pens for Sir Thomas's next literary undertaking.   In the further distance are several feathered creatures, which are probably meant for poetical swans, but which bear a painful likeness to prosaic geese.   At the foot of the picture in one corner we have Apollo, playing on his lyre; and on the ground in front are a half-starved dragon and a snake, writhing in impotent rage, as they witness the triumph of Sir Thomas. We can hardly be mistaken in concluding that these last are symbolical representations of envious and carping critics.

CHAPTER IV

EPIGRAMS: DIVINE AND MORAL, AND THE TRISSOTETRAS

N 1641, Sir Thomas Urquhart published his first work—a volume of poems, entitled "EPIGRAMS: DIVINE AND MORAL,"[1] and dedicated to the Marquis of Hamilton. The poems are divided into three books, two of which contain forty-five epigrams, while the third contains forty-four. Most of them are in iambic pentameters, and are for the greater part sextets in form; but though the versification is occasionally smooth, these compositions do little credit to the Muse who inspired them. They are, without an exception, pointless; and an epigram without a point is about as useless and exasperating as a needle without one.[2] It is

---

[1] "EPIGRAMS: DIVINE AND MORAL. *By Sir Thomas Urchard, Knight.* London: Printed by Barnard Alsop and Thomas Fawcet, in the Yeare 1641."

[2] It is only fair, however, to Urquhart to remember that his idea of an Epigram was probably different from ours. In modern times point or "bite" is regarded as essential to such kind of compositions. The original idea of them was that they should contain a single distinct thought, and be brief enough to serve as inscriptions.

somewhat remarkable that in his prose compositions
the imagination of Sir Thomas seems quite un-
fettered, while in his poems it is under some such
restraining influence as a strait-waistcoat is said
to exercise upon a certain class of patients.

A wild legend, the origin of which is unknown,
but which is utterly baseless, asserts that Urquhart
" was laureated poet at Paris before he was three
and twenty years of age." [1] We could hardly
conceive of any responsible authorities being so far
" left to themselves " as to do a deed like this. The
story may be either the misapplication to Urquhart
of some vague tradition of one of the feats of his
hero, the Admirable Crichton, or of what he himself
has actually recorded of the poet, Arthur Johnston.[2]

A modern critic, who has given Urquhart a full
measure of praise, finds himself unable to say a
word in favour of his poems. " This slender
volume," he remarks, " gives not the slightest
promise of talent. Its stanzas are indistinguished
and indistinguishable. There is no reason why anyone should have written them, but, on the other
hand, there is no reason why anyone should not.
They express the usual commonplaces : the inevit-
ableness of death, and the worth of endeavour. A
mildly Horatian sentiment is dressed up in the
tattered rags of Shakespearianism, and the surprise
is that the author, whose prose is restrained by no
consideration of sound or sense, should have deemed
it worth while to print so tame a collection of
exercises." [3]

[1] Granger's *Biographical History*, iii. 160.
[2] *Works*, p. 263.   [3] Charles Whibley, *New Review*, July 1897.

A favourable specimen of the *Epigrams* is the following from the first book :—

"HOW DIFFICULT A THING IT IS TO TREAD IN THE PATHES OF VERTUE.

"The way to vertue's hard, uneasic, bends
  Aloft, being full of steep and rugged alleys ;
For never one to a higher place ascends,
  That always keeps the plaine, and pleasant valleyes :
    And reason in each human breast ordaines
    That precious things be purchased with paines."

Or take this from the opposite page :—

"WHEN A TRUE FRIEND MAY BE BEST KNOWNE.

"As the glow-worme shines brightest in the darke
  And frankincense smells sweetest in the fire ;
So crosse adventures make us best remarke
  A sincere friend from a dissembled lyer ;
    For some, being friends to our prosperity,
    And not to us, when it failes, they decay."

The fault of obscurity, of which the poet Browning has been accused, could not be laid to the charge of Sir Thomas Urquhart. Nor can it be said of him that he neglects truths that are obvious, and occupies himself in discovering and bringing forward those that are recondite. The sentiments to which he gives utterance seem those which spontaneously occur to the average mind : on reading the subject of the poem, as given in the title, and then the poem itself, we think

"A said whot a owt to 'a said,"

and we come away without any feverish mental agitation or accelerated movement of pulse.[1]

[1] A school-girl once wrote in a copy of *Moral Tales*, which she used for her Italian lessons, that they were "moral to the last

8

The sentiments which, from his own account, had, on more occasions than one, filled his mind, are expressed in the piece entitled "THE GENEROUS SPEECH OF A NOBLE CAVALLIER AFTER HE HAD DISARMED HIS ADVERSARY AT THE SINGLE COMBAT." They are as follows :—

> "Though with my raper, for the guerdon
>   Your fault deserveth, I may pierce ye,
>   Your penitence in craving pardon,
>   Transpassions my revenge in mercy ;
>   And wills me both to end this present strife,
>   And give you leave in peace t' enjoy your life."

Another Epigram, which one critic regards as Urquhart's *chef d'œuvre* in this kind of composition, is the following :—

> "Take *man* from *woman*, all that she can show
>   Of her own proper, is nought else but *wo*."[1]

In a letter of commendation prefixed to his next work, *The Trissotetras*, Sir Thomas Urquhart says of himself : "This Mathematicall tractate doth no lesse bespeak him a good Poet and Orator, then [than] by his elaboured poems he hath showne himselfe already a good Philosopher and Mathematician." This self-criticism is all that could be desired. A degree." The same may be said of Sir Thomas Urquhart's *Moral Epigrams*.

[1] This reminds one of Alice's subtraction sum. "Take a bone from a dog. What remains ? . . . The dog's temper would remain" (*Through the Looking-Glass*, chap. ix.). A somewhat different and more sombre turn of thought than the above was suggested to Southey's Dr Dove by the resemblance between the words. "*Woman*," he says, "evidently meaning either *man's woe* —or abbreviated from *woe to man*, because by woman was woe brought into the world" (*The Doctor*, chap. ccviii.).

work on mathematics that proves an author's possession of poetical and rhetorical gifts, and a volume of poetry which leads one to think that the singer is an accomplished mathematician, are gifts with which the world is but seldom favoured, and as it is likely that their merits will not instantly be observed, the zeal of the author in calling our attention to them is by no means unnecessary. But when he goes on to say, still speaking of himself in the third person, " The Muses never yet inspired sublimer conceptions in a more refined stile then [than] is to be found in the accurate strain of his most ingenious Epigrams," we feel that he is less felicitous. His first shot has hit the blank, but the second is wide of the target altogether.

In his dedication of the volume to " the Marquis of Hamilton, Earle of Arren and Cambridge, etc.," he describes its contents as " but flashes of wit." A modern reader will probably, however, be inclined to think that this modest opinion of them is far too flattering. At times there is a faint suggestion of a possible gleam of brightness, but this is instantly followed by Egyptian darkness, and one is reminded of a revolving light that has somehow gone wrong.

The volume closes with the somewhat liturgical formula, " Here end the first three Bookes of Sir Thomas Vrchard's Epigrams," and with a doxology, the latter being almost the only trace of matter in it to justify the use of " Divine " in the title. The author was evidently prepared to go on with more " bookes " of the kind, if he got any encouragement from publishers or public, but, probably, both thought it about time for him to stop. The fact that, in five years after this volume of poems had appeared, a second edition should apparently have been brought out, would seem at first to indicate that there must have been some little run upon the *Epigrams*. But the truth of the matter is, that one "William Leake" had evidently got the "remainder," and issued them in 1646 with a new title-page.

In the Introductory Notice to Sir Theodore Martin's edition of Rabelais, some information is given concerning a folio volume of unpublished Epigrams by Urquhart, which is still in existence.[1] It consists of ten books, called after Apollo and the Muses, each containing 110 Epigrams, except the last, which has 113. The MS. is dedicated to the Marquis of Hamilton; but, in addition to this, each book has a separate dedication to some one of the author's political associates or friends. The persons thus honoured are the Marquis of Huntly, the Earl of Arundel, the Earl of Northumberland, the Earl of Pembroke, the Earl of Dorset, the Earl of Holland, the Earl of Newcastle, the Earl of Stafford, Lord Craven, and Lord Gaurin (Gowran). According to the custom of that time, the reader finds his progress barred by several prefaces, respectively named, in this instance, as the "Isagoge," or "Introduction," the "Premonition," and the "Prolog," and cannot get away without a

---

[1] The title is as follows :—" *Ten Books of Epigrams: the Curiositie whereof, for Conception, stile, instruction, and Other mixtures of show and substance, being no lesse fruitfull then [than] pleasing to the diligent Peruser,* are *entitled* APOLLO *and the* MUSES. *Written by the Right Worshipfull* SIR THOMAS URCHARD, *Knight.*" The volume is now in the possession of Professor Ferguson, of Glasgow University. From it our specimen of his handwriting is taken.

The invocation
To Apollo,
and the Muses.

Grave Pythian knight, sing that to rown the Top
of Laurel aimers, goe some hand in hand
With the Nine Systers of th' Aonian kind,
Whose residence is setled on the tops
of Helicon, and Pindus, I demand
from yow, and them this favour, that some drops
be poured in me out of Hipporrène,
to æternize the offspring of my Veine.

Fac-simile of Sir Thomas Urquhart's handwriting considerably reduced.

"Corollarie," an "Animadversion," several extra leaves of verses, "A Table for the more easie finding out of such Epigrams as treat of one subject," an "Index," and a "List of proper names." For one of these latter he has reason to be grateful to Sir Thomas, for the "Index" is a glossary of "the harshest and most difficult words contained in the preceding Epigrams."

The general character of the unpublished Epigrams does not seem to be higher than that of those which have seen the light of day, and consequently there is little likelihood of any anxiety being expressed by the general public for a sight of them. Some of them also are of a sportive turn, and are more in accordance with the standard of taste and manners which prevailed in the middle of the seventeenth century than with that of our own day. From the "Animadversion" it seems that Urquhart "contryved, blocked, and digested these eleven hundred epigrams in a thirteen weeks tyme." This surely breaks the record in the matter of speed in producing epigrams. Had the results been better, one would have had more pleasure in supporting Sir Thomas against all-comers.

The second literary venture made by Sir Thomas Urquhart was the publication of a scientific work, entitled "THE TRISSOTETRAS" [1]—a treatise which

----

[1] The title-page, according to the custom of the time, gives a somewhat elaborate account of the contents of the volume. It runs as follows :—"THE TRISSOTETRAS : Or, *A most Exquisite Table* for Resolving all manner of Triangles, whether plain or sphericall, Rectangular or Obliquangular, with greater facility, then [than] ever hitherto hath been practised : Most necessary for all such as would attaine to the exact knowledge of Fortification, Dyaling, Naviga-

professed to simplify trigonometry. Yet, notwithstanding the statement on the title-page that the new method of working problems in that department of mathematical science would be found invaluable by soldiers, sailors, architects, astronomers, and others, the volume seems to have dropped at once into the depths of oblivion, without even having produced a ripple upon the surface of the waters. No one is known to have read it or to have been able to read it. Lord Bacon, indeed, says that things solid and weighty are drowned in the river of time, while things that are light and blown-up are carried down by its current.[1] A very comfortable theory would this be for those of us who write books that are found unreadable and drop at once out of notice, if only some trustworthy person could be found who would certify to the truth of Lord Bacon's assertion.

The editor of the Maitland Club edition of Sir Thomas Urquhart's Works has some qualms of conscience about reprinting this treatise. With a touch of humour, which only true Philistines will fully appreciate, he says that some apology may

tion, Surveying, Architecture, the Art of Shadowing, taking of Heights and Distances, the use of both the Globes, Perspective, the skill of making Maps, the Theory of the Planets, the calculating of their motions, and all other Astronomicall Computations whatsoever. Now lately invented, and perfected, explained, commented on, and, with all possible brevity and perspicuity, in the hiddest and most re-searched mysteries, from the very first grounds of the Science it selfe, proved, and convincingly demonstrated. By Sir Thomas Urquhart of Cromartie, Knight. Published for the benefit of those that are mathematically affected. *London*, Printed by James Young. 1645."

[1] *Advancement of Learning.*

appear necessary, *even to an Antiquarian Club*,[1] for reprinting a work apparently so unintelligible and useless ; and accordingly he shelters himself behind the opinion of Mr Wallace, the Professor of Mathematics in the University of Edinburgh at that time (1834). " I have," says Mr Wallace, who had been asked to examine the work, " looked at Sir Thomas Urquhart's *Trissotetras*, but I hardly know what to think of it. The book is not absolute nonsense, but is written in a most unintelligible way,[2] and so as never book was written before nor since. On this account it is truly a literary curiosity. There appears to have been a perverted ingenuity exercised in writing it, and I imagine that, with some patience, the author's plan might be understood, but I doubt if any man would take the trouble ; for, after he had overcome the difficulty, there is nothing to reward his labour. I presume the object of the author was to fix the rules of Trigonometry in the memory, but no writer since his time has adopted his invention. Indeed, I do not observe the least mention of his book in the history of mathematical science. Yet, for his time, he seems not to have been a bad mathematician. Urquhart speaks in terms of great praise of Napier, yet not greater than he deserved. I infer from this that he was well acquainted with the subject as then known. The book in question is certainly a *curious*, if not a

---

[1] The italics are ours.

[2] Sir Theodore Martin remarks that this conclusion nearly resembles that of Socrates, upon being asked his opinion of the book of Heraclitus the Obscure. " Those things," he said, " which I understood were excellent; I imagine so were those I understood not ; but they require a diver of Delos " (*Rabelais*, p. xviii.).

valuable relic of Scottish genius in the olden time, and it is a good specimen of the pedantry and fantastic taste of the Author. If, therefore, by reprinting his works, it be intended to give a true portraiture of him, *The Trissotetras* should on that account, and I see no better reason, again pass through the press." [1]

The volume is dedicated " To the right honourable and most noble lady, my dear and loving mother, the Lady Dowager of Cromartie." The " Epistle Dedicatory " is couched in the high-flown language which others would have had difficulty in concocting, but which seems to flow with ease from the lips of Sir Thomas. " Thus, Madam," he says, " unto you doe I totally belong; but so as that those exteriour parts of mine, which by birth are from your Ladiship derived, cannot be more fortunate in this their subjection, notwithstanding the egregious advantages of bloud and consanguinity thereby to them accruing, then [than] my selfe am happy, as from my heart I doe acknowledge it, in the just right your Ladiship hath to the eternall possession of the never-dying powers of my soule." The following passage from the same " Epistle " reminds one of the adulatory terms in which Sir Walter Raleigh and Spenser addressed Queen Elizabeth : " By vertue of your beloved society, your neighbouring Countesses, and other great dames of your kindred and acquaintance, become more illustrious in your imitation [*i.e.* in imitation of you]; amidst whom, as Cynthia amongst the obscurer planets, your Ladiship shines, and darteth

[1] *Works,* p. xvi.

the angelick rayes of your matchlesse example on
the spirits of those who by their good Genius have
been brought into your favourable presence to be
enlightened by them." The concluding passage in
his Dedication is still more remarkable: "I will here,"
he says, "in all submission, most humbly take my
leave of your Ladiship, and beseech Almighty God
that it may please his Divine Majesty so to blesse
your Ladiship with continuance of dayes, that the
sonnes of those whom I have not as yet begot, may
attaine to the happinesse of presenting unto your
Ladiship a braine-babe of more sufficiencie and consequence." [1]

The ordinary reader who looks into the volume
cannot fail to be appalled by the new and mysterious
terms with which its pages are crowded. Words
like " proturgetick," "quadrobiquadræquation," " sindiforall," "cathetobasall," "loxogonosphericall," and
" zetetick," are freely used, and many others equally
hard and thorny. Even the author himself finds
it necessary to append to the work a glossary,
containing an explanation of a number of the
words of which he had made use. " Being certainly
perswaded," he says, " that a great many good spirits
[*i.e.* worthy souls] ply Trigonometry that are not
versed in the learned tongues, I thought fit for their
encouragement to subjoyne here the explication of
the most important of those Greek and Latin termes,
which for the more efficacy of expression I have
made use of in this Treatise." [2]

In some cases, however, the " explication," instead
of dispelling the darkness, only renders it more

---

[1] *Works*, pp. 55–57.   [2] *Ibid.* p. 131.

visible, as when, *e.g.*, we are told that "*cathetobasall* is said of the concordances of loxogonosphericall moods, in the datas of the perpendicular and the base, for finding out of the maine quæsitum." "*Inversionall*," we are told, "is said of the concordances of those moods which agree in the manner of their inversion; that is, in placing the second and fourth termes of the analogy, together with their indowments, in the roomes of the first and third, and contrariwise." Probably only those who are able to follow the statement that "*oppoverticall* is said of those moods which have a catheteuretick concordance in their datas of the same cathetopposites and verticall angles," will be qualified to give an intelligent assent to the statement that "*sindiforall* is said of those moods the fourth terme of whose analogie is onely illatitious to the maine quæsitum."[1]

Besides the Epistle of Dedication to the author's mother, there are two Epistles and some Latin verses addressed to the reader. The former of these last-mentioned Epistles is signed by Sir Thomas, and consists of a glowing tribute of respect to Napier, the inventor of logarithms. "To write of Trigonometry," he says, "and not make mention of the illustrious Lord Neper[2] of Marchiston,

[1] The author of the above sentences is one of the very few persons in history or fiction known to us who would have been qualified to join in the conversation of the pleasant company in Illyria, when they began "to speak of Pigrogromitus, and of the Vapians passing the equinoctial of Queubus" (*Twelfth Night*, Act II. Sc. iii.)—the allusion to which has caused so many German commentators on Shakespeare to spend sleepless nights in their libraries.

[2] John Napier, of Merchiston (1550–1617), who published his invention in 1614. Our author calls him Lord Napier, but we are to understand the title as simply equivalent to "*laird*." He calls

the inventer of Logarithms, were to be unmindfull of him that is our daily benefactor; these artificiall numbers by him first excogitated and perfected, being of such incomparable use,[1] that by them we may operate more in one day, and with lesse danger of errour, then [than] can be done without them in the space of a whole week; a secret which would have

himself on one of his title-pages *Baro Merchistonii*, but that phrase is merely the designation of the superior of a barony, or lord of a manor. In the old Scottish Parliament men of this rank sat as *" lesser barons."*

[1] The subject of logarithms is perhaps one of those things which the ordinary reader might safely be presumed to know something about. In these days of higher education for women, it would be an act of impertinence to provide information on this point for that class of our readers. The following explanations are, therefore, intended for those members of the inferior sex whose education on the mathematical side has been neglected. The idea of logarithms arose in the mind of Napier from the wish to simplify the processes of multiplication and division, by making addition and subtraction take their place. To effect this, connect together a series of numbers increasing by arithmetical progression with a series increasing by multiplication or by mathematical progression.

Thus:					
0.	1.	5.	32.	10.	1024.
1.	2.	6.	64.	11.	2048.
2.	4.	7.	128.	12.	4096.
3.	8.	8.	256.	13.	8192.
4.	16.	9.	512.	14.	16384.

To multiply, say, 64 by 256, that is, to find the products of the 6th and 8th powers of 2, we must take the $(6+8)$th or 14th power, which from the table is 16384. To divide 8192 by 256, or the 13th power of 2 by the 8th, we must take the $(13-8)$th or 5th power, which from the table is 32. By means of this principle calculations can be made by persons whose business it is to do so, and stored up apart for use. The vast saving to mental labour by this simple and beautiful adjustment of numbers may be estimated by a glance at any collection of tables of logarithms. In a science like astronomy, progress would be terribly impeded if calculations had to be conducted by the ordinary methods.

beene so precious to antiquity that Pythagoras, all the seven wise men of Greece, Archimedes, Socrates, Plato, Euclid, and Aristotle, had, if coævals, joyntly adored him, and unanimously concurred to the deifying of the revealer of so great a mystery." He concludes with the splendid sentence that Napier's "immortall fame, in spite of time, will out-last all ages, and look eternity in the face." [1]

The second Epistle to the reader is of a very startling kind. It professes to be by some one whose initials are J. A., and it is written in commendation of the book and its author, but there can be no doubt that it is the production of Sir Thomas himself. He could no more disguise his style of writing than Sir Piercie Shafton could lay aside his Euphuistic English. After reading the laudatory sentences bestowed upon the inventor of logarithms, it is very amusing to find J. A. remarking of Sir Thomas Urquhart, that "the praise he hath beene pleased to confer on the learned and honourable Neper, doth, without any diminution, in every jot as duly belong unto himselfe." [2] As all our author's eulogies are constructed on a vast scale, it is not surprising to read that the new method of measuring triangles, as compared with the old, is like the sea-journey between the Pillars of Hercules ("commonly called the Straits of Gibraltar"), as compared with the land-journey from the one to the other. In the one case, we have a short voyage of not more than six hours' sail; in the other case, a walk of some seven thousand long miles. The two concluding paragraphs of the Epistle are so

[1] *Works*, p. 59.   [2] *Ibid.* p. 61.

extraordinary and so characteristic of our author,
that we must be allowed to quote them at length.

"The secret unfolded in the following book," says
J. A., " is so precious, that [the author's] countrey
and kindred would not have been more honoured
by him had he purchased [procured] millions of
gold, and severall rich territories of a great and
vast extent, then [than] for this subtile and divine
invention, which will out-last the continuance of
any inheritance, and remaine fresh in the under-
standings of men of profound literature, when
houses and possessions will change their owners,
the wealthy become poor, and the children of the
needy enjoy the treasures of those whose heires are
impoverished.   Therefore, seeing for the many-fold
uses thereof in divers arts and sciences, in speculation and practice, peace and war, sport and earnest,
with the admirable furtherances we reape by it in
the knowledge of sea and land, and heaven and
earth, it cannot be otherwise then [than] permanent, together with the Author's fame, so long as
any of those endure; I will, God willing, in the
ruines of all these, and when time it selfe is expired,
in testimony of my thankfulnesse in particular for
so great a benefit, after the resurrection there be
any complementall [complimentary] affability, ex-
presse myselfe then as I doe now, The Author's most
affectionate, and most humbly devoted servant, J. A."[1]

Why our author should have resorted to this
device for recommending himself and his book, we
cannot tell.   Perhaps he felt that some strong
affirmations were needed in the case.   Probably he

[1] *Works*, p. 63.

agreed with the old saying that, if you wish work to be thoroughly done, you had better do it yourself. The moral aspect of the matter we leave in the hands of our readers for discussion.

In five Latin elegiac couplets of a very neat and polished kind, Alexander Ross [1] recommends *The Trissotetras* to the reader, and assures the author that Scotia, whom by his writings he was exalting to the stars, looked down upon him with a benignant smile. Ross himself is now only known to most of us from the mention made of him in *Hudibras*, in the well-known passage—

> "There was an ancient sage philosopher
> Who had read Alexander Ross over."

It is to be feared that Alexander Ross had not performed the same feat with regard to Sir Thomas Urquhart's treatise; for his verses [2] would have

---

[1] Alexander Ross (1590–1654) was a believer in centaurs and griffins, in nations of giants and pygmies, and also, of course, in witches. In short, a pretty accurate statement of his intellectual creed might be constructed by turning into the articles of a confession of faith the list of "Vulgar Errors" controverted by Sir Thomas Browne. It is interesting to know that he was probably the last person in Scotland who heard the voice of the water-kelpie. "One day," he says, "travelling before day with some company near the river Don in Aberdeen, we heard a great noise and voices calling to us. I was going to answer, but was forbid by my company, who told me they were spirits, who never are heard there but before the death of somebody; which fell out too true, for the next day a gallant gentleman was drowned, with his horse offering to swim over" (Quoted in *Lives of Eminent Men of Aberdeen*, by J. Bruce).

[2] They begin—

> "Si cupis ætherios tutò peragrare meatus,
> Et sulcare audes si vada salsa maris," etc.

A friend, who knows

been equally appropriate if the subject of them had been a flying-machine or a water-tricycle invented by his friend.

At the end of the glossary in which the hardest words in *The Trissotetras* are explained, the author addresses a word in season to the persons into whose hands his book may fall. He expects that " learned and judicious mathematicians " will welcome it, and he promises them more of the same kind. His dignified attitude towards carping critics is very impressive. " But as for such," he says, " who, either understanding it not, or vain-gloriously being accustomed to criticise on the works of others, will presume to carp therein at what they cannot amend, I pray God to illuminate their judgments and rectifie their wits, that they may know more and censure lesse; for so by forbearing detraction, the venom whereof must needs reflect upon themselves, they will come to approve better of the endeavours of those that wish them no harme." [1]

" Himself to sing and build the lofty rhyme,"

has given me the following metrical translation of Ross's verses :—

" Wouldst thou in safety trace ethereal ways,
  Or plough with daring keel the briny deep ;
  Shouldst thou earth's wide expanses long to span,
  Come hither, make this learned book thine own.
  By it, without Dædalian wings, canst fly,
  And without Neptune, through the depths canst swim ;
  By it thou canst subdue the Lybian heat,
  And bear the cruel cold of Scythian skies.
  On, Thomas ! Scotia, whom unto the stars
  Thy writings raise, will yet rejoice in thee."

[1] *Works*, p. 146. *N.B.*—The attention of professional critics is respectfully directed to the above passage.

CHAPTER V

ΠΑΝΤΟΧΡΟΝΟΧΑΝΟΝ, OR THE PEDIGREE

NE of the most characteristic of Sir Thomas Urquhart's works is his *ΠΑΝΤΟΧΡΟΝΟΧΑΝΟΝ* : or, A Peculiar PROMPTUARY of TIME.[1] This contains a complete pedigree of the Urquhart family from the creation of the world down to the year A.D. 1652. Prefixed to it is a letter to the reader by " a well-wisher," whose initials are G. P., into whose hands the pedigree had fallen by mere chance, and who had thought himself bound in duty to the public to see it safely through the press. According to the statements of this disinterested philanthropist, the work in question was but one of a large number of papers of very great importance, forming part of the author's baggage,

[1] The full title of the work is as follows :—ΠΑΝΤΟΧΡΟΝΟΧΑΝΟΝ : or, A Peculiar PROMPTUARY of TIME ; Wherein (not one instant being omitted since the beginning of motion) is displayed A most exact DIRECTORY for all particular *Chronologies* in what Family soever : And that by deducing the true Pedigree and Lineal descent of the most ancient and honourable name of the VRQVHARTS, in the house of CROMARTIE, since the Creation of the world, until this present yeer of God, 1652. London, Printed for Richard Baddeley, and are to be sold at his shop, within the Middle-Temple-Gate, 1652.

which he had to abandon after the battle of Worcester. It is the habit, we know, of impecunious and importunate wayfarers to carry about with them documents of interest to which they solicit attention; but why a man in Sir Thomas Urquhart's position should have gone on a campaign, encumbered by various unpublished works in manuscript, it is difficult to say. Perhaps the simplest explanation is that he was different from other people.

The soldiers of Cromwell, we were told, made but light of this portion of the enemy's baggage, after " the fatal blowe given to the Royal party at Worcester"; indeed, but for " a surpassing honest and civil officer of Colonel Pride's regiment," the pedigree of the Urquharts would have been used by " a file of musquettiers to afford smoak to their pipes of tobacco." [1]

The fame of Sir Thomas as an author and as a soldier moved G. P., as he tells us, to commit this treatise to the press. With considerable ingenuity he remarks that, though the author is now in prison as a Royalist, he understands that his position is by no means " so desperate as that he thereby will be much endangered." If any doubt up to this point existed as to who G. P. might be, it is set at rest by the terms in which he pleads for favourable conditions being granted to the prisoner. " It is humbly desired," he says, " and, as I believe, from the hearts of all that are acquainted with him, that the greatest State in the world stain not their glory by being the Atropos to cut the thred of that

[1] *Works*, p. 151.

9

which Saturne's sithe hath not been able to mow in the progress of all former ages, especially in the person of him whose inward abilities are like to produce effects conducible to the State of as long continuance for the future." [1]   Only Sir Thomas Urquhart himself had the secret of what we may call the "spacious" manner of self-eulogy, which by its very grandeur seems lifted up above all such petty feelings as pride or vanity.

The concluding passage in the address to the reader is also worth quoting, as it illustrates the magnanimous spirit in which the captive deprecates severity towards himself on the ground of the injury which would thereby redound to the State. " Considering," it says, " how formerly he hath been a Mæcenas to the scholar, a patron to the souldier, a favourer of the marchant, a protector of the artificer, and upholder of the yeoman, it were a thousand pities that by the austerity of a State, which dependeth in both its *esse* and *bene esse* upon the flourishing of these worthy professions, effects so advantagious thereto, should, by not conferring deserved courtesies on him, be extinguished in the very brood." [2]

In the *True Pedigree and Lineal Descent of the Most Ancient and Honourable Family of the Urquharts in the House of Cromartie*, we have a brief but surprisingly complete history of the family from the time of Adam [3] down to A.D. 1652. The

---

[1] *Works*, p. 152.   [2] *Ibid.* p. 152.

[3] Poor Sir Thomas thought that he was going back to the beginning when he traced his descent up to Adam, or, to be more exact, to the red earth of which the "protoplast" was made.

line runs through the Sethite and not the Cainite branch of the human race, and, among the sons of Noah, it passes through Japhet.   The story is told of a marginal note being found in the history of some ancient Highland family, to the effect that " about this time the Flood took place."   Something like this is to be found in the document before us, for, under the date B.C. 2893, Sir Thomas adds to a mention of his ancestor Noah, a remark to the effect that " the Universal Deluge occurred in the six hundreth yeer compleat of his age."

The good fortune of his ancestors in their inheritances, marriages, and friendships is very remarkable.   To one of them, Japhet, fell the inheritance of " all the regions of Europe "; Japhet's grandson Penuel was " a most intimate friend of Nimrod, the mighty hunter and builder of Babel "; while his great-grandson Tycheros was chosen by " Orpah, the daughter of Sabatius Saga, Prince of the Armenians, to be her husband, because of his gallantry and good success in the wars." [1]

The name Urquhart came into use at the comparatively late period of B.C. 2139, when the family had been in existence for over eighteen hundred years.   It was first borne by Esormon. " He," we are told, " was soveraign Prince of Achaia. For his fortune in the wars, and affability in conversation, his subjects and familiars surnamed him

The late Charles Darwin carried back the pedigree of man a prodigious length, though he lowered its quality.   There can be little doubt that our author would have disdained to accept what used to be called "the lower animals" as, in any sense, ancestors of mankind, or, at any rate, of the dignified family of Urquhart.

[1] *Works*, p. 156.

οὐροχάρτος, that is [to] say, fortunate and well-beloved. After which time, his posterity ever since hath acknowledged him the father of all that carry the name of Urquhart.[1] He had for his arms, three banners, three ships, and three ladies, in a field *d'or*, with a picture of a young lady above the waste, holding in her right hand a brandished sword, and a branch of myrtle in the left, for crest; and for supporters, two Javanites, after the souldier-habit of Achaia, with this motto in the scroll of his coat-armour, ταῦτα τὰ τρία ἀξιοθέατα; that is, These three are worthy to behold. Upon his wife Narfesia, who was soveraign of the Amazons, he begot Cratynter."[2]

The habits of the Urquharts to form alliances and friendships with persons afterwards famous in

---

[1] In one respect, at any rate, we have legitimate ground of triumph over our ancestors—we spell better than they did. Charles Lamb once lent a volume of the old dramatists to a friend, and asked him his opinion of it. The reply was that it contained a considerable amount of bad spelling! The name Urquhart, as thus written, occurs here in Sir Thomas's "Pedigree," and is, doubtless, the correct form of the name. In the Latinised shape of Urquhardus it occurs on the register of the University of Aberdeen, at which our author studied. Yet Urchard seems to have been

> "The name our valiant Knight
> To all his challenges did write."

The unbridled licence in the matter of spelling prevalent at that period is still further illustrated by the historian Gordon, who wrote the *History of Scots Affairs*, and who gives us the name in the form of Wrqhward! This, one would think, was as far as it was possible to get in the way of bad spelling, without altogether taking leave of the sounds to be expressed by alphabetical signs. After it the spelling Wrwhart, as we find it in an Act of Parliament of 1663, seems rather poor.

[2] *Works*, p. 156.

sacred and secular history is very marked. Thus, one of them, Phrenedon Urquhart, "was in the house of the Patriarch Abraham at the time of the destruction of Sodom and Gomorrha." At a later period, another, named Hypsegoras Urquhart, married a daughter of Herculus Lybius ; while a descendant of theirs, Pamprosodos Urquhart, married Termuth, " who was that daughter of Pharaoh Amenophis which found Moses among the bulrushes, and brought him up as if he had been her own childe."

Another ancestor, Molin Urquhart (c. B.C. 1534), married Panthea, " the daughter of Deucalion and Pyrrha, of whom Ovid maketh mention in the first of his Metamorphoses." The genealogist goes on to say that " in that part of Africk which, after his name, is till this hour called Molinea, by cunning and valour together he killed in one morning three lions ;[1] the heads whereof, when in a basket, presented to his lady Panthea, so terrified her, that (being quick with childe) for putting her right hand to her left side, with this sudden exclamation, O Hercules, what is this ? the impression of three lions' heads was found upon the left side of the childe as soon as he was born." In consequence of this incident, the three banners, three ships, and three ladies in the Urquhart arms were exchanged for three lions' heads.

A century later, we find that Propetes Urquhart married Hypermnestra, " the choicest of Danaus' fifty daughters." This must have been some time after the little affair happened for which forty-nine of her sisters were condemned to draw water in

[1] *Works*, p. 159.

sieves; for, as every schoolboy knows, the fifty
daughters of Danaus were married to their cousins,
the fifty sons of Ægyptus, and all of them, but one,
at the bidding of their father, murdered their
husbands on the evening of the marriage-day.
Hypermnestra, however, had pity upon her cousin
and husband, Lynceus, and spared him.[1]   He must
have died shortly after, probably from natural
causes, as it is recorded in the work before us that
she married Propetes Urquhart, and became the
mother of Euplocamos Urquhart.

[1] Horace gives us the speech in which she told Lynceus of his
danger, and urged him to make his escape—

> " ' Wake ! ' to her youthful spouse she cried,
>   ' Wake ! or you yet may sleep too well :
> Fly—from the father of your bride,
>   Her sisters fell :
> They, as she-lions bullocks rend,
>   Tear each her victim : I, less hard,
> Than these, will slay you not, poor friend,
>   Nor hold in ward :
>
> Me let my sire in fetters lay
>   For mercy to my husband shown :
> Me let him ship from hence away,
>   To climes unknown.
> Go ; speed your flight o'er land and wave,
>   While Night and Venus shield you ; go
> Be blest : and on my tomb engrave
>   This tale of woe.' "
>   *Odes*, iii. 11 (Conington's Translation).

Her sad forebodings concerning her own fate, it is satisfactory to
know, were not fully realised.   Perhaps she was shipped away to
Cromartie, or Ireland, or Portugal, or Africa, or wherever it was
that the head of the Urquhart family was then reigning.   Instead
of Lynceus having the melancholy satisfaction of putting an
inscription on her tombstone, it is probable that she performed
that office for him.

The thought of what the family to which Hypermnestra belonged were capable when their blood was up, must, one would think, have cast a slight shadow of apprehension upon the married life of Propetes Urquhart. A more cheerful tone must have pervaded that of his descendant Cainotomos Urquhart, for he, we are told, "took to wife Thymelica, the daughter of Bacchus, in recompense of his having accompanied him in the conquest of the Indies." Further interesting particulars, which are not elsewhere recorded, are related of this ancestor of Sir Thomas. On his return from the expedition in which he assisted Bacchus to conquer India, he "passed through the territories of Israel, where, being acquainted with Debora the Judge and Prophetess, he received from her a very rich jewel, which afterwards by one of his succession was presented to Pentasilea, that Queen of the Amazons that assisted the Trojans against Agamemnon."

Their son Rodrigo Urquhart (c. B.C. 1295) was, we are told, invited over by his kindred the Clanmolinespick,[1] the principal clan in Ireland, and "bore rule there with much applause and good success"—the one solitary instance of the kind, we suppose, which is to be found in the history of that "most distressful country." "From him," it is said,

---

[1] Clanmolinespick is, we believe, more correctly *clann-maol-an-easbuig* (the last pronounced *espick*), and means "the clan" or "family of the servant of the bishop." They are probably the Irish ancestors of the Macmillans of Knapdale in Argyleshire. The word "*maol*," "a tonsured servant," occurs in Malise (*maol-Josa*), "a servant of Jesus," a family name of the old Earls of Strathearn; and *easbuig* in Gillespie or Gillespic, "a servant" or "gillie of the bishop."

" is descended the Clanrurie,[1] of which name there were twenty-six rulers and kings of Ireland before the days of Ferguse the first, King of Scots in Scotland."

A slight degree of uncertainty hangs about the identity of the wife of Mellessen Urquhart (*c.* B.C. 1049). Her name was Nicolia, and before her marriage she " travelled from the remote Eastern countries to have experience of the wisdom of Solomon, and by many [2] is supposed to have been the Queen of Sheba." Her husband, however, must have considered that, though she loved wisdom, she had not acquired much of it, or, at any rate, of the kind which is needed for bringing up a young family; for the historian goes on to say that " Mellessen Urquhart nevertheless sent some of his children to Ireland and Britain, to be brought up with the best of his own father and mother's kindred."

Amongst other celebrated persons who had the honour of being enrolled amongst the ancestors of Sir Thomas Urquhart are Pothina, a niece of Lycurgus ; Æquanima, the sister of Marcus Coriolanus : Diosa, the daughter of Alcibiades ; and Tortolina, the daughter of King Arthur. It is observable that for a good many generations immediately preceding the author's time, the ladies who figure in the genealogy are of comparatively

---

[1] Clanrurie is "the clan" or "family of Roderick." These are the Macrories and Fullartons, their eponym having been Rory or Roderick, one of the two sons of Reginald, whose father in almost prehistoric times was Somerled, Lord of the Isles. They settled in Bute and Arran, and about Ardnamurchan and the islands there.

[2] This phrase—" by many "—is very delightful.

SCULPTURED STONE SHOWING URQUHART'S COAT OF ARMS

lowly birth—seldom, indeed, do they reach the rank of an earl's daughter. Either the supply of princesses was by this time somewhat exhausted, or the demands of the Urquharts were less exorbitant. The high-spirited character of the most remarkable scion of the family who drew up the genealogy forbids us to think that, with the lapse of time, they had suffered any diminution of courage. It rather seems as though the world had entered upon a less heroic stage. Perhaps, like Sir Thomas Browne in a later age, they had concluded that "it was too late to be ambitious, for the great mutations of the world were acted."

In the time of Vocompos (A.D. 775) a further change took place in the arms of the Urquharts, which gave them their final form. "Vocompos," we learn, "was the first in the world that had the bears' heads to his arms, being induced to exchange, by the instigation of King Solvatius, his arms of three lions' heads, for the three bears' heads, razed, because of the great exploit, in presence of the King, done by him and his two brothers, in killing, one morning, three wild bears, in the Caledonian forrest: the supporters were also changed into two greyhounds: the crest and impress remaining still the same as it was since the days of Astioremon." [1]

---

[1] *Works*, p. 168. A curious stone lintel now at Kinbeakie gives a representation of the Urquhart coat of arms, such as it was in Sir Thomas's own time. It was no doubt executed at his orders and under his direction, for inscribed on it are the names of some of those worthies who appear in the above genealogical history. The representation which we give of this stone is from a photograph specially taken for the illustration of this work. As the porch in the wall of which the slab is set is very narrow, it was impossible,

An alleged ancestor of our author, William de
even with the use of a wide-angle lens, to get a more satisfactory photograph than that which is here reproduced. Our
readers will therefore kindly excuse the distortion of shape
which is only too apparent, and accept as a measure of compensation the vividness with which the details of the engraved
stone are brought out. "This singular relic," says Hugh
Miller, "which has, perhaps, more of character impressed upon it
than any other piece of sandstone in the kingdom, is about five
feet in length by three in breadth, and bears date A.M. 5612,
A.C. 1651. On the lower and upper edges it is bordered by a plain
moulding, and at the ends by belts of rich foliage, terminating in
a chalice or vase. In the upper corner two knights in complete
armour on horseback, and with their lances couched, front each
other, as if in the tilt-yard. Two Sirens playing on harps occupy the
lower. In the centre are the arms—the charge on the shield three
bears' heads, the supporters two greyhounds leashed and collared,
the crest a naked woman holding a dagger and palm, the helmet
that of a knight, with the beaver partially raised, and so profusely
mantled that the drapery occupies more space than the shield and
supporters, and the motto MEANE WEIL, SPEAK WEIL, AND DO
WEIL. Sir Thomas's initials, S. T. V. C., are placed separately,
one letter at the outer side of each supporter, one in the centre of
the crest, and one beneath the label; while the names of the more
celebrated heroes of his genealogy, and the eras in which they
flourished, occupy in the following inscription the space between
the figures :—ANNO ASTIOREMONIS, 2226; ANNO VOCOMPOTIS,
3892; ANNO MOLINI, 3199; ANNO RODRICI, 2958; ANNO CHARI,
2219; ANNO LUTORCI, 2000; ANNO ESORMONIS, 3804. It is
melancholy enough that this singular exhibition of family pride
should have been made in the same year in which the family received its deathblow—the year of Worcester battle" (*Scenes and
Legends of the North of Scotland*, chap. vii.). The arms of the
Urquhart family in their later form, as associated with those of the
Meldrum and Seton families, are given in the 1774 edition of the
ΠΑΝΤΟΧΡΟΝΟΧΑΝΟΝ, and are as follows :—"*Arms*, Or, three
Bears-heads, erazed, gules, langued azure. *Crest*, a demy Otter
issuing from the wreath sable, crowned with an antique Crown, or,
holding betwixt his paws a crescent gules. *Motto* above, *Per mare
et Terras*, and below, *Mean, speak, and do well*. *Supporters*, two
grayhounds, proper collared gules, and leashed." There can be no
doubt that the Urquhart arms should be the three *bears'* heads,

Monte Alto (Mouat),[1] took part in the patriotic resistance of Scotland against English oppression which is associated with the names of Bruce and Wallace, and the faint local traditions of that time partly corroborate Urquhart's statements. "This William," he says, "caried himself so lovingly towards King Robert, that when almost all Scotland was possest by King Edward's faction, and his lands at Cromartie altogether overrun by them, and his house garrisoned and victualed with three yeers provision of all necessaries for one hundred men, he by a stratagem gained the castle, and with the matter of fourty men, keept it out against the forces of Edward for the space of seven yeers and a half, during which time all his lands there were totally wasted, and his woods burnt; so that, having nothing then he could properly call his own but the mote-hill onely of Cromartie, which he fiercely maintained against the enemies, he was agnamed *Gulielmus de Monte Alto.* At last William Wallace

though they are often described as three *boars'* heads. The records of 1742 and 1760 in the Lyon Register make this quite certain. Probably the close resemblance between the two words is the principal cause of the confusion with regard to the matter which exists. In the sculptured coat of arms, of which we give a representation, the heads certainly have a superficial resemblance at least to those of boars. A correspondent who takes an interest in this question remarks, however, that "though the heads have tusks worthy of any boar, they (*i.e.* the heads) are set at right angles to the necks in a way in which no boar could be represented." On the other hand, the snouts of the animals have that distinctly *retroussé* shape which we associate with pigs, both wild and domesticated. The question is, therefore, not so simple as at first sight it appears, and can scarcely be adequately dealt with in a mere footnote. Accordingly we leave our readers to discuss and settle the difficulty.

[1] See p. 4, *supra.*

came to his relief, but, as I conceive, it was the brother's son of the renowned William, who in a little den [or hollow] within two miles of Cromartie, till this hour called Wallace Den, killed six hundred of King Edward's unfortunate forces. Afterwards, raising the siege from about the mote-hill of Cromartie by the assistance of his namesake the other William, the shire of Cromarty was totally purged of the enemy."[1]

Tradition, according to Hugh Miller, is silent respecting the siege, but relates many details of the battle. The Scottish forces lay in ambuscade in the ravine or hollow which is still, or was until recently, called by Wallace's name, and attacked a large body of English troops on their way to join some of their countrymen, who were encamped on the peninsula of Easter Ross. The English were surprised and panic-struck, and left six hundred dead on the field of battle. The survivors were unacquainted with the country, and were under the impression that there was continuous land between them and their countrymen on the opposite shore. "They were only undeceived," we are told, "when, on climbing the southern Sutor, where it rises behind the town, they saw an arm of the sea more than a mile in width, and skirted by abrupt and dizzy precipices, opening before them. The spot is still pointed out where they made their final stand; and a few shapeless hillocks, that may still be seen among the trees, are said to have been raised above the bodies of those who fell; while the fugitives, for they were soon beaten from this

[1] *Works*, p. 170.

position, were either driven over the neighbouring precipices, or perished amidst the waves of the Firth." [1]

Sir Thomas does not let us off easily. After subjecting our credulity to a severe strain by one kind of statement, he unexpectedly increases the tension by another. Thus he says that an ancestor in the fifteenth century, Thomas Urquhart, had by his wife Helen Abernethie, daughter of Lord Salton, five-and-twenty sons, who grew up to manhood, and eleven daughters, all of whom found husbands. It would only have been kind of him to have reduced these numbers a little. But on one point he has spared us : we are not asked to believe that there were others who died in infancy.

In a postscript Sir Thomas Urquhart explains that he has just given his readers a sketch of the history of his family, but hopes to furnish them with a complete narrative as soon as he obtains his release from his parole, and is at liberty to attend to this and to other matters of greater importance. The thought of the delightful book in store for mankind is so attractive to him that he cannot help dilating upon it. "In the great chronicle of

---

[1] *Scenes and Legends of the North of Scotland*, Hugh Miller, p. 48. This battle is supposed to be mentioned by Blind Harry, who has celebrated the achievements of Wallace in the following uncouth lines :—

> "Wallace raid throw the northland into playne.
> At Crummade feill Inglismen thai slew.
> The worthi Scottis till hym thus couth persew.
> Raturnd agayne and come till Abirdeyn,
> With his blith ost apon the Lammess ewyn "
> (vii. 1084–88).

the House of Urquhart," he continues, "the aforesaid Sir Thomas purposeth, by God's assistance, to
make mention of the illustrious families from thence
descended, which as yet are in esteem in the
countries of Germany, Bohemia, Italy, France, Spain,
England, Scotland, Ireland, and several other nations
of a warmer climate, adjacent to that famous terri-
tory of Greece, the lovely mother of this most
ancient and honourable stem."[1]   He also intends
not to omit the name of any family with which at
any time the aforesaid house has contracted alliance.

The concluding paragraph is very amusing; for
in it our author promises to give proof of the statements he has made, by quoting from the works
of respectable chroniclers of past ages, though the
degree of certainty which the reader may thereby
expect to reach falls short of that given by Holy
Writ or the works of Euclid.   "And finally," he
says, "for confirmation of the truth in deriving of
his extraction from the Ionian race of the Prince of
Achaia, and in the deduction of all the considerable
particulars of the whole story, [the author] is resolved
to produce testimonies of Arabick, Greek, Latin, and
other writers of such authentick approbation, that
we may boldly from thence infer consequences of
no less infallible verity then [than] any that is not
grounded on faith by means of a Divine illumina-
tion, as is the story of the Bible, or on reason, by
vertue of the unavoidable inference of a necessary
concluding demonstration, as that of the Elements
of Euclid; which being the greatest evidence that
in any narration of that kinde is to be expected,

[1] *Works*, p. 174.

the judicious reader is bid farewel, from whom the Author for the time most humbly takes his leave." [1]

It is needless to say that the scheme of filling out the sketch of the history of the Urquhart family was never carried out, if ever it had been seriously entertained by Sir Thomas; and we are left in ignorance of the names of the Arabic, Greek, Latin, and other authors on whose testimony our belief in the authenticity of the narrative was to have been firmly based.   In the absence of this our judgment is left in suspense, unless, indeed, we conclude that, as the genealogy begins and ends with the names of actual persons,[2] the intermediate part is not likely to have been a mere fabrication. If the links are sound in the places where we can test them, it requires no very great exercise of credulity to believe that they are the same throughout.

Matthew Arnold on one occasion laid down the principle, that a book should either " edify the uninstructed," or "inform the instructed."   Sir Thomas Urquhart's " *ΠΑΝΤΟΧΡΟΝΟΧΑΝΟΝ* " certainly justifies its existence according to this standard of judging literature; for if it does not serve to edify the uninstructed, it *does* inform the

[1] *Works*, p. 175.

[2] The editor of the 1774 edition of the Tracts of Sir Thomas Urquhart says that he had compared the genealogy with the records kept by the Lord Lyon of Scotland, which go back as far as the reign of Alexander II. (A.D. 1214–1249), and had found it strictly correct from that period.   In Appendix I., which contains the lists of names of Sir Thomas's ancestors, we have taken the liberty of indicating the names on which reliance can be placed, by printing them in italics (see p. 211).

instructed, since the information it contains is not to be found in any other quarter.[1]

One's faith in the credibility of his narrative is, however, a little shaken by finding that in the second book of his favourite author, Rabelais, the genealogy of the giant Pantagruel is carried up to a period far beyond the Flood. It may be a mere coincidence, but it is one of those coincidences that make us very thoughtful.[2]

At the time when Sir Thomas Urquhart wrote, Scotland was supposed to have had a dynasty of kings and a connected political history dating far

---

[1] Sir Thomas is said to have remarked about "*the Pedigree*," that by the first generation of readers it would be received with scoffs, that the second generation would have their doubts about it, but that the third generation would be heavily inclined to believe it. Time has moved somewhat more slowly, however, than he anticipated, and probably but few of us have as yet got past the second stage.

[2] In the article on Crichton in the *Biographia Britannica*, Dr Kippis subjects our author to grave censure (see p. 158). With respect to Urquhart's present work he says: "Of his total disregard to truth there is incontestible evidence in another work of his, entitled *The True Pedigree*, etc. In this work it is almost incredible what a number of falsities he has invented, both with respect to names and facts. Perhaps a more flagrant instance of imposture and fiction was never exhibited; and the absurdity of the whole pedigree is beyond the power of words to express. It can only be felt by those who have perused the Tract itself." It is to be feared that Dr Kippis was mentally akin to the Irish bishop who remarked of *Gulliver's Travels* when it appeared, that "all was not gospel that was in that book."

Some one has said that the names of Urquhart's ancestors, at any rate on the male side, are very likely those of the giants and heathen in the *Amadis of Gaul*; and certainly Famongomadan, Cartadaque, Madanfabul, Arcalaus, and Basagante remind one of chiefs and heroes of the Cromartie line. In the female line the resemblance is much closer; for Asymbleta, Eromena, and Gonima distinctly recall the Darioleta, Brisena, and Madasima of the romance.

back before the birth of Christ. The impudent fictions of Hector Boece, whose history of Scotland was published in 1526, had been accepted by the public, and were regarded as genuine facts even by such literary personages as Erasmus and Paulus Jovius. Perhaps Sir Thomas thought that a credulity which had endured the considerable strain which Boece had put upon it might be trusted to bear a still greater weight. Indeed, he interwove the story of his family with that which was current as the genuine history of his native land.

According to the mythical history of Scotland, Gathelus, a Grecian prince, having quarrelled with his father Miol, took refuge in Egypt, and married Scota, a daughter of the Pharaoh who perished in the Red Sea. The young people came west and founded Portugal (*i.e.* Port of Gathelus), and then journeyed north to Scotland, bringing with them, as part of their baggage, the coronation-stone yet to be seen in Westminster Abbey. Their descendant Fergus, "the father of a hundred kings," was the founder of the Scottish monarchy. These shadowy persons appear again, "with the moonlight streaming through them," and play their parts in the genealogy of the Urquharts.

Some have thought that Sir Thomas believed devoutly in the genealogy himself, and was the dupe of his own imagination. One would be sorry to form so low an opinion of his mental endowments. If the book in question were not an elaborate joke, it can only have been intended to impose upon the English people by convincing them of the extraordinary dignity and grandeur of their captive.

10

If this were indeed the case, he must have had an humbler opinion of the intellectual faculties possessed by the average Englishman than even the majority of his fellow-countrymen entertain.

A very amusing reference to this book of Sir Thomas Urquhart's is to be found in the Decisions of the Court of Session, under date of 23rd to 25th January, 1706.[1] In that year an action was brought by the Earl of Sutherland against the Earls of Crawford, Errol, and Marischal, to determine the question of precedency in the rolls of Parliament. The pursuer asserted that he was lineally descended from an Earl of Sutherland living in 1275, while his opponents' ancestors were not Earls till about 1399. The pursuer laid stress upon the fact that, in 1630, a formal inquiry into this matter had been held at Inverness, and that the decision had been in his favour. The persons who conducted the inquiry were, he said, of undoubted credit, and well versed in the particulars investigated, and "might have had good information from old men and writs, which in the course of time and through accidents had long disappeared." The advocate for the defenders replied that the "Chancellor of the Inquest" had been Sir Thomas Urquhart, who might have traced the pursuer's descent from Noah, as he had deduced his own genealogy from Adam, and that the decision arrived at was of no more value than "his fanciful derivation of his own pedigree. For the members of the Inquest seemed to have sworn rashly upon matters of greater

[1] Fountainhall, *Decisions*, ii. 265 and 315 ; Morrison, *Dictionary of Decisions*, xxvii. 11304.

antiquity than they could certainly know." "It is true," was the pursuer's reply, "the defender in his gaiety objects against Sir Thomas Urquhart as an ill genealogist; and it is owned that his derivation from Adam and Noah was fantastic enough, and indeed but *lusus ingenii;* but, after all, the defender's criticism will not hinder him to pass for a most knowing gentleman." The case was decided in favour of the Earl of Sutherland, so far as some of his contentions were concerned. But it is somewhat curious that his advocate overlooked the fact that the Sir Thomas Urquhart of 1630, who had been the " Chancellor of the Inquest," was not the author of the book containing the genealogy of the Urquharts, but that it was written by his son. It is quite possible, however, that it was a matter of notoriety that the elder Sir Thomas had been a believer in the long pedigree which his more famous son had, years after, elaborated and published.[1]

[1] In some ways the elder Sir Thomas reminds us of the pedantic and undignified monarch, James VI., from whom he received knighthood. Both were the first Protestants of their respective houses, both were attached to prelacy rather than to Presbyterianism, and both were wasteful and slovenly in money matters. If the above conjecture be well founded, they had a further point of resemblance to each other, in their interest in fabulous genealogies. And it may be said of them both that they prepared a series of misfortunes for their chivalrous, high-spirited sons.

CHAPTER VI

ΕΚΣΚΥΒΑΛΑΥΡΟΝ : or, THE JEWEL, and
LOGOPANDECTEISION : or, THE UNIVERSAL
LANGUAGE.

IR THOMAS URQUHART'S previous excursions into literature had been of a somewhat tentative kind, and calculated to whet the desire of a judicious reader for him to enter upon more serious undertakings. He had appeared in the world of letters in several different aspects,—as a a man of science, and as the representative and poet, as historian of a family which, for long descent and glorious achievements, could not be rivalled, if his statements concerning it were to be credited,—but no one could forecast, from what he had already published, the nature of his next literary exploit.

The volume which followed the Pedigree of the Urquharts has the strange name above printed,[1]

---

[1] Its title-page is as follows :—ΕΚΣΚΥΒΑΛΑΥΡΟΝ : Or, The Discovery of A MOST EXQUISITE JEWEL, more precious then [than] DIAMONDS inchased in Gold, the like whereof was never seen in any age; found in the kennel of *Worcester*-streets, the day after the Fight, and six before the Autumnal Equinox, *anno* 1651. Serving in this place, To Frontal a VINDICATION of the honour of SCOTLAND, from that Infamy, whereinto the Rigid *Presbyterian*

but most of those who have occasion to mention it more than once find it more convenient to call it "The Jewel." [1] Its contents are of such a character that one who had read it carefully would find it difficult to state off-hand or in a single sentence what they were. A Scottish Divinity professor of somewhat erratic habits began, on one occasion, a

party of that Nation, out of their Covetousness and ambition, most dissembledly hath involved it. *Distichon ad Librum sequitur, quo tres ter adæquant Musarum numerum, casus et articuli.*

voc.   nom.   1 abl.   2 abl.   dat.
O thou'rt a Book in truth with love to many,

3 abl.   4 abl. acc.   gen.
Done by and for the free'st spoke Scot of any.

Efficiens et finis sunt sibi invicem causæ. LONDON, Printed by Ja: Cottrel; and are to be sold by *Rich. Baddeley*, at the Middle-Temple-gate. 1652.

[1] ΕΚΣΚΤΒΑΛΑΤΡΟΝ is supposed to be the Greek for "*Gold out of the dirt.*" Dr Irving, the author of a very carefully-written memoir of Sir Thomas Urquhart, in his *Lives of Scottish Writers*, vol. ii., is a little puzzled by this extraordinary name. The latter part of it was, he thought, perhaps connected with αὔριον—"to-morrow"—in allusion to the fact that this "exquisite Jewel" was taken out of the kennel *the morrow* after the battle of Worcester. But the word is evidently αὖρον—the Lat. *aurum*, "gold." In the "Postilla" to the Pedigree of the Urquharts, our author says that "the shire of Cromartie . . . hath the names of its towns, villages, hamlets, dwellings, promontories, hillocks, temples, dens, groves, fountains, rivers, pools, lakes, stone heaps, akers, and so forth, of pure and perfect Greek." We need not be surprised that Sir Thomas's Greek has more affinity with the vernacular form of the language current in the Cromartie of his time than with the Attic of the age of Pericles,

"*For Greke oj Athenes was to him unknowë.*"

Probably in this northern dialect of the Greek tongue αὖρον was used instead of the more classical χρυσός. Another indication of the difference between the Cromartian and Attic forms of speech is given by Sir Thomas in the same treatise in the name Ἀλεξάνδηρ, which Thucydides would have written Ἀλέξανδρος.

lecture in which he was to deal with several miscellaneous items, with the words, " Gentlemen, my subject to-day will be hotch-potch." This is an exact description of *The Jewel*, and those to whom nature has given the mental apparatus needed for appreciating Sir Thomas Urquhart will rejoice and not repine at the fact that the feeding laid before them is of a confused character. Accordingly no logical sequence will be allowed to mar the symmetry of this chapter in which *The Jewel* is described.

The main contents of the work are lists of the ancestors, male and female, of the Urquhart family from the beginning down to the year 1652, taken from the Pedigree ; a narrative of the sad fate that overtook the author's manuscripts after the battle of Worcester ; some pages of one of them which contained a scheme for a Universal Language : a denunciation of the " unjust usurpation of the Presbyterian Clergy, and the judaical practices of some merchants " by which discredit had been cast upon the Scottish name ; an account of Scotsmen famous for martial exploits or for learning during the previous half-century : a statement of personal wrongs inflicted upon the author by ministers of his own parishes : arguments in favour of the union of Scotland and England ; and apologies for the simple and unadorned strain in which the work is written. All through the volume Sir Thomas is spoken of in the third person, and the signature of " Christianus Presbyteromastix " is attached to the preface, or " the Epistle Liminary," as it is called, but there is scarcely any attempt made to keep up the pretence of anonymity. The object of the writer is to try to obtain for the prisoner of war restoration to complete liberty and the enjoyment of his property, and he seeks to correct the evil impression, which the conduct of certain persons in Scotland had produced upon the English people, by narrating the martial and literary achievements of more worthy representatives of his nation.

The rapidity with which the work had been produced is described by the writer in the following terms. " Laying aside all other businesses," he says, " and cooping my self up daily for some hours together, betwixt the case and the printing press, I usually afforded the setter copy at the rate of above a whole printed sheet in the day ; which, although by reason of the smallness of a Pica letter, and close couching thereof, it did amount to three full sheets of my writing ; the aforesaid setter, nevertheless (so nimble a workman he was), would in the space of twenty-four hours make dispatch of the whole, and be ready for another sheet. He and I striving thus who should compose fastest, he with his hand, and I with my brain ; and his uncasing of the letters, and placing them in the composing instrument, standing for my conception ; and his plenishing of the gally, and imposing of the form, encountering with the supposed equi-value of my writing, we would almost every foot or so jump together in this joynt expedition, and so neerly overtake other in our intended course, that I was oftentimes, (to keep him doing), glad to tear off parcels of ten or twelve lines apeece, and give him them, till more

were ready;[1] unto which he would so suddenly put
an order, that almost still, before the ink of the
written letters was dry, their representatives were,
(out of their respective boxes), ranked in the compos-
ing-stick; by means of which great haste, I writing
but upon the loose sheets of cording-quires, which, as
I minced and tore them, looking like pieces of waste
paper, troublesome to get rallyed, after such dis-
persive scattredness, I had not the leisure to read
what I had written, till it came to a proof, and
sometimes to a full revise.   So that by vertue of
this unanimous contest, and joint emulation betwixt the theoretick and practical part, which of us
should overhye other in celerity, we in the space of
fourteen working daies compleated this whole book,
(such as it is), from the first notion of the brain to
the last motion of the press; and that without any
other help on my side, either of quick or dead, (for

[1] Sir Egerton Brydges, Bart., an author who combines a great
many of the peculiarities of the two Sir Thomas Urquharts, the
father and the son, and who has recorded his experiences in an
Autobiography, lays stress in like manner upon this quality of
speed in composition.   Thus he says of his little novel, *Mary de
Clifford* (published in 1792), "it was written with a fervent
rapidity, which no one seems to believe;—begun in October, 1791,
and the sheets sent to the press by the post, as fast as they were
scribbled."   The passage in which he refers to the vexations to
which he had been subjected is worth quoting, on account of its
similarity to our Sir Thomas's story.   "I have suffered," he says,
"a hundred times more disappointments, and crosses, and insults,
and wrongs, and deprivations, than Chatterton, yet my spirit,
though bent and sunk, was never broken.   I am calm and defiant,
though not hopeful, in proportion as the storm presses me;—and
what trials have I not undergone?   I do not mean to relate all
these trials; it would involve the conduct of obscure individuals,
many of whom are still living" (*Autobiography*, pp. 8, 9).

books I had none, nor possibly would I have made
use of any, although I could have commanded
them), then [than] what, (by the favour of God),
my own judgment and fancy did suggest unto
me." [1]

The account which our author gives of the
plunder of his manuscripts after the battle of
Worcester, and of the strange series of accidents
by which some of the documents which make up
The Jewel were preserved, is so odd and amusing that it would be a pity to deprive our readers
of it, though it is related by Sir Thomas at great
length. " No sooner," he says, " had the total rout
of the regal party at Worcester given way to the
taking of that city, and surrendring up of all the
prisoners to the custody of the marshal-general
and his deputies, but the liberty, customary at
such occasions to be connived at in favours of
a victorious army, imboldened some of the new-
levied forces of the adjacent counties to confirm
their conquest by the spoil of the captives. For
the better atchievement of which designe, not
reckoning those great many others that in all the
other corners of the town were ferreting every
room for plunder, a string or two of exquisite snaps
and clean shavers [snappers-up and plunderers ?]
(if ever there were any), rushing into Master Spilsbury's house, (who is a very honest man, and hath
an exceeding good woman to his wife), broke into
an upper chamber, where finding, (besides scarlet
cloaks, buff suits, arms of all sorts, and other such
rich chaffer, at such an exigent escheatable to the

[1] *Works*, p. 181.

prevalent soldier [1]), seven large portmantles ful of precious commodity ; in three whereof, after a most exact search for gold, silver, apparel, linen, or any whatever adornments of the body, or pocket implements, as was seized upon in the other four, not hitting on any things but manuscripts in folio, to the quantity of six score and eight quires and a half, divided into six hundred fourty and two quinternions and upwards, the quinternion consisting of five sheets, and the quire of five and twenty ; besides some writings of suits in law, and bonds, in both worth above three thousand pounds English, they in a trice carried all whatever els was in the room away save those papers, which they then threw down on the floor as unfit for their use ; yet immediately thereafter, when upon carts the aforesaid baggage was put to be transported to the country, and that by the example of many hundreds of both horse and foot, whom they had loaded with spoil, they were assaulted with the temptation of a new booty, they apprehending how useful the paper might be unto them, went back for it, and bore it straight away ; which done, to every one of those their camarads whom they met with in the streets, they gave as much thereof, for packeting up of raisins, figs, dates, almonds, caraway, and other such like dry confections and other ware, as was requisite ; who, doing the same themselves, did together with others kindle pipes of tobacco with a great part thereof, and threw out all the remainder upon the streets. . . . .

---

[1] *I.e.* at such an extremity liable to be forfeited to the victorious soldier.

" Of those dispersedly-rejected bundles of paper, some were gathered up by grocers, druggists, chandlers, pie-makers, or such as stood in need of any cartapaciatory utensil, and put in present service, to the utter undoing of all the writing thereof, both in its matter and order.   One quinternion, nevertheless, two days after the fight on the Friday morning, together with two other loose sheets more, by vertue of a drizelling rain, which had made it stick fast to the ground, where there was a heap of seven and twenty dead men lying upon one another, was by the command of one Master Braughton taken up by a servant of his ; who, after he had (in the best manner he could) cleansed it from the mire and mud of the kennel, did forthwith present it to the perusal of his master ; in whose hands it no sooner came, but instantly perceiving by the periodical couching of the discourse, marginal figures, and breaks here and there, according to the variety of the subject, that the whole purpose was destinated for the press, and by the author put into a garb befitting either the stationer or printer's acceptance ; yet because it seemed imperfect, and to have relation to subsequent tractates, he made all the enquiry he could for trial whether there were any more such quinternions or no ; by means whereof he got full information that above three thousand sheets of the like paper, written after that fashion, and with the same hand, were utterly lost and imbezzeled, after the manner aforesaid ; and was so fully assured of the misfortune, that to gather up spilt water, comprehend the windes within his fist, and recover those papers again, he thought would be a work of one and the same labour and facility." [1]

The anonymous personage who gives the above account says that he heard of Mr Braughton's discovery of these remarkable documents, and also of "the great moan made for the loss of Sir Thomas Urquhart's manuscripts," and, putting the two facts together, resolved to ask Sir Thomas if the papers found at Worcester belonged to him. He examined them, and identified them as part of the preface to a grammar and lexicon of a Universal Language, of which he was the inventor. The loss of a work of such a size and of such great importance did not greatly depress him. He stated that if he got but encouragement and time, freedom and the enjoyment of his ancestral estates, he doubted not but that he could supply the missing sheets—the originals of which had come to such base uses and disastrous fate at Worcester. The papers, therefore, found by Mr Braughton are published in order that the readers may see the reasonableness of giving Sir Thomas what he asked, in view of the astounding benefits which he would in return confer upon them. This is put with great clearness and brevity in a couplet prefixed to the above narrative :

> " He should obtain all his desires,
> Who offers more than he requires."

The fragment of the treatise concerning the Universal Language, which was picked up out of the gutter of Worcester streets, wiped clean, and

[1] *Works*, pp. 189, 190.

presented to the public in *The Jewel*, was re-published with additions in Sir Thomas Urquhart's next work, so that we may here pass it over without further notice and allude to some of the other matters treated of.

In order to vindicate the honour of his country, Sir Thomas Urquhart tells at considerable length of the fame won by various compatriots of his in war in every part of Europe, during the earlier half of the seventeenth century, and he draws the attention of his readers to the fact that, at no battle in the period named, were all the Scots that fought overthrown and totally routed. The explanation of this statement is that there were always Scots on both sides, so that, if some were defeated and taken prisoners, others of that nation were victorious and givers of quarter. This part of the work is of great historical value, and, as Burton remarks, is not liable to the reproach of Urquhart's usual wandering profuseness of language—its leading defect, on the other hand, being its too great resemblance at times to a muster-roll.

The choicest and most remarkable passage in Sir Thomas Urquhart's original works is, undoubtedly, the description he gives in *The Jewel* of his fellow-countryman "the Admirable Crichton," who belonged to the latter part of the sixteenth century. In an appendix [1] our readers may find a long extract from it, in which that hero's feats are related. But for fear of making the appendices out of all proportion to the size of this volume, the whole sketch might have been given. To most people the name

[1] Appendix II. p. 215.

of "the Admirable Crichton" is now a mere proverbial phrase to describe a universal genius, and
whether the person who bore it is a historical or a
mythical character, is a matter of some uncertainty.
If any who are possessed of only this amount of
information on the subject seek for more by reading
our author's description of Crichton, the probability is that they will decide that he is quite
mythical. The extraordinary flightiness, turgidity,
and bombast which mark the narrative, in spite of
its many conspicuous merits, make it seem a mere
piece of burlesque, rather than a genuine history ; [1]
and yet there is ample evidence of an unimpeach-
able kind of the truthfulness of the main statements which it contains. Sir Thomas Urquhart's
narrative was for a long time one of the principal
sources of information concerning the brilliant
young Scotchman, and the result was that a general
disbelief in the whole history became prevalent.[2]

[1] "This part is written in a euphuistic, rhapsodical vein, and
affords an indication of the saturation of Urquhart's mind with the
style of Rabelais. It might almost be pieced together from the
meeting of Pantagruel with the Limousin scholar, the discomfiture
of Thaumast by Panurge, and the meeting of Pantagruel and his
party with Queen Entelechia" (W. F. Smith's Introduction to
Rabelais).

[2] Dr Kippis, the editor of the *Biographia Britannica, or Lives
of the Most Eminent Persons who have Flourished in Great Britain
and Ireland* (1789), had a bad time in writing the notice of
Crichton that appears in it. He says that he entered upon the
task with diffidence, and even with anxiety. On the one hand,
he was desirous not to detract from Crichton's real merit, and, on
the other, he wished to form a just estimate of the truth of the
facts which are recorded concerning him. Part of his perturbation
of mind was due to the indignation which he felt towards our
author, whose narrative of Crichton's adventures he regarded as

As Burton says, "It was from the hands of Sir Thomas Urquhart that the world accepted of an idol which, after a period of worship, it cast down, but so hastily, as it was discovered, that it had again to be set up, but rather in surly justice than the old devout admiration."[1] Tytler, in his *Life of the Admirable Crichton*, gives full proof from contemporary writers that the accomplishments and feats ascribed to that personage are authentic.

James Crichton was born in 1560, of a noble family, at Eliock, in Perthshire. At the age of ten he became a student at St. Andrews, then the most famous university in Scotland. Before he was fifteen years of age he graduated as Master of Arts,

utterly untrustworthy. At an early stage in the article he remarks : "And here it must be observed that no credit can be granted to any facts which depend upon the sole authority of Sir Thomas Urquhart. . . . I must declare my full persuasion that Sir Thomas Urquhart is an author whose testimony to facts is totally unworthy of regard ; and it is surprising that a perusal of his works does not strike every mind with this conviction. His productions are so inexpressibly absurd and extravagant, that the only rational judgment which can be pronounced concerning him is, that he was little, if at all, better than a madman. To the character of his having been a madman must be added that of his being a liar. Severe as this term may be thought, I apprehend that a diligent examination of the treatise which contains the memorials concerning Crichton would show that it is strictly true." The censure uttered by Dr Kippis is very severe, but some excuse for him is easily found. He was anxious to make his dictionary of biography a mine of facts on which the public could rely with absolute confidence ; and he saw before him the danger of quoting as an authority a writer like Urquhart, who so palpably elongated facts and embroidered them with fancies. His opinion with regard to the *Pedigree* of the Urquharts is given on p. 144.

[1] *The Scot Abroad*, p. 256. In the *Adventurer*, No. 81, Dr Johnson has reproduced Sir Thomas Urquhart's narrative of the career of Crichton, but has toned down its glowing colours.

and stood third in order of merit among the students of his year. After leaving the university he spent three years in the pursuit of learning, devoting himself to one after another of the various branches of the science and philosophy of his time, until he had gone through nearly the whole of them ; and, by force of natural ability, aided, no doubt, by intense application, he acquired the use of ten different languages.

Some time probably in the year 1578 he began his foreign travels, with the desire not only to enlarge his experience of the world, but also to display the extent of his learning in those public disputations which were still in fashion at the continental universities. In form and countenance he is said to have been a perfect model of manly beauty ; whilst in all the accomplishments of his time he was as well versed as in the branches of learning. He was a skilful swordsman, a bold rider, a graceful dancer, a sweet singer, and a cultivated musician. Soon after his arrival in Paris he set up, in accordance with a custom of the time, in various parts of the city, challenges to literary and philosophic disputation, and announced that he would present himself on a certain day at the College of Navarre, to answer any questions that might be put to him " in any science, liberal art, discipline, or faculty, whether practical or theoretic," and this in any one of twelve specified languages—Hebrew, Syriac, Arabic, Greek, Latin, Spanish, French, Italian, English, Dutch, Flemish, or Sclavonian. Our readers may find in the appendix a full narrative in Sir Thomas Urquhart's inimitable style of this extraordinary episode. Though Crichton seemed to make no preparation for the learned encounter, to which he had challenged the most scholarly men in France, he acquitted himself in such a manner as to astonish all beholders, and to receive the congratulations of the president and professors of the University of Paris. From this display of his intellectual powers and acquirements, as well as from the brilliant figure he cut at the balls and tournaments, which were such favourite employments of the Court of France at that time, he acquired the title by which he is now universally known—that of "the Admirable Crichton."[1]

It is worth while to compare the passage in Rabelais which describes the similar feats of the giant Pantagruel with the account Sir Thomas Urquhart gives of Crichton's intellectual tournaments.[2] To us there seems something very

---

[1] The reader will remember that this simply meant the "Wonderful Crichton"—this use of the word "admire" being now archaic.

[2] The passage in Rabelais is as follows :—"Pantagruel . . . would one day make trial of his knowledge. Thereupon in all the Carrefours, that is, throughout all the foure quarters, streets and corners of the city, he set up Conclusions to the number of nine thousand seven hundred sixty and foure,* in all manner of learning, touching in them the hardest doubts that are in any science. And first of all, in the Fodder-street† he held disputes

---

* Pico della Mirandola in the winter of 1486-87 offered to maintain at Rome 900 theses *de omni scibili* (W. F. S.).

† *Rue de la Feurre* (near the Place Maubert) was the street in Paris where the poorer students used to lodge. It got its name because straw served them for beds and furniture. Dante says in *Par.* x. 137 :

> "Essa è la luce eterna di Sigieri,
> Che, leggendo nel vico degli strami,
> Sillogizzò invidiosi veri." (*Ibid.*).

ridiculous in the practice of posting up placards on the walls, challenging all-comers to disputation, but in the sixteenth century it would not necessarily appear in this light. Rabelais, indeed, laughed at it; but then he laughed at many things which the people of his time did not think absurd. John Hill Burton is of the opinion that Sir Thomas Urquhart, in describing the way in which Crichton conducted himself on the field which had witnessed Pantagruel's feats, had the ridicule of Rabelais in view, and that, in spite of his laudations, we

against all the Regents or Fellowes of Colledges, Artists or Masters of Arts, and Oratours, and did so gallantly, that he overthrew them, and set them all upon their tailes. He went afterwards to the Sorbonne, where he maintained argument against all the Theologians or Divines, for the space of six weeks, from foure a clock in the morning until six in the evening, except an interval of two houres to refresh themselves, and take their repast. And at this were present the greatest part of the Lords of the Court, the Masters of Requests, Presidents, Counsellors, those of the Accompts, Secretaries, Advocates, and others : as also the Sheriffes of the said town, with the Physicians and Professors of the Canon-Law. Amongst which it is to be remarked, that the greatest part were stubborn jades, and in their opinions obstinate ; but he took such course with them, that, for all their ergo's and fallacies, he put their backs to the wall, gravelled them in the deepest questions, and made it visibly appear to the world, that, compared to him, they were but monkies, and a knot of mufled calves. Whereupon everybody began to keep a bustling noise, and talk of his so marvellous knowledge, through all degrees of persons in both sexes, even to the very laundresses, brokers, rostmeat-sellers, penknife-makers, and others, who, when he past along in the street, would say, This is he ! in which he took delight, as Demosthenes the prince of Greek oratours did when an old crouching wife, pointing at him with her fingers, said, That is the man " * (ii. chap. 10).

---

* Cf. "At pulchrum est, digito monstrari, et dicier : Hic est" (*Pers.* i. 28). (*Ibid.*)

cannot help having the impression that his tongue
is all the time in his cheek. We think that this
is unfair to Sir Thomas. There is no reason why
those who looked on in admiration at a real tourna-
ment should not also enjoy seeing a burlesque
one. So that it is quite possible that our author
smiled while he translated the French satire, and
that he glowed with honest pride and admiration
as he recounted his fellow-countryman's exploits
before the University of Paris.

After serving for a couple of years in the French
army, Crichton journeyed into Italy, and in the
month of August, 1580, arrived in Venice. He
made the acquaintance of the famous printer, Aldus
Manutius, who introduced him to the principal
men of learning and note in that city. Here he
maintained the reputation he had acquired in Paris,
and lives of him were written and published. From
Venice he proceeded to Padua, and from thence to
the Court of Mantua, where the adventure occurred
with which Sir Thomas Urquhart begins the
narrative of his celebrated fellow-countryman's
exploits, namely, the defeat and death of the travelling bravo, whose challenge he had accepted. Sir
Thomas is the only authority for this incident in
Crichton's history. As there is no reason to believe
that he invented it, we are at liberty to suppose
that he found it in some one of the lives of
Crichton which he met with in his Italian travels,
but which has not come down to us, or that he
heard of it from some of those who witnessed it.
For, as Urquhart was born only twenty-three years
after Crichton's death, he must, in the course of

his continental travels, have met some who were his contemporaries.[1]

In consequence of this achievement, and also of the brilliant reputation acquired by Crichton, he was appointed by the Duke of Mantua, companion and tutor to his son, Vincenzio de Gonzaga, a young man of some literary culture, but of furious temper and dissolute morals. Very soon after, Crichton met his death in a tragical manner. He was walking home one evening in the streets of Mantua, from a visit to his mistress, and was playing a guitar, when suddenly he was attacked by a riotous party of men in masks, whom, however, he speedily put to flight. He seized the leader of the party, overpowered him, and tore off his mask, and found to his horror that it was his own pupil, the son of the Duke of Mantua. He instantly dropped upon one knee, and, in a spirit of romantic devotion, took his sword by the blade, and presented its hilt to the prince. Vincenzio, heated with wine, irritated at his discomfiture, and also, it is said by some, inspired by jealousy, took the sword and plunged it into Crichton's heart. The brilliant young Scotsman was but twenty-two years of age when he thus met his fate.

The narrative which Sir Thomas Urquhart gives of the death of his hero is marked by the same richness of description as is to be found in the

[1] He says in reference to the whole history of Crichton: "The verity of this story I have here related, concerning this incomparable Crichton, may be certified by above two thousand men yet living, who have known him" (*Works*, p. 244). There can scarcely have been so many, unless centenarians were much commoner then than now.

account of his exploits as a scholar, a swordsman, and an actor. In language of astonishing luxuriance and frequent happiness of phrase, he enlarges upon the incidents of the last evening of Crichton's life, and depicts the tender intercourse of the lovers before the sudden and bloodly close of their courtship. With a minuteness which, as Tytler remarks, reminds one of the multitude of particulars by the enumeration of which Mrs Quickly sought to bring to Falstaff's remembrance his promise to marry her,[1] Sir Thomas Urquhart depicts the lovers in the " alcoranal paradise " in which they were embowered on that evening. " Nothing," he says, " tending to the pleasure of all the senses was wanting ; the weather being a little chil and coldish, they on a blue velvet couch sate by one another towards a char-coale fire burning in a silver brasero, whilst in the next room adjacent thereto a pretty little round table of cedar wood was a covering for the supping of them two together ; the cates prepared for them, and a week

---

[1] " Thou didst swear to me upon a parcel-gilt goblet, sitting in my Dolphin-chamber, at the round table, by a sea-coal fire, upon Wednesday in Wheeson week, when the prince broke thy head for liking his father to a singing-man of Windsor ; thou didst swear to me then, as I was washing thy wound, to marry me and make me my lady thy wife. Canst thou deny it ? Did not goodwife Keech, the butcher's wife, come in then and call me gossip Quickly ? coming in to borrow a mess of vinegar ; telling us she had a good dish of prawns ; whereby thou didst desire to eat some ; whereby I told thee they were ill for a green wound ? And didst thou not, when she was gone down stairs, desire me to be no more so familiarity with such poor people ; saying that ere long they should call me madam ? And didst thou not kiss me, and bid me fetch thee thirty shillings ? I put thee now to thy book-oath : deny it, if thou canst " (*2 Henry IV*. ii. i.).

before that time bespoke, were of the choisest dainties and most delicious junkets that all the territories of Italy were able to afford, and that deservedly, for all the Romane Empire could not produce a completer paire to taste them." [1]

A tragical note rings through the description of the lamentation of the hapless girl over her murdered lover. " She, rending her garments and tearing her haire, like one of the Graces possest with a Fury, spoke thus : ' O villains ! what have you done ? you vipers of men, that have thus basely slaine the valiant Crichtoun, the sword of his own sexe and the buckler of ours, the glory of this age, and restorer of the lost honour of the Court of Mantua : O Crichtoun, Crichtoun ! ' " [2]

The sequel of the story is in the same vein of florid eloquence. " The whole court," says Sir Thomas, " wore mourning for him full three quarters of a yeer together. His funeral was very stately, and on his hearse were stuck more epitaphs, elegies, threnodies, and epicediums, then [than], if digested into one book, would have outbulk't all Homer's works ; some of them being couched in such exquisite and fine Latin, that you would have thought great Virgil, and Baptista Mantuanus, for the love of their mother-city, had quit the Elysian fields to grace his obsequies ; and other of them, besides what was done in other languages, composed in so neat Italian, and so purely fancied, as if Ariosto, Dante, Petrark, and Bembo had been purposely resuscitated, to stretch even to the utmost their poetick vein to the honour of this

---

[1] *Works*, p. 234.   [2] *Ibid*. p. 243.

brave man; whose picture till this hour is to be seen in the bed-chambers or galleries of the most of the great men of that nation, representing him on horseback, with a lance in one hand and a book in the other; and most of the young ladies likewise, *that were anything handsome*,[1] in a memorial of his worth, had his effigies in a little oval tablet of gold hanging 'twixt their breasts, and held, for many yeers together, that metamazion, or intermammilary ornament, an as necessary outward pendicle for the better setting forth of their accoutrements, as either fan, watch, or stomacher. My lord Duke, upon the young lady that was Crichtoun's mistres and future wife, although she had good rents and revenues of her own by inheritance, was pleased to conferr a pension of five hundred ducats a yeer. The Prince also bestowed as much on her during all the days of his life, which was but short, for he did not long enjoy himself after the cross fate of so miserable an accident. The sweet lady, like a turtle bewailing the loss of her mate, spent all the rest of her time in a continual solitariness." [2]

After giving a long list of his fellow-countrymen who had won fame in foreign lands by their valour,

[1] The italics are ours.

[2] *Works*, p. 224. At one of Charles Lamb's Wednesday evenings in Mitre Court Building, Hazlitt tells us, "the name of the Admirable Crichton was suddenly started as a splendid example of *waste* talents, so different from the generality of his countrymen." A North Briton present declared himself descended from that prodigy of learning and accomplishment, and said he had family plate in his possession as vouchers for the fact, with the initials engraved upon them of A. C.—"Admirable Crichton!" A phrenological report upon this gentleman by Charles Lamb would have enlarged "the public stock of harmless pleasure."

learning, or skill, in order to put to silence those who maligned his nation, Sir Thomas Urquhart takes up a less pleasing topic—that of contemporary politics. In the plainest and most forcible manner he repudiates the whole policy of the dominant party in Scotland, and declares that a true Royalist or Malignant like himself had much more in common with an Independent, than either of them had with a Presbyterian ; and he enlarges upon the turbulent disloyalty with which so many of the last-named party had, in his opinion, conducted themselves towards their sovereigns since Queen Mary's time, evidently in forgetfulness for the moment that his newly - found friends, the Independents, had executed Charles I. and abolished monarchy.

His account of the mode in which the Presbyterian or " Consistorian " party were in the habit of treating their kings is very amusing. " Of a king," he says, " they onely make use for their own ends, and so they will of any other supreme magistracie that is not of their own erection. Their kings are but as the kings of Lacedemon, whom the Ephors presumed to fine for any small offence ; or as the puppy [puppet] kings, which, after children have trimmed with bits of taffata, and ends of silver lace, and set them upon wainscoat cupboards besides marmalade and sugar-cakes, are oftentimes disposed of, even by those that did pretend so much respect unto them, for a two-peny custard, a pound of figs, or mess of cream. Verily, I think they make use of kings in their Consistorian State, as we do of card kings in playing at the hundred ; any one whereof, if there

be appearance of a better game without him, and
that the exchange of him for another incoming card
is like to conduce more for drawing of the stake, is
by good gamesters without any ceremony discarded :
or as the French on the Epiphany-day use their
Roy de la Febve, or king of the bean ; whom, after
they have honoured with drinking of his health,
and shouting *Le Roy boit, le Roy boit*, they make pay
for all the reckoning ; not leaving him sometimes
one peny, rather then [than] that the exorbitancie
of their debosh should not be satisfied to the full.
They may be likewise said to use their king as the
players at nine-pins do the middle kyle, which they
call the king ; at whose fall alone they aim, the
sooner to obtain the gaining of their prize ; or
as about Christmas we do the King of Misrule,
whom we invest with that title to no other end
but to countenance the bacchanalian riots and
preposterous disorders of the family where he is
installed.   The truth of all this appears by their
demeanour to Charles the Second, whom they
crowned their king at Sterlin, and who, though
he be for comeliness of person, valour, affability,
mercy, piety, closeness of counsel, veracity, foresight,
knowledge, and other vertues both moral and intellectual, in nothing inferior to any of his hundred
and ten predecessors, had nevertheless no more rule
in effect over the Presbyterian Senate of Scotland,
then [than] any of the six foresaid mock-kings had
above those by whom they were dignified with the
splendour of royal pomp." [1]

[1] *Works*, p. 277. The charity which "believeth all things and
hopeth all things," or the credulity which persuades itself of the

The passage in *The Jewel* which tells of the faults
of the clergy, as illustrated by the conduct of the
ministers of the parishes of which Sir Thomas was
patron, has already been given in these pages, and
therefore need not be repeated here; but room
must be found for the paragraph in which he
denounces those who by their covetousness had cast
a slur upon the Scottish name. The art of writing
such English perished with him, its inventor; and
one cannot be too thankful for such a passage as
the following. "Another thing there is," he says,
" that fixeth a grievous scandal upon that nation in
matter of philargyrie, or love of money, and it is
this: There hath been in London, and repairing to
it, for these many years together, a knot of Scotish
bankers, collybists, or coine-coursers, of traffickers
in merchandise to and againe, and of men of other
professions, who by hook and crook, *fas et nefas*,
slight and might, (all being as fish their net could
catch), having feathered their nests to some purpose,
look so idolatrously upon their Dagon of wealth, and
so closely, (like the earth's dull center), hug all unto
themselves, that for no respect of vertue, honour,
kinred, patriotism, or whatever else, (be it never so

truth of the things which it wishes to believe, is manifest in Sir
Thomas Urquhart's estimate of the character of Charles II. Less
charitable or more impartial critics are probably inclined to the
opinion that the existence in that sovereign of a number of the
above-mentioned virtues was as mythical as that of a good many of
his "hundred and ten predecessors." So far as "comeliness" is
concerned, Charles II. at a later period had a much humbler view of
the matter than Sir Thomas here expresses. For he complained
that when they wished to represent a villain on the stage they
made up a figure somewhat like himself. See Cibber's *Apology*,
p. 111.

recommendable), will they depart from so much as one single peny, whose emission doth not, without any hazard of loss, in a very short time superlucrate beyond all conscience an additionall increase to the heap of that stock which they so much adore; which churlish and tenacious humor hath made many that were not acquainted with any else of that country, to imagine all their compatriots infected with the same leprosie of a wretched peevishness, whereof those *quomodocunquizing* clusterfists and rapacious varlets have given of late such cannibal-like proofs, by their inhumanity and obdurate carriage towards some, (whose shoe-strings they are not worthy to unty), that were it not that a more able pen then [than] mine will assuredly not faile to jerk them on all sides, in case, by their better demeanour for the future, they endeavour not to wipe off the blot wherewith their native country, by their sordid avarice and miserable baseness, hath been so foully stained, I would at this very instant blaze them out in their names and surnames, notwithstanding the vizard of Presbyterian zeal wherewith they maske themselves, that like so many wolves, foxes, or Athenian Timons, they might in all times coming be debarred the benefit of any honest conversation." [1]

After suggesting a number of ways in which the tone of society in Scotland might be raised and sweetened—one of which is the establishment of " a free schoole and standing library in every parish " [2]—Sir Thomas proceeds to argue in a very

[1] *Works*, p. 212.

[2] His unhappy prejudices against the Presbyterian clergy are

sensible and convincing manner for complete union between Scotland and England. The subject is introduced by lengthy quotations from speeches by Bacon, delivered by him in Parliament as far back as the year 1608, in which the advantages of such an arrangement are set forth.

The style of our author is seen at its worst in the peroration to *The Jewel*, in which he apologizes for the comparative simplicity, if not baldness, by which, in the opinion of some, it might be thought to be characterised. " I could truly," he says, " have enlarged this discourse with a choicer variety of phrase, and made it overflow the field of the reader's understanding, with an inundation of greater eloquence ; and that one way, tropologetically, by metonymical, ironical, metaphorical, and synecdochical instruments of elocution, in all their several kinds, artificially affected, according to the nature of the subject, with emphatical expressions in things of great concernment, with catachrestical in matters of meaner moment ; attended on each side respectively with an epiplectick and exegetick modification ; with hyperbolical, either epitatically or hypocoristically, as the purpose required to be elated or extenuated, with qualifying metaphors, and accompanied by apostrophes ; and lastly, with allegories of all sorts, whether apologal, affabulatory, parabolary, ænigmatick, or paræmial. And on the other part, schematologetically adorning the proposed

---

irrepressible, for immediately after suggesting "a standing library in custody of the minister of the parish," he adds, "with this proviso, that none of the books should be embezeled by him or any of his successors" (*Works*, p. 282).

theam with the most especial and chief flowers of
the garden of rhetorick, and omitting no figure either
of diction or sentence, that might contribute to the
ear's enchantment, or perswasion of the hearer.   I
could have introduced, in case of obscurity, synony-
mal, exargastick, and palilogetick elucidations; for
sweetness of phrase, antimetathetick commutations
of epithets; for the vehement excitation of a matter,
exclamation in the front, and epiphonemas in the
reer.   I could have used, for the promptlier stirring
up of passion, apostrophal and prosopopœial diversions; and, for the appeasing and settling of them,
some epanorthotick revocations, and aposiopetick
restraines.   I could have inserted dialogismes,
displaying their interrogatory part with communi-
catively pysmatick and sustentative flourishes; or
proleptically, with the refutative schemes of anticipation and subjection, and that part which concerns
the responsory, with the figures of permission and
concession.   Speeches extending a matter beyond
what it is, auxetically, digressively, transitiously, by
ratiocination, ætiology, circumlocution, and other
wayes, I could have made use of; as likewise with
words diminishing the worth of a thing, tapinotically,
periphrastically, by rejection, translation, and other
meanes, I could have served myself." [1]

[1] We have reason to be thankful to Sir Thomas for his kindness
in refraining from the style of composition which he here indicates,
for we can scarcely credit his assurance that the results would have
been less terrifying than the description of the processes by which
they would have been reached.   There is no need for an apology,
for he has really done pretty well as it is.   Mr Ruskin had once a
vision of ten thousand school-inspectors assembled on Cader Idris.
What horror would seize such a company, if they were treated as a

He goes on for a long time in this strain, and
is at pains to explain that, if the work had been
written in this more elaborate manner, it would not
necessarily have been found tedious even by young
ladies. "I could have presented it to the imagination," he says, "in so spruce a garb, that spirits
blest with leisure, and free from the urgency of
serious employments, would happily have bestowed
as liberally some few houres thereon as on the
perusal of a new-coined romance, or strange history
of love adventures. For although the figures and
tropes above rehearsed seem in their *actu signato*, (as
they signifie meer notional circumstances, affections,
adjuncts, and dependencies on words), to be a little
pedantical, and to the smooth touch of a delicate
ear somewhat harsh and scabrous, yet in their
exerced act, (as they suppone for things reduplicat-
ively as things in the first apprehension of the
minde, by them signified), I could, even in far abstruser
purposes, have so fitly adjusted them with apt and
proper termes, and with such perspicuity couched
them, as would have been suitable to the capacities
of courtiers and young ladies,[1] whose tender hearing,
for the most part, being more taken with the in-

class in elementary English, and the above passage were read out
as an exercise in dictation ! Nay, it is to be feared that even the
more august assembly in Dover House, the Lords of Education
themselves, would be panic-stricken at such a task.   Only
Macaulay's "school-boy" would probably be found to enter upon
it with unblenched countenance, and to accomplish it successfully.

[1] This reminds us of Bottom the weaver. "I will roar that I
will do any man's heart good to hear me. . . . [Yet not to frighten
the ladies.] I will aggravate my voice so that I will roar you as
gently as any sucking dove : I will roar you an 'twere any nightingale" (*Midsummer-Night's Dream*, I. ii.).

sinuating harmony of a well-concerted period, in its isocoletick and parisonal members, then [than] with the never-so-pithy a fancy of a learned subject, destitute of the illustriousness of so pathetick ornaments, will sooner convey perswasion to the interior faculties from the ravishing assault of a well-disciplined diction, in a parade of curiously-mustered words in their several ranks and files then [than] by the vigour and fierceness of never so many powerful squadrons of a promiscuously-digested elocution into bare logical arguments; for the sweetness of their disposition is more easily gained by undermining passion then [than] storming reason, and by the musick and symmetry of a descourse in its external appurtenances, then [than] by all the puissance imaginary of the ditty or purpose disclosed by it." [1]

The last of Sir Thomas Urquhart's original works was his " LOGOPANDECTEISION, or an INTRODUCTION TO THE UNIVERSAL LANGUAGE," a portion of which, as already mentioned, had been embedded in the conglomerate mass of *The Jewel*. The idea of a universal language was not originated by Urquhart, for it is said that something of the kind had been planned a generation earlier by the celebrated William Bedell (1570–1642), the Bishop of Kilmore and Ardagh, who is better known for promoting the translation of the Bible into the Irish tongue. We are told by Burnet, who wrote his life, that he had in his diocese a clergyman named Johnston, a man of ability, but, unfortunately, of "mercurial wit." In order to give him adequate employment, and to

---

[1] *Works*, pp. 292, 293.

keep him, we suppose, out of mischief, Bedell planned out a scheme for a universal character, which should be understood by all nations as readily as the Arabic numerals or the figures in geometry, and started Johnston upon the task of completing it.   He made, we are told, considerable progress with the scheme, but his labours were interrupted, and the results of them destroyed, by the frightful rebellion of 1641.

The *Logopandecteision*[1] is divided into six books, which bear names of the remarkable kind which seem to come so readily to Urquhart's tongue, and are so hard to be compassed by the tongues of others.   The "Epistle Dedicatorie" is an elaborate piece of writing, and is animated by considerable bitterness of spirit.   It is addressed to Nobody— the person who has assisted him in his labours, pitied him in his sorrows, and relieved him in his penury.   It is only the first book—entitled "Neaudethaumata, or Wonders of the New Speech" —which makes a pretence of dealing with the professed subject of the volume, and of laying the

---

[1] *Logopandectcision,* or an INTRODUCTION to the UNIVERSAL LANGUAGE.   Digested into these Six several Books, Neaudethaumata, Chrestasebeia, Cleronomaporia, Chryseomystes, Neleodicastes, and Philoponauxesis.   By Sir Thomas Urquhart of *Cromartie,* Knight.   Now lately contrived and published, both for his own utilitie, and that of all pregnant and ingenious Spirits. *Credere quaerenti nonne haec justissima res est?   Qui non plura cupit, quam ratio ipsa jubet.   Englished thus,* To grant him his demands, were it not just?   Who craves no more, then [than] reason sayes he must. *London.*   Printed, and are to be sold by *Giles Calvert* at the *Black Spread Eagle* at the West-end of *Pauls;* and by *Richard Tomlins* at the Sun and Bible near Pye-corner. 1653.

great scheme before the reader. Much to the gratification of the judicious student of the work, Urquhart rambles off in the remaining books into autobiographical details, from which we have already gleaned heavily in the earlier chapters of this volume, and the only connexion between them and the Universal Language is that they show the difficulties which prevented the author from carrying out his plan. The sources from which these difficulties arose are vaguely indicated in the titles of the books: thus, the second is called "Chrestasebeia, or Impious Dealing of Creditors": the third, "Cleronomaporia, or the Intricacy of a Distressed Successor or Apparent Heir"; the fourth, "Chryseomystes, or the Covetous Preacher"; and the fifth, "Neleodicastes, or the Pitiless Judge." While the sixth book is entitled "Philoponauxesis, or Furtherance of Industry," and tells of the marvellous benefits which would accrue to all branches of trade, manufacture, and industry in Scotland, if the writer's demands were granted, and he were at liberty to carry out the multitudinous schemes with which his mind was filled. The volume concludes with requests or "proquiritations" from thirty-two distinct petitioners, who modestly conceal themselves from public notice under the shelter of the initial letters of their names, that the State would, for the various weighty reasons which they allege, grant the desire of Sir Thomas to be set free, and to be established in possession of the estates and honours which his family had enjoyed from time immemorial. This section of the work suggests failure in ingenuity on the part of the author, for few persons above the condition of idiocy could surely be found capable of believing that the reasons and initials alike were anything else than the concoction of Sir Thomas himself.

Very slight indeed can be the notice which we are able to give of the proposed Universal Language, the description of which, as set forth in the early part of the *Logopandecteision,* is more like an incoherent dream than anything else. There is no evidence that Sir Thomas Urquhart ever really made a grammar or vocabulary of the new language. Indeed, he writes about it in such a manner as to lead one to think that he had made no way in the real working out of the scheme, but merely dreamed of what he was going to do. In the new tongue which was to supersede all others there were to be twelve parts of speech, all words would have at least ten synonyms, nouns and pronouns would have eleven cases and four numbers—singular, dual, plural, and redual—and verbs would have four voices, seven moods, and eleven tenses. "In this tongue," says the author, "there are eleven genders,[1] wherein," he truthfully adds, "it exceedeth

---

[1] Eleven genders seem nine more than are necessary, and the use of such a large number suggests to one that in Sir Thomas's Universal Language the distinctions in question were to receive an undue amount of attention. At the same time, fault has been found with our English language for being somewhat defective in accentuating these distinctions; and an attempt to correct this shortcoming, to a certain extent, has been made by Southey in *The Doctor.* He proposed to anglicise the orthography of the female garment, "which is indeed the sister to the shirt," and then to utilise the hint offered in its new form : thus *Hemise* and *Shemise.* In letter-writing every person knows that male and female letters have a distinct character ; they should therefore, he thought, be generally distinguished thus, *Hepistle* and *Shepistle.* And as

all other languages." "Every word in this language," we are told, "signifieth as well backward as forward, and however you invert the letters, still shall you fall upon significant words, whereby a wonderful facility is obtained in making of anagrams. . . . Of all languages, this is the most compendious in complement, and consequently fittest for courtiers and ladies. . . . As its interjections are more numerous, so are they more emphatical in their respective expression of passions, then [than] that part of speech is in any other language whatsoever." [1] And finally Sir Thomas vouches for its conciseness in a hyperbole which it would be difficult to excel. "This language," he says, "affordeth so concise words for numbering, that the number for setting down, whereof would require in vulgar arithmetic more figures in a row then [than] there might be grains of sand containable from the center of the earth to the highest heavens, is in it expressed by

there is the same marked difference in the writing of the two sexes, he proposed *Penmanship* and *Penwomanship*. Erroneous opinions in religion being promulgated in this country by women as well as men, the teachers of such false doctrine may be divided into *Heresiarchs* and *Sheresiarchs*, so that we should speak of the *Heresy* of the Quakers and the *Sheresy* of Joanna Southcote's people. The troublesome affection of the diaphragm, which every one has experienced, is, upon the same principle, to be called, according to the sex of the patient, *Hecups*, or *Shecups*, which, upon the principle of making our language truly British, is better than the more classical form of *Hiccups* and *Haccups*. In its object-ive use the word becomes Hiscups or Hercups; and in like manner Histerics should be altered into Herterics, the complaint never being masculine. It is perhaps a little surprising that this suggestion should have lain before the British public for half a century, and have been left unutilised.

[1] *Works*, pp. 316–318.

two letters."[1]   A considerable revenue might be
secured if the rule found at the end of some of
Grimm's *Household Tales* were applied to this statement, and strictly enforced : " Whosoever does not
believe this must pay a thaler."   In a very innocent
manner our author excuses himself for the extravagant praise he has poured out upon his own
invention.   " Why it is," he exclaims, " I should
extoll the worth thereof, without the jeopardy of
vaine glory, the reason is clear and evident, being
necessitated . . . to merchandise it for the redin-
tegrating of an ancient family, it needeth not be
thought strange, that in some measure I descend
to the fashion of the shop-keepers, who, to scrue
up the buyer to the higher price, will tell them no
better can be had for mony, 'tis the choicest ware
in England, and if any can match it, he shall have
it for nought . . . [And so] I went on in my
laudatives, to procure the greater longing, that an
ardent desire might stir up an emacity [a pro-
pensity to buy], to the furtherance of my proposed
end."   One is obliged sadly to assent to his further
statement   about   such   conduct — " whereof . . .
there wanteth not store of presidents [precedents]." [2]

Hugh Miller, animated by the patriotic zeal
which prompts one North Briton to stand by
another, and with the desire to make out the best
case possible for one who was not only a fellow-
countryman, but also a fellow-townsman, speaks in
high terms of Urquhart's inventive powers as displayed in the *Logopandecteision*.   " The new chemical
vocabulary," he says, " with all its philosophical

---

[1] *Works*, pp. 316–318.   [2] *Ibid.* p. 332.

ingenuity, is constructed on principles exactly similar to those which he divulged more than a hundred years prior to its invention, in the preface to his Universal Language."[1]   This is a statement which it is rather difficult to understand.   The only indication of the nature of the new tongue which we can glean from Sir Thomas's description of it, is that every letter of every word in it would have a meaning, so that when anyone who knew the principles of the language heard a word for the first time, he would understand it.[2]   Now, of course, it is true that anyone who knows the principle of the nomenclature of salts, to which, we suppose, Hugh Miller refers, can tell a good deal about a

---

[1] *Scenes and Legends*, chap. vii.

[2] A somewhat similar project was described in the Marquis of Worcester's *Century of the Names and Scantling of* . . . *Inventions* (1663), in which the steam-engine is anticipated. The passage is as follows :—"32.   How to compose an universal character, methodical, and easie to be written, yet intelligible in any language : so that if an English-man write it in English, a Frenchman, Italian, Spaniard, Irish, Welsh, being scholars, yea, Grecian or Hebritian, shall as perfectly understand it in their owne Tongue, as if they were perfect English, distinguishing the Verbs from the Nouns, the Numbers, Tenses, Cases as properly expressed in their own Language as it was written in English."

A writer in *Blackwood's Magazine* in 1820 affirms that he has good reasons for believing that the above volume was really by Sir Thomas Urquhart, and was dishonestly put forth as the work of the Marquis of Worcester.   He does not give us any of his reasons.   The style of the little volume bears no resemblance to that of our author, and this fact is of itself almost conclusive proof that Sir Thomas Urquhart had nothing to do with it.   The Scottish knight could scarcely open his lips without revealing his identity.   It is rather difficult to believe, too, that a manuscript lost by Sir Thomas in the streets of Worcester should have been picked up by the Marquis of Worcester.   The coincidence would be a very extraordinary one.

salt from the name of it, say, nitrate of potassium, KNO_3, but it would be impossible to invent a systematic nomenclature of which this would not be true.

The same author is also very much impressed by the fact that the new language was to contain the dual, and regards this, on Lord Monboddo's authority, as a proof of philosophical acumen on the part of the inventor. He does not take any notice of the "redual," which the language was also to contain, and which might have been taken as an indication of double-distilled wisdom. Lord Monboddo (1714–1799) says of the Greek language that if there "were nothing else to convince him of its being a work of philosophers and grammarians, its dual number would of itself be sufficient; for as certainly as the principles of body are the point, the line, and the surface, the principles of number are the monad and the duad, though philosophers only are aware of the fact." The idea that this venerated instrument for the expression or conceal-ment of thought was the concoction of a committee of primitive sages, and that they deliberately in-vented the dual, and added it as another spike to the *chevaux - de - frise* through which our young people, of both sexes, have to struggle[1] on their way to the Temple of Learning, is truly revolting. One would not like to think that the ancient

---

[1] Hear Heine's angry allusions to his early scholastic experiences, in which he suggests another and less honourable origin of the Greek tongue: "Vom Griechischen will ich gar nicht sprechen—ich ärgere mich sonst zu viel. Die Mönche im Mittelalter hatten so ganz Unrecht nicht, wenn sie behaupteten, dass das Griechische eine Erfindung des Teufels sei" (*Das Buch Le Grand*, vii.).

Greeks were quite so malicious as to do a thing like that. It is more probably the case that, like other Aryans,[1] they received the dual as part of the inheritance of the past, handed down to them, and retained it; while in some of the cognate languages [1] it was gradually rubbed off, very much in the same way as Lord Monboddo's men lost their tails, when they gave up their arboreal habits, and betook themselves to sedentary occupations.

[1] Sanskrit, Old Persian, Lithuanian, and old Slavonic have the dual both in declension and conjugation, and in the first of these it is used much more frequently than in Greek. Faint traces of it in declension are to be found in Teutonic speech, though in conjugation it is only in the Gothic that the dual is used. In old Gaelic the dual is a regular feature of declension, but not of conjugation.

CHAPTER VII

HE foundation on which Sir Thomas Urquhart's literary fame securely rests is his translation into English of the first three books of the works of Rabelais. Of these the first and second appeared in two separate volumes in the year 1653—exactly a century after the death of the great French satirist—and the third was published by Pierre Antoine Motteux in 1693, long after Sir Thomas's own death.[1]

[1] The title-page of the first book does not contain Sir Thomas Urquhart's name, but on it is his motto ("Mean, speak, and do well"). It runs as follows :—"The first Book of the Works of MR. FRANCIS RABELAIS, Doctor in Physick : Containing Five Books of the Lives, Heroick Deeds, and Sayings of GARGANTUA and his Sonne PANTAGRUEL. Together with the Pantagrueline Prognostication, the Oracle of the divine Bacbuc, and response of the bottle. Hereunto are annexed the Navigations unto the sounding Isle and the Isle of the Apedefts : as likewise the Philosophical cream with a Limosin Epistle. All done by Mr. Francis Rabelais, in the French Tongue, and now faithfully translated into English. εὐνοεῖ εὐλογε καὶ εὔπραττε. London, Printed for Richard Baddeley, within the Middle Templegate. 1653." On the title-page of the second book are the translator's initials, S. T. V. C. (Sir Thomas Urquhart of Cromartie). While on that of the third book we have his name in full : "Now faithfully translated into English by the unimitable pen of Sir Thomas Urwhart, Kt. and Bar. The Trans-

The difficulty, singularity, and obscurity of the writings of Rabelais had probably been hindrances in the way of their being presented to the English public in their own tongue ; for, though the register of the Stationers' Company preserves a record of two attempts at translation, these seem to have been but fragmentary, and to have dropped still-born from the press.   The works themselves are not known to be extant, and nothing more than the bare name of them survives.

The difficulties which lie in the way of the ordinary reader who wishes to become acquainted with the·works of Rabelais are very considerable.[1] The fantastical style of the satirist, his countless allusions to contemporary persons and events, his

lator of the Two First Books.   Never before Printed.   London : Printed for Richard Baldwin, near the Oxford Arms in Warwick Lane, 1693." Copies of the first and second books of the above date are in the British Museum, but erroneously catalogued—not under Urquhart, but only under C., S. T. V.   A second edition of them both seems from the Bodleian Catalogue to have been published in 1664.   Both are very rare, it is said, owing to the destruction caused by the fire of London in 1666.

[1] For those who are not special students, adequate information concerning Rabelais and extracts from his works are to be got in Sir Walter Besant's luminous and charming volume in the series of Foreign Classics for English Readers (Blackwood), and in Morley's *Universal Library* (Routledge).   In one of his poems Browning describes the steps taken by a reader to banish the memory of a dreary pedant, whose book he had been perusing.   He says :

> "Then I went indoors, brought out a loaf,
>   Half a cheese, and a bottle of Chablis ;
> Lay on the grass, and forgot the oaf
>   Over a jolly chapter of Rabelais."

Some have turned over Rabelais and searched for the jolly chapter in vain, and have, perhaps, attributed their failure to the want of a bottle of Chablis.

out-of-the-way learning, the care with which he conceals at such length the seriousness of his purpose, and the incredible grossness of manners which so often disfigures his pages, are obstacles which can with difficulty be surmounted. The last-mentioned characteristic is, indeed, a grave and in-grained fault, which must for ever be a slur upon the writer's fame. Yet we may say of him what Don Pedro says of Benedick, "The man doth fear God howsoever it seems not in him by some large jests he will make": or what Mrs Blower in *St Ronan's Well* says of her deceased husband, "He was a merry man, but he had the root of the matter in him for a' his light way of speaking." Coleridge —"the brother," according to Mr Birrell, "whose praise is throughout all the churches"—speaks of Rabelais in very high terms indeed; "Beyond a doubt," he says, "he was among the deepest, as well as boldest thinkers of his age. His buffoonery was not merely Brutus' rough stick, which contained a rod of gold: it was necessary as an amulet against the monks and legates.[1] Never was there a more plausible, and seldom, I am persuaded, a less appropriate line than the thousand times quoted

'Rabelais laughing in his easy chair'

of Mr Pope. The caricature of his filth and zany-

[1] This is somewhat doubtful. The Sorbonne and the Parliaments might have been moved by ultra-orthodox opponents to prosecute Rabelais on this account. The true explanation seems to be that the form of his book was popular, and the popular French litera-ture of the Middle Ages—fableaux, farces, and burlesque romances —can hardly be exceeded in the matter of coarseness (*Ency. Brit.*, "Rabelais").

ism show how fully he both knew and felt the danger in which he stood. I could write a treatise in praise of the moral elevation of Rabelais' work, which would make the church stare and the conventicle groan,[1] and yet would be truth, and nothing but the truth. I class Rabelais with the great creative minds of the world, Shakespeare, Dante, Cervantes, etc."

François Rabelais was born in Touraine, according to the date usually given, and which there is no reason to question, in the same year as Luther and Raphael, A.D. 1483, and died in Paris in 1553. His father had a small estate, and was an apothecary (or, as some say, a tavern-keeper) in the town of Chinon, at the foot of the castle where, three centuries before, our Henry II. had died, and whither, a little more than fifty years before François was born, Joan of Arc had come with promises of supernatural aid to Charles VII. He was the youngest of five sons, and, as was often the case in those days, was provided for by being made a monk, while the other members of the family divided amongst them the paternal estate. In one passage in his works he speaks of mothers who "cannot bear their children nor brook them in their houses nine, nay often not seven years, but by putting a shirt over their robe, and by cutting a few hairs on the top of their head . . . they transform

---

[1] This is surely an early allusion to the superior sensitiveness on some points of the "*Nonconformist Conscience*." The fact alluded to should inspire joy rather than call forth sneers, for when a conscience becomes sensitive on some points there are reasonable hopes of its becoming sensitive on others.

them into birds," *i.e.*, get rid of them as soon as possible, and thrust them into monasteries. This seems to have been his own sad fate.

In course of time, after the schoolboy period of his life was past, he entered the order of Franciscan monks at the convent of Fontenay-le-Comte in Poitou, and took holy orders; and it was here, during the next fifteen years (1509–1524), that he devoted himself to the acquisition of everything in the shape of literature or learning, and laid the foundation of the astonishing erudition which his works display. His long residence in the monastery had inspired Rabelais with a deep hatred of monasticism and monks, and, after being allowed to exchange the Franciscan for the Benedictine order, he laid down the regular habit and took that of a secular priest, and left the convent without the sanction of his superior—a breach of ecclesiastical discipline which exposed him to severe censure. After wandering hither and thither in the pursuit of medical knowledge, he entered the University of Montpellier, graduated as a physician, and practised there with credit and success. After being Hospital Physician at Lyons, he spent some time in Rome, as a medical attendant upon Jean du Bellay, Bishop of Paris. While here he succeeded in making his peace with the Church, and by a papal Bull (17th January 1536) was allowed to return to the Benedictine order and to practise physic according to canonical rules, *i.e.*, to charge no fees and to use neither fire nor knife. This release from ecclesiastical disabilities allowed him to be appointed to a place in the abbey of St Maur-des-Fosses, near

Paris.   After another period of exile and wandering
he was nominated curé of Meudon, an office which he
resigned after two years.   Three months afterwards
he died in Paris (9th April, 1553), and was buried
in the cemetery of the parish of St Paul's.

The publication of the satirical writings of
Rabelais was spread over a long series of years,
from 1532 or 1533, when the first instalment,
in his *Gargantua*, was brought out, down to
1564, eleven years after his death, when the
fifth and concluding book of his *Pantagruel* was
issued in its entirety.   The main object of his
satire was what used to be called " the intolerance,
superstition, and disgusting follies and vices of the
Romish Church," but, incidentally, pretenders to
knowledge of every kind come under his lash.   For
when imposture, folly, and humbug grow too rank
and noisome, there arise, it can scarcely be by accident, men like Lucian, Rabelais, and Voltaire, whose
calling it is to cut them down.   That theirs is an
ill-requited office is sufficiently plain from the odium
which, in spite of their beneficent labours, is often
associated with their names.   " [Hast thou] only a
torch for burning, no hammer for building ? " says
the somewhat wearisome Herr Teufelsdröckh to
the last named of these satirists, " take our thanks,
then, and—thyself away." [1]   Yet the torch for
burning is as necessary as the hammer for building,
if the site for the Temple of Truth is to be prepared.   It may well be that burning down and
rooting up are needed before building can be begun,
and some of those who have endeavoured to benefit

[1] *Sartor Resartus*, chap. ix.

mankind have felt themselves called to the one sort of work rather than to the other.

The form which Rabelais chooses for the framework of his satire is the burlesque adventures of the giant Gargantua, of whom many legends were current in Touraine, and of his son Pantagruel, sometimes spoken of as also a giant, and at others as a wise and virtuous prince of ordinary proportions. Along with the strange, tangled, and chaotic story of their exploits the writer from time to time enunciates admirable ideas, which must have seemed revolutionary to his contemporaries, and some of which even we have not yet realised.

The translation of Rabelais by Sir Thomas Urquhart is his great literary achievement. "It is impossible," says Tytler, "to look into it without admiring the air of ease, freshness, and originality which the translator has so happily communicated to his performance. All those singular qualifications which unfitted Urquhart to succeed in serious composition—his extravagance, his drollery (?), his unbridled imagination, his burlesque and endless epithets—are in the task of translating Rabelais transplanted into their true field of action, and revel through his pages with a licence and buoyancy which is quite unbridled, yet quite allowable. Indeed, Urquhart and Rabelais appear, in many points, to have been congenial spirits, and the translator seems to have been born for his author."[1]

As might have been expected, the translation is not marked by painful exactness of rendering. On the contrary, evidences of carelessness and in-

[1] *Life of Crichton*, p. 182.

accuracy are by no means uncommon, but yet the work is, as some one calls it, "one of the most perfect transfusions of an author from one language to another,[1] that ever man accomplished." The great merits of the translation consist in its preserving the very air and style of the original, and in the astonishing richness of vocabulary which it manifests. Where Rabelais invents a word, Sir Thomas invents one, or two, or three; and if the former has a list of twenty or thirty epithets, the latter has no hesitation in supplying his readers with forty or sixty, which seem quite as good as the original stock which he thus enlarges. Sometimes, too, as Mr W. F. Smith, a very distinguished student of Rabelais, remarks, "in translating a single word of the French he often empties all the synonyms given by Cotgrave into his version."

Mr Tytler, in the above-quoted criticism on Urquhart's translation, speaks of the peculiarities of his style as "revelling through his pages with a licence and buoyancy which is quite unbridled, yet quite allowable." One is obliged to demur to the last adjective. A translator, like a compositor, should be under some obligation to adhere to the text before him; and, as a matter of fact, the success of Urquhart's version is occasionally interfered with by this same "unbridled revelling." The style of Rabelais is graphic and vigorous, and

[1] In addition to any aid Urquhart may have received from friends who were intimately acquainted with the French language, he was deeply indebted to Cotgrave's French Dictionary, published in 1611, and dedicated to "Sir William Cecil, Knight, Lord Burghley, and sonne and heir apparant unto the Earle of Exeter," i.e., the grandson of Queen Elizabeth's Lord Burghley.

at times exceedingly graceful, and occupies a high place in French literature. Any tampering with it, therefore, in the way of alteration or addition, was not likely to be an improvement.

But, even after all deductions are made, the praise bestowed upon Urquhart's work has been fully deserved. "The buoyancy and unembarrassed sweep of its general character," says Sir Theodore Martin, "which gives his Rabelais more the look of an original than of a translation, its rich and well-compacted diction, the many happy turns of phrase that are quite his own, have fairly earned for it the high estimation in which it has long been held. His task was one of extreme difficulty, and there have perhaps been few men besides himself that could have brought to it the world of omnigenous knowledge which it required. It was apparently Urquhart's ambition to realise in his own person the ideal of human accomplishment, to be at once

> 'Complete in feature and in mind,
> With all good grace to grace a gentleman.'

He had left no source of information unexplored, few aspects of life unobserved, and, in the translation of Rabelais, he found full exercise for his multiform attainments. Ably as the work has been completed by Motteux, one cannot but regret that the worthy Knight of Cromarty had not spared him the task." [1]

The merits of the translation can scarcely be exhibited in selections torn from their context, and perhaps only partly intelligible; but perhaps the

[1] *Rabelais*, p. xxi.

following may be welcome to the reader. Let us take these extracts from the graceful and charming sketch of the Abbey of Thelema, which was to be different from all other monastic communities, and was to be the home of a society of young people living together in all innocence and joy, free from sordid cares, and devoted to the studies, exercises, and accomplishments which are appropriate to refined and noble spirits.

"'First, then,' said Gargantua, 'you must not build a wall about your convent, for all other abbies are strongly walled and mured about. . . . Moreover, seeing there are certain convents in the world, whereof the custome is, if any woman come in, I mean chaste and honest women, they immediately sweep the ground which they have trod upon;[1] therefore was it ordained, that if any man or woman, entered into religious orders, should by chance come within this new abbey, all the roomes should be thoroughly washed and cleansed through which they had passed. And because in all other monasteries and nunneries all is compassed, limited, and regulated by houres, it was decreed that in this new structure there should be neither clock nor dial, but that, according to the opportunities and incident occasions, all their hours should be disposed of; for,' said Gargantua, 'the greatest losse of time, that I know, is to count the hours. What good comes of it? Nor can there be any greater dotage in the world then [than] for one to guide and direct his courses by the sound of a bell, and not by his owne judgement and discretion.'

[1] *I.e.* the Carthusians : like their impudence !

13

"Item, Because at that time they put no women into nunneries, but such as were either purblind, blinkards, lame, crooked, ill-favoured, misshapen, fooles, senselesse, spoyled, or corrupt ; nor en-cloystered any men, but those that were either sickly, ill-bred lowts, simple sots, or peevish trouble-houses ; . . . therefore was it ordained, that into this religious order should be admitted no women that were not faire, well featur'd, and of a sweet disposition ; nor men that were not comely, per-sonable, and well conditioned.

"Item, Because in the convents of women men come not but under-hand, privily, and by stealth, it was therefore enacted, that in this house there shall be no women in case there be not men, nor men in case there be not women.

"Item, Because both men and women, that are received into religious orders after the expiring of their noviciat or probation-year, were constrained and forced perpetually to stay there all the days of their life, it was therefore ordered, that all whatever, men or women, admitted within this abbey, should have full leave to depart with peace and contentment, whensoever it should seem good to them so to do.

"Item, for that the religious men and women did ordinarily make three vows, to wit, those of chastity, poverty, and obedience, it was therefore constituted and appointed, that in this convent they might be honourably married, that they might be rich, and live at liberty.

"In regard of the legitimat time of the persons to be initiated, and years under and above which they were not capable of reception, the women were to be admitted from ten till fifteen, and the men from twelve till eighteen." [1]

After an elaborate description of the magnificence of the abbey and of its endowments, and of the apparel worn by the members of the new order, we are told of "*how the Thelemites were governed, and of their manner of living.*" "All their life," we read, "was spent not in lawes, statutes, or rules, but according to their own free will and pleasure. They rose out of their beds, when they thought good; they did eat, drink, labour, sleep, when they had a minde to it, and were disposed for it. None did awake them, none did offer to constrain them to eat, drink, nor to do any other thing; for so had Gargantua established it. In all their rule, and strictest tie of their order, there was but this one clause to be observed,

DO WHAT THOU WILT;

Because men that are free, well-borne, well-bred, and conversant in honest companies, have naturally an instinct and spurre that prompteth them unto vertuous actions, and withdraws them from vice, which is called honour. Those same men when by base subjection and constraint they are brought under and kept down, turn aside from that noble disposition, by which they formerly were inclined to vertue, to shake off and break that bond of servitude, wherein they are so tyrannously inslaved: for it is agreeable with the nature of man to long after things forbidden, and to desire what is denied us.[2]

[1] Book i. chap. 52.

[2] "*Nitimur in vetitum, semper cupimus negata*" (Ovid, Amor. iii. 4, 17).

"By this liberty they entered into a very laudable emulation, to do all of them what they saw did please one. If any of the gallants or ladies should say, Let us drink, they would all drink. If any one of them said, Let us play, they all played. If one said, Let us go a-walking into the fields, they went all. If it were to go a-hawking or a-hunting, the ladies mounted upon dainty, well-paced nags, seated in a stately palfrey saddle,[1] carried on their lovely fists, miniardly begloved every one of them, either a sparhawk, or a laneret, or a marlin, and the young gallants carried the other kinds of hawkes. So nobly were they taught, that there was neither he nor she amongst them but could read, write, sing, play upon several musical instruments, speak five or sixe several languages, and compose in them all very quaintly, both in verse and prose. Never were seen so valiant knights, so noble and worthy, so dextrous and skilful both on foot and a horseback, more brisk and lively, more nimble and quick, or better handling all manner of weapons then [than] were there. Never were seene ladies so proper[2] and handsome, so miniard and dainty, lesse froward, or more ready with their hand, and with their needle, in every honest and free action belonging to that sexe, then [than] were there. For this reason, when the time came, that any man of the said abbey, either at the request of his parents, or for some other cause, had a minde to go out of it, he

---

[1] *Avec leur palefroy guorrier*—rather, "with their prancing palfrey." Guorrier from Gr. γαῦρος—haughty.

[2] Cf. Heb. xi. 23, "a proper child."

carried along with him one of the ladies, namely, her whom he had before that chosen for his mistris,[1] and [they] were married together. And if they had formerly in Theleme lived in good devotion and amity, they did continue therein and increase it to a greater height in their state of matrimony: and did entertaine that mutual love till the very last day of their life, in no lesse vigour and fervency, then [than] at the very day of their wedding."[2]

Such is the dream which floated before the mind of Rabelais, but, unhappily, it is still an airy fancy, and has never received a local habitation and a name. Mrs Grundy, the vegetarians, the teetotallers, the anti-tobacco people, and the enemies of " rational costume " have up to the present forbidden the erection of any such building.

One of the most prominent figures in the story of Pantagruel is his favourite, Panurge, who is a rogue, a drunkard, a coward, and a malicious scoundrel, but who yet, like Falstaff, in spite of all his moral deficiencies, manages to appear as an amusing personage. Into his lips is put, with a fine disregard of congruity, an eloquent speech, which begins in praise of debt, and ends by setting forth the interdependence of all things in the universe. Panurge is represented as having threescore and three ways of making money, and two hundred and fourteen of spending it, so that he is always poor, and his sovereign Pantagruel remonstrates with him on account of his prodigal habits.

He replies as follows : " Be still indebted to some-

---

[1] *Celle laquelle l'auroit prins pour son devot*—rather, "her, who had chosen him as her devoted servant."

[2] Book i. chap. 57.

body or other, that there may be somebody always
to pray for you; [to pray] that the giver of all
good things may grant unto you a blessed, long,
and prosperous life ; fearing, if fortune should deal
crossly with you, that it might be his chance to
come short of being paid by you, he will always
speak good of you in every company, ever and
anon purchase new creditors unto you ; to the end,
that through their means you may make a shift by
borrowing from Peter to pay Paul,[1] and with other
folk's earth fill up his ditch. When of old in the
region of the Gauls, by the institution of the
Druids,[2] the servants, slaves, and bondmen were
burnt quick at the funerals and obsequies of their
lords and masters, had not they fear enough, think
you, that their lords and masters should die ? For,
per force, they were to die with them for company.
Did not they uncessantly send up their supplica-
tions to their great God Mercury,[3] as likewise unto
Dis, the Father of Wealth,[4] to lengthen out their
days, and preserve them long in health ? Were
not they very careful to entertain them well,
punctually to look unto them, and to attend them
faithfully and circumspectly ? For by those means
were they to live together at least until the hour
of death. Believe me your creditors with a more
fervent devotion will beseech [Providence] to pro-

---

[1] Fr. *faire versure* = Lat. *facere versuram* (Cic. Att. v. 1, § 2), to
borrow money to pay another debt (F. W. S.).

[2] Caes. B. G. vi. 19.

[3] "*Deum maxime Mercurium colunt*" (B. G. vi. 17) (*Ibid.*).

[4] "*Galli se omnes ab Dite patre prognatos dicunt*" (B. G. vi. 18).
Dis is called *père des escus*, as identical with Plutus, the god of
hidden wealth (*Ibid.*).

long your life, they being of nothing more afraid
than that you should die. . . . I, in this only
respect and consideration of being a debtor, esteem
myself worshipful, reverend, and formidable.   For,
against the opinion of most philosophers, that of
nothing ariseth nothing, yet, without having
bottomed on so much as that which is called the
First Matter [Primary Matter], did I out of nothing
become such [a] maker and creator, that I have
created—what?—a gay number of fair and jolly
creditors.   Nay, creditors, I will maintain it, even
to the very fire itself exclusively,[1] are fair and
goodly creatures.   Who lendeth nothing is an
ugly and wicked creature. . . . You can hardly
imagine how glad I am, when every morning I
perceive myself environed and surrounded with
brigades of creditors,—humble, fawning, and full of
their reverences.   And whilst I remark that, as I
look more favourably upon, and give a chearfuller
countenance to one than to the other, the fellow
thereupon buildeth a conceit that he shall be the first
dispatched, and the foremost in the date of payment; and he valueth my smiles at the rate of
ready money. . . . I have all my life-time held
debt to be as an union or conjunction of the
heavens with the earth, and the whole cement
whereby the race of mankind is kept together;[2] yea,

[1] *Exclusively, i.e.,* "I will affirm it, but not go to the stake for
it" (F. W. S.).

[2] A fine passage in one of South's *Sermons* was evidently suggested by the above chapter in Rabelais. "The World is maintained by Intercourse; and the whole Course of Nature is a great
Exchange, in which one good Turn is and ought to be the stated
Price of another. If you consider the Universe as one Body, you

of such vertue and efficacy, that, I say, the whole pro-
geny of Adam would very suddenly perish without it."

He then goes on to describe a world in which
there are no debtors and no debts. There will be no
regular course among the planets, but all will be in
disorder. Jupiter, reckoning himself to be nothing
indebted to Saturn, will go near to thrust him out
of his place; Saturn and Mars will combine to
promote the confusion; Mercury, being debtor to
no one, will no longer serve any; Venus, because
she shall have lent nothing, will no longer be
venerated. "The moon," he says, "will remain

shall find Society and Conversation to supply the Office of the
Blood and Spirits; and it is Gratitude that makes them circulate.
Look over the whole Creation, and you shall see that the Band or
Cement that holds together all the Parts of this great and glorious
Fabric is Gratitude, or something like it: you may observe it in
all the Elements, for does not the Air feed the Flame? and does not
the Flame at the same time warm and enlighten the Air? Is not
the Sea always sending forth, as well as taking in? And does not
the Earth quit scores with all the Elements, in the noble Fruits
and Productions that issue from it? And in all the Light and
Influence that the Heavens bestow upon this lower World, though
the lower World cannot equal their Benefaction, yet with a Kind
of grateful Return, it reflects those Rays that it cannot recompense:
so that there is some Return however, though there can be no
Requital. . . . In short, Gratitude is the great Spring that sets all
the Wheels of Nature agoing; and the whole Universe is supported
by giving and returning, by Commerce and Commutation. And
now, thou ungrateful Brute, thou Blemish to Mankind, and
Reproach to thy Creation; what shall we say of thee, or to what
shall we compare thee? For thou art an Exception from all the
visible World; neither the Heavens above nor the Earth beneath
afford anything like thee: and therefore, if thou wouldest find thy
Parallel, go to Hell, which is both the Region and the Emblem of
Ingratitude; for besides thyself, there is nothing but Hell that
is always receiving and never restoring" (I. SERM. xi. "Of the
odious Sin of Ingratitude").

bloody and obscure. For to what end should the sun impart unto her any of his light?[1] He owed her nothing. Nor yet will the sun shine upon the earth, nor the stars send down any good influence,[2] because the terrestrial globe hath desisted from sending up their wonted nourishment by vapours and exhalations, wherewith Heraclitus said, the Stoicks proved, Cicero maintained, they were cherished and alimented. . . . No rain will descend upon the earth, nor light shine thereon; no wind will blow there, nor will there be in it any summer or harvest. . . . Such a world without lending will be no better than a dog-kennel, a place of contention and wrangling. . . . Men will not then salute one another; it will be but lost labour to expect aid or succour from any, or to cry fire, water, murther, for none will put to their helping hand. Why? He lent no money, there is nothing due to him. Nobody is concerned in his burning, in his shipwrack, in his ruine, or in his death; and that because he hitherto hath lent nothing, and would never thereafter have lent anything. In short, Faith, Hope, and Charity would be quite banish'd from such a world—for men are born to relieve and assist one another."

---

[1] "Nec fratris radiis obnoxia surgere Luna" (Virg. *Georg.* i. 396) (F. W. S.).

[2] *Influence*, much used as an astrological term. Cf. Milton:

"taught the fix'd
Their *influence* malignant when to shower."

Par. Lost, x. 662.

"Bending one way their precious *influence*."

Hymn on the Nativity, 71.
(*Ibid.*).

" But, on the contrary," he went on to say, " be pleased to represent unto your fancy another world, wherein every one lendeth, and every one oweth, all are debtors, and all creditors. O how great will that harmony be, which shall thereby result from the regular motions of the heavens! Methinks I hear it every whit as well as ever Plato did.[1]   What sympathy will there be amongst the elements! O how delectable then unto nature will be our own works and productions! Whilst Ceres appeareth loaden with corn, Bacchus with wines, Flora with flowers, Pomona with fruits, and Juno fair in a clear air, wholsom and pleasant. I lose myself in this high contemplation. Then will among the race of mankind, peace, love, benevolence, fidelity, tranquillity, rests, banquets, feastings, joy, gladness, gold, silver, single money [small change], chains, rings, with other ware, and chaffer of that nature, be found to trot from hand to hand. No suits at law, no wars, no strife, debate, nor wrangling; none will be there an usurer, none will be there a pinch-penny, a scrape-good wretch, or churlish hard-hearted refuser. Will not this be the golden age in the reign of Saturn?—the true idea of the Olympick regions, wherein all [other] vertues cease,

---

[1] *Plato* never pretends that the "music of the spheres" can be heard. He adopts the theory to some extent from the Pythagoreans. Aristotle (*de Cœlo*, ii. 9), that the noise caused by the movements of the heavenly bodies is so prodigious and continuous, that, being accustomed to it from our birth, we do not notice it. The only notice in Plato that can be construed into a statement about audible music of the spheres is in *Rep.* x., where he speaks of a siren standing upon each of the circles of the planetary system uttering one note in one tone; and from all the eight notes there results a single harmony (F. W. S.).

charity alone ruleth, governeth, domineereth, and triumpheth ?   All will be fair and goodly people there, all just and vertuous.   O happy world !   O people of that world most happy !   Yea, thrice and four times blessed is that people !   I think in very deed that I am amongst them." [1]

In one curious passage Sir Thomas Urquhart amplifies the text of the author whom he translates, and supplies his readers with an astonishing list of onomatopœic words, many of which will probably be new to those who have not come across this passage before.   Rabelais has nine of these words, but the translator [2] enlarges the list to seventy-one.   Pantagruel is arguing against fasting and solitude as aids to a contemplative life, and quotes the authority of his father Gargantua.

"He [Gargantua] gave us also," he said, " the example of the philosopher, who, when he thought most seriously to have withdrawn himself unto a solitary privacy, far from the rusling clutterments of the tumultuous and confused world, the better to improve his theory, to contrive, comment, and ratiocinate, was, notwithstanding his uttermost endeavours to free himself from all untoward noises, surrounded and environ'd about so with the barking of currs [bawling of mastiffs, bleating of sheep, prating of parrets, tatling of jack-daws, grunting of swine, girning of boars, yelping of

---

[1] Book iii. chaps. 3, 4.

[2] It is quite possible that Motteux, who published the third book of Rabelais after Urquhart's death, is responsible for some of the interpolations.

foxes, mewing of cats, cheeping of mice, squeaking of weasils, croaking of frogs, crowing of cocks, kekling of hens, calling of partridges, chanting of swans, chattering of jays, peeping of chickens, singing of larks, creaking of geese, chirping of swallows, clucking of moorfowls, cucking of cuckos, bumling of bees, rammage of hawks, chirming of linots, croaking of ravens, screeching of owls, whicking of pigs, gushing of hogs, curring of pigeons, grumbling of cushet-doves, howling of panthers, curkling of quails, chirping of sparrows, crackling of crows, nuzzing of camels, wheening of whelps, buzzing of dromedaries, mumbling of rabets, cricking of ferrets, humming of wasps, mioling of tygers, bruzzing of bears, sussing of kitnings, clamring of scarfes, whimpring of fullmarts, boing of buffaloes, warbling of nightingales, quavering of meavises, drintling of turkies, coniating of storks, frantling of peacocks, clattering of mag-pyes, murmuring of stock-doves, crouting of cormorants, cigling of locusts, charming of beagles, guarring of puppies, snarling of messens, rantling of rats, guerieting of apes, snuttering of monkies, pioling of pelicanes, quecking of ducks], yelling of wolves, roaring of lions, neighing of horses, crying of elephants, hissing of serpents, and wailing of turtles, that he was much more troubled than if he had been in the middle of the crowd at the fair of Fontenay or Niort."[1]   In spite of the amplification of the

---

[1] Book iii. chap. 13. *Fontenay le Comte* in Lower Poitou and *Niort* were noted for their busy yearly fairs. There can be doubt that the above passage was suggested to Rabelais by what St Jerome records of the experience of St Hilarion in the desert. "Sic atten-

original text of Rabelais, two of the sounds are
omitted—"the braying of asses," and the noise
made by grass-hoppers (*sonnent les cigales*), which
we might have called "chirping," if the swallows
and sparrows had not taken possession of that term.

As already stated, the first two books were all
that were published in the lifetime of Sir Thomas
Urquhart. They appeared as separate volumes in
1653. The unsold stock of each was reissued in

tuatus," he says, "[jejunio et vigiliis], et in tantum exeto corpore, ut
ossibus vix haereret, quadam nocte cœpit infantum audire vagitus,
balatus pecorum, mugitus boum, planctum quasi mulierum, leonum
rugitus, murmur exercitus, et prorsus variarum portenta vocum,"
etc. (*Vita Sancti Hilarionis*). In Burton's *Anatomy of Melancholy* (iii. 4. 1. 2) there is the following reference to the same
passage: "Monks, Anachorites, and the like, after much empti-
ness become melancholy, vertiginous, they think they hear
strange noises, confer with Hob-goblins, Devils. . . . *Hilarion*,
as *Hierome* reports in his life, and *Athanasius of Antonius*, was so
bare with fasting, *that the skin did scarce stick to the bones;* for
want of vapours (*sic*) he could not sleep, and for want of sleep
became idle-headed, *heard every night infants cry, Oxen low,
Wolves howl, Lions roar* (*as he thought*), *clattering of chains,
strange voices, and the like illusions of Devils.*" It is probable
also that Rabelais had read the following passage in the *Life of
Geta*, by Ælius Spartianus (*c.* A.D. 317): "Familiare illi fuit
has quæstiones grammaticis proponere, ut dicerent, singula
animalia quomodo vocem emitterent, velut, Agni balant, porcelli
grunniunt, palumbes minurriunt, ursi saeviunt, leones rugiunt,
leopardi rictant, elephanti barriunt, ranæ coaxant, equi hinniunt,
asini rudunt, tauri mugiunt, easque de veteribus approbare." Nor
is it likely that Rabelais was unacquainted with the verses in Teofilo
Folengo's (1491–1544) *Merlini Cocaii Macaronicon*, which run thus :

"Nam Leo rugitum mittit, Lupus ac ululatum,
    Bos boat, et nitrescit equus, Gallusque cucullat,
    Sguavolat et Gattus, baiat Canis, Ursus adirat,
    Raucagat Oca, rudit Mullus, sed raggiat Asellus ;
    Denique quodque animal propria cum voce gridabat."
                                                Macaronea, xx.

1664, in one volume, an additional title-page, an extra preface, and a life of Rabelais being prefixed to them. The volume became very scarce, and in 1693–94 Pierre Antoine Motteux, a Frenchman, who was master of exceedingly racy and idiomatic English, published an edition containing the third book. This was extremely inaccurate, so far as typography was concerned, and gave the public the version of Sir Thomas Urquhart with certain unspecified changes made by the editor in order to impart to it additional "smartness." In 1708 Motteux published a complete translation of Rabelais, the version of the fourth and fifth books being supplied by himself,[1] as supplementary to Urquhart's work. After the death of Motteux, a somewhat pretentious editor named Ozell[2] brought out the combined versions, with notes principally taken from the French of Duchat, and this has

---

[1] In the introduction to this volume Motteux says that Sir Thomas Urquhart was "a learned physician." It is difficult to understand what could have given rise to such a statement. Sir Thomas had many projects for the benefit of the human race, but there is no evidence of his ever having cherished that of combating disease. One cannot help thinking of the magniloquent terms in which he would have extolled his remedies, if the fates had led him to the concoction of patent medicines. It is doubtful, however, whether he would have had what is technically known as "a good bed-side manner." It is quite possible that Motteux simply meant that Sir Thomas was well acquainted with medical science, and not that he was a physician by profession. Yet his words have often been understood as asserting the latter. Thus we find the erroneous statement in Granger's *Biographical Dictionary*, the Amsterdam (1741) edition of Rabelais, and Sir John Hawkins' *Life of Johnson*, p. 294.

[2] Both Ozell and Motteux figure in Pope's *Dunciad*, in i. 296, and ii. 412, respectively.

been reprinted time after time since its first appearance in 1737.

At least seventeen editions of Urquhart's work, either by itself or with Motteux's supplementary matter, have been issued since his day, and there is no sign of its fame waxing dim through the lapse of time ; and therefore the immortality after which he longed has in a measure been won by him. And so, once more before we take our leave of him, we look again into the twilight of the past, and see his striking figure—the soldier, the scholar, and the author—crowned with the wreath which his own hands have placed upon his brows, but which succeeding generations declare him worthy to bear.

APPENDICES

APPENDIX I

THE NAMES OF THE CHIEFS OF THE NAME OF
URQUHART, AND OF THEIR PRIMITIVE FATHERS;
as by Authentick Records and Tradition they
were from time to time through the various
Generations of that Family successively conveyed, till the present yeer 1652 (p. 143).

The ancestors of Sir Thomas, for whose existence there is evidence apart
from his assertions, are indicated by their names being printed in italics. If
the editor of the *Tracts* (1774) were to be believed, the italics would have to
begin with George, No. 138 in the list. The fact that the names in this list are
more numerous than those in the list which follows, is to be explained by
brothers succeeding each other occasionally, when there was no son to inherit
the dignity of chieftainship.

1. *Adam.*	24. Phrenedon.
2. *Seth.*	25. Zameles.
3. *Enos.*	26. Choronomos.
4. *Cainan.*	27. Leptologon.
5. *Mahalaleel.*	28. Aglætos.
6. *Jared.*	29. Megalonus.
7. *Enoch.*	30. Evemeros.
8. *Methusalah.*	31. Callophron.
9. *Lamech.*	32. Arthmios.
10. *Noah.*	33. Hypsegoras.
11. *Japhet.*	34. Autarces.
12. *Javan.*	35. Evages.
13. Penuel.	36. Atarbes.
14. Tycheros.	37. Pamprosodos.
15. Pasiteles.	38. Gethon.
16. Esormon.	39. Holocleros.
17. Cratynter.	40. Molin.
18. Thrasymedes.	41. Epitomon.
19. Evippos.	42. Hypotyphos.
20. Cleotinus.	43. Melobolon.
21. Litoboros.	44. Propetes.
22. Apodemos.	45. Euplocamos.
23. Bathybulos.	46. Philophon.

47. Syngenes.
48. Polyphrades.
49. Cainotomos.
50. Rodrigo.
51. Dicarches.
52. Exagastos.
53. Denapon.
54. Artistes.
55. Thymoleon.
56. Eustochos.
57. Bianor.
58. Thryllumenos.
59. Mellessen.
60. Alypos.
61. Anochlos.
62. Homognios.
63. Epsephicos.
64. Eutropos.
65. Coryphæus.
66. Etoimos.
67. Spudæos.
68. Eumestor.
69. Griphon.
70. Emmenes.
71. Pathomachon.
72. Anepsios.
73. Auloprepes.
74. Corosylos.
75. Detalon.
76. Beltistos.
77. Horæos.
78. Orthophron.
79. Apsicoros.
80. Philaplus.
81. Megaletor.
82. Nomostor.
83. Astioremon.
84. Phronematias.
85. Lutork.
86. Machemos.
87. Stichopæo.
88. Epalomenos.
89. Tycheros (2).
90. Apechon.
91. Enacmes.
92. Javan (2).
93. Lematias.

94. Prosenes.
95. Sosomenos.
96. Philalethes.
97. Thaleros.
98. Polyænos.
99. Cratesimachos.
100. Eunæmon.
101. Diasemos.
102. Saphenus.
103. Bramoso.
104. Celanas.
105. Vistoso.
106. Polido.
107. Lustroso.
108. Chrestander.
109. Spectabundo.
110. Philodulos.
111. Paladino.
112. Comicello.
113. Regisato.
114. Arguto.
115. Nicarchos.
116. Marsidalio.
117. Hedumenos.
118. Agenor.
119. Diaprepon.
120. Stragayo.
121. Zeron.
122. Polyteles.
123. Vocompos.
124. Carolo.
125. Endymion.
126. Sebastian.
127. Lawrence.
128. Olipher.
129. Quintin.
130. Goodwin.
131. Frederick.
132. Sir Jaspar.
133. Sir Adam.
134. Edward.
135. Richard.
136. Sir Philip.
137. Robert.
138. George.
139. James.
140. David.

141. Francis.
142. William.
143. *Adam.*
144. *John.*
145. *Sir William.*
146. *William.*
147. *Alexander.*

148. *Thomas.*
149. *Alexander.*
150. *Walter.*
151. *Henry.*
152. *Sir Thomas.*
153. Sir Thomas.

THE NAMES OF THE MOTHERS OF THE CHIEFS OF THE NAME OF URQUHART, AS ALSO OF THE MOTHERS OF THEIR PRIMITIVE FATHERS. The authority for the truth thereof being derived from the same Authentick Records and Tradition on which is grounded the above-written Genealogie of their male collaterals.

1. *Eva.*
2. Shifka.
3. Mahla.
4. Bilha.
5. Timnah.
6. Aholima.
7. Zilpa.
8. Noema.
9. Ada.
10. Titea.
11. Debora.
12. Neginothi.
13. Hottir.
14. Orpah.
15. Axa.
16. Narfesia.
17. Goshenni.
18. Briageta.
19. Andronia.
20. Pusena.
21. Emphaneola.
22. Bonaria.
23. Peninah.
24. Asymbleta.
25. Carissa.
26. Calaglais.
27. Theoglena.
28. Pammerisla.

29. Floridula.
30. Chrysocomis.
31. Arrenopas.
32. Tharsalia.
33. Maia.
34. Roma.
35. Termuth.
36. Vegeta.
37. Callimeris.
38. Panthea.
39. Gonima.
40. Ganymena.
41. Thespesia.
42. Hypermnestra.
43. Horatia.
44. Philumena.
45. Neopis.
46. Thymelica.
47. Ephamilla.
48. Porrima.
49. Lampedo.
50. Teleclyta.
51. Clarabella.
52. Eromena.
53. Zocallis.
54. Lepida.
55. Nicolia.
56. Proteusa.

57. Gozosa.
58. Venusta.
59. Prosectica.
60. Delotera.
61. Tracara.
62. Pothina.
63. Cordata.
64. Aretias.
65. Musurga.
66. Romalia.
67. Orthoiusa.
68. Recatada.
69. Chariestera.
70. Rexenora.
71. Philerga.
72. Thomyris.
73. Varonilla.
74. Stranella.
75. Æquanima.
76. Barosa.
77. Epimona.
78. Diosa.
79. Bonita.
80. Aretusa.
81. Bendita.
82. Regalletta.
83. Isumena.
84. Antaxia.
85. Bergola.
86. Viracia.
87. Dynastis.
88. Dalga.
89. Eutocusa.
90. Corriba.
91. Præcelsa.
92. Plausidica.
93. Donosa.
94. Solicælia.
95. Bontadosa.
96. Calliparia.
97. Creleuca.
98. Pancala.
99. Dominella.
100. Mundala.
101. Pamphais.

102. Philtrusa.
103. Meliglena.
104. Philetium.
105. Tersa.
106. Dulcicora.
107. Gethosyna.
108. Collabella.
109. Eucnema.
110. Tortolina.
111. Ripulita.
112. Urbana.
113. Lampusa.
114. Vistosa.
115. Hermosina.
116. Bramata.
117. Zaglopis.
118. Androlema.
119. Trastevole.
120. Suaviloqua.
121. Francoline.
122. Matilda.
123. Allegra.
124. Winnifred.
125. Dorothy.
126. Lawretta.
127. Genivieve.
128. Marjory.
129. Jane.
130. Anne.
131. Magdalen.
132. Girsel.
133. Mary.
134. Sophia.
135. Eleonore.
136. Rosalind.
137. Lillias.
138. *Brigid.*
139. *Agnes.*
140. *Susanna.*
141. *Catherine.*
142. *Helen.*
143. *Beatrice.*
144. *Elizabeth.*
145. *Elizabeth.*
146. *Christian.*

APPENDIX II

THE ADMIRABLE CRICHTON (p. 157).

"To speak a little now of his compatriot Crichtoun, I hope will not offend the ingenuous reader; who may know, by what is already displayed, that it cannot be heterogeneal from the proposed purpose, to make report of that magnanimous act atchieved by him at the Duke of Mantua's court, to the honour not only of his own, but to the eternal renown also of the whole Isle of Britain; the manner whereof was thus:

"A certain Italian gentleman, of a mighty, able, strong, nimble, and vigorous body, by nature fierce, cruell, warlike, and audacious, and in the gladiatory art so superlatively expert and dextrous, that all the most skilful teachers of Escrime, and fencing-masters of Italy, (which in matter of choice professors in that faculty, needed never as yet to yeild to any nation in the world), were by him beaten to their good behaviour, and by blows given in, which they could not avoid, enforced to acknowledge him their over comer; bethinking himself, how, after so great a conquest of reputation, he might by such means be very suddenly enriched, he projected a course of exchanging the blunt to sharp, and the foiles into tucks. And in this resolution providing a purse full of gold, worth neer upon four hundred pounds English money, traveled alongst the most especial and considerable parts of Spaine, France, the Low-

Countryes, Germany, Pole, Hungary, Greece, Italy, and other places, where ever there was greatest probability of encountring with the eagerest and most atrocious duellists. And immediately after his arrival to any city or town that gave apparent likelihood of some one or other champion that would enter the lists and cope with him, he boldly challenged them with sound of trumpet, in the chief market-place, to adventure an equal sum of money against that of his, to be disputed at the sword's point who should have both. There failed not several brave men, almost of all nations, who, accepting of his cartels, were not afraid to hazard both their person and coine against him; but, (till he midled with this Crichtoun), so maine was the ascendant he had above all his antagonists, and so unlucky the fate of such as offered to scuffle with him, that all his opposing combatants, (of what state or dominion soever they were), who had not lost both their life and gold, were glad, for the preservation of their person, (though sometimes with a great expence of blood), to leave both their reputation and mony behind them. At last, returning homewards to his own country, loaded with honor and wealth, or rather the spoile of the reputation of those forraginers, whom the Italians call Tramontani, he, by the way, after his accustomed manner of abording other places, repaired to the city of Mantua, where the Duke, (according to the courtesie usually bestowed on him by other princes), vouchsafed him a protection and savegard for his person; he (as formerly he was wont to do, by beat of drum, sound of trumpet, and several printed papers, disclosing his designe, battered on all the chief gates, posts, and pillars of the town), gave all men to understand, that his purpose was to challenge, at the single rapier, any whosoever of that city or country, that durst be so bold as to fight with him, provided he would deposite a bag of five hundred Spanish pistols

over against another of the same value, which he
himself should lay down, upon this condition, that
the enjoyment of both should be the conqueror's
due.   His challenge was not long unanswered, for
it happened, at the same time, that three of the most
notable cutters in the world, (and so highly cryed up
for valour, that all the bravos of the land were
content to give way to their domineering, how
insolent soever they should prove, because of their
former constantly obtained victories in the field),
were all three together at the court of Mantua, who,
hearing of such a harvest of five hundred pistols to
be reaped, (as they expected), very soon, and with
ease, had almost contested amongst themselves for
the priority of the first encounterer, but that one of
my Lord Duke's courtiers moved them to cast lots
for who should be first, second, and third, in case
none of the former two should prove victorious.
Without more adoe, he whose chance it was to
answer the cartel with the first defiance, presented
himself within the barriers, or place appointed for
the fight, where, his adversary attending him, as soon
as the trumpet sounded a charge, they jointly fel to
work ; and, (because I am not now to amplifie the
particulars of a combat), although the dispute was
very hot for a while, yet, whose fortune it was to be
first of the three in the field, had the disaster to be
first of the three that was foyled ; for, at last, with
a thrust in the throat, he was killed dead upon the
ground.   This, nevertheless, not a whit dismayed the
other two, for, the nixt day, he that was second in
the roll gave his appearance after the same manner
as the first had done, but with no better success ; for
he likewise was laid flat dead upon the place, by
means of a thrust he received in the heart.   The last
of the three, finding that he was as sure of being
engaged in the fight as if he had been the first in
order, pluckt up his heart, knit his spirits together,

and, on the day after the death of the second, most
couragiously entering the lists, demeaned himself for
a while with great activity and skill; but at last, his
luck being the same with those that preceded him,
by a thrust in the belly, he within four and twenty
hours after gave up the ghost.   These (you may
imagine), were lamentable spectacles to the Duke and
citie of Mantua, who, casting down their faces for
shame, knew not what course to take for reparation
of their honour.   The conquering duellist, proud of
a victory so highly tending to both his honour and
profit, for the space of a whole fortnight, or two
weeks together, marched daily along the streets of
Mantua, (without any opposition or controulment),
like   another   Romulus   or   Marcellus   in   triumph;
which, the never too much to be admired Crichtoun
perceiving, to wipe off the imputation of cowardise
lying upon the court of Mantua, to which he had
but even then arrived, (although formerly he had
been a domestick thereof), he could neither eat nor
drink till he had first sent a challenge to the conqueror, appelling him to repair with his best sword
in his hand, by nine of the clock in the morning of
the next day, in presence of the whole court, and in
the same place where he had killed the other three,
to fight with him upon this quarrel, that in the court
of Mantua there were as valiant men as he; and, for
his better encouragement to the desired undertaking,
he assured him that, to the aforesaid five hundred
pistols, he would adjoyn a thousand more, wishing
him to do the like, that the victor, upon the point of
his sword, might carry away the richer bootay.   The
challenge, with all its conditions, is no sooner accepted
of, the time and place mutually condescended upon,
kept accordingly, and the fifteen hundred pistols
hinc inde deposited, but of the two rapiers of equal
weight, length, and goodness, each taking one, in
presence of the Duke, Dutchess, with all the noble-

men, ladies, magnificos, and all the choicest of men,
women, and maids of that citie, as soon as the signal
for the duel was given, by the shot of a great piece
of ordnance of threescore and four pound ball, the
combatants, with a lion-like animosity, made their
approach to one another, and, being within distance,
the valiant Crichtoun, to make his adversary spend his
fury the sooner, betook himself to the defensive part;
wherein, for a long time, he shewed such excellent
dexterity in warding the other's blows, slighting his
falsifyings, in breaking measure, and often, by the
agility of his body, avoiding his thrust, that he
seemed but to play, while the other was in earnest.
The sweetness of Crichtoun's countenance, in the
hotest of the assault, like a glance of lightning on
the hearts of the spectators, brought all the Italian
ladies on a sudden to be enamoured of him; whilst
the sternness of the other's aspect, he looking like an
enraged bear, would have struck terrour into wolves,
and affrighted an English mastiff. Though they
were both in their linens, (to wit, shirts and drawers,
without any other apparel), and in all outward con-
veniences equally adjusted, the Italian, with re-
doubling his stroaks, foamed at the mouth with a
cholerick heart, and fetched a pantling breath: the
Scot, in sustaining his charge, kept himself in a
pleasant temper, without passion, and made void his
designes; he alters his wards from tierce to quart:
he primes and seconds it, now high, now lowe, and
casts his body, (like another Prothee), into all the
shapes he can, to spie an open on his adversary, and
lay hold of an advantage, but all in vain; for the
invincible Crichtoun, whom no cunning was able to
surprise, contrepostures his respective wards, and,
with an incredible nimbleness of both hand and foot,.
evades the intent and frustrates the invasion. Now
is it, that the never before conquered Italian, finding
himself a little faint, enters into a consideration that

he may be over-matched; whereupon a sad apprehension of danger seizing upon all his spirits, he
would gladly have his life bestowed on him as a gift,
but that, having never been accustomed to yield,
he knows not how to beg it.   Matchless Crichtoun,
seeing it now high time to put a gallant catastrophe
to that so long dubious combat, animated with a
divinely inspired servencie to fulfil the expectation
of the ladies, and crown the Duke's illustrious hopes,
changeth his garb, falls to act another part, and,
from defender, turn assailant; never did art so grace
nature, nor nature second the precepts of art with so
much liveliness, and such observancie of time, as
when, after he had struck fire out of the steel of his
enemie's sword, and gained the feeble thereof with
the fort of his own, by angles of the strongest position,
he did, by geometrical flourishes of straight and
oblique lines, so practically execute the speculative
part, that, as if there had been Remoras and secret
charms in the variety of his motion, the fierceness of
his foe was in a trice transqualified into the numbness
of a pageant.   Then was it that, to vindicate the reputation of the Duke's family, and expiate the blood
of the three vanquished gentlemen, he alonged a
stoccade *de pied ferme;* then recoyling, he advanced
another thrust, and lodged it home; after which,
retiring again, his right foot did beat the cadence of
the blow that pierced the belly of this Italian, whose
heart and throat being hit with the two former
stroaks, these three franch bouts given in upon the
back of the other; besides that, if lines were imagined
drawn from the hand that livered them, to the places
which were marked by them, they would represent a
perfect isosceles triangle, with a perpendicular from
the top angle cutting the basis in the middle; they
likewise give us to understand, that by them he was
to be made a sacrifice of atonement for the slaughter
of the three aforesaid gentlemen, who were wounded

in the very same parts of their bodies by other such three venees as these, each whereof being mortal; and his vital spirits exhaling as his blood gushed out, all he spoke was this, That seeing he could not live, his comfort in dying was, that he could not dye by the hand of a braver man : after the uttering of which words, he expiring, with the shril clareens of trumpets, bouncing thunder of artillery, bethwacked beating of drums, universal clapping of hands, and loud acclamations of joy for so glorious a victory, the aire above them was so rarified by the extremity of the noise and vehement sound, dispelling the thickest and most condensed parts thereof, that (as Plutarch speakes of the Grecians, when they raised their shouts of allegress up to the very heavens at the hearing of the gracious proclamations of Paulus Æmilius in favour of their liberty), the very sparrows and other flying fowls were said to fall to the ground for want of aire enough to uphold them in their flight.

"When this sudden rapture was over, and all husht into its former tranquility, the noble gallantry and generosity, beyond expression, of the inimitable Crichtoun, did transport them all againe into a new exstasie of ravishment, when they saw him like an angel in the shape of a man, or as another Mars, with the conquered enemie's sword in one hand, and the fifteen hundred pistols he had gained in the other, present the sword to the Duke as his due, and the gold to his high treasurer, to be disponed equally to the three widows of the three unfortunate gentlemen lately slaine, reserving only to himself the inward satisfaction he conceived, for having so opportunely discharged his duty to the House of Mantua.

"The reader perhaps will think this wonderful; and so would I too, were it not that I know, (as Sir Philip Sydney sayes), that a wonder is no wonder in a wonderful subject, and consequently not in him, who for

his learning, judgement, valour, eloquence, beauty,
and good-fellowship was the perfectest result of the
joynt labour of the perfect number of those six
deities, Pallas, Apollo, Mars, Mercury, Venus, and
Bacchus, that hath been seen since the dayes of
Alcibiades; for he was reported to have been in-
riched with a memory so prodigious, that any sermon,
speech, harangue, or other manner of discourse of an
hour's continuance, he was able to recite without
hesitation, after the same manner of gesture and
pronuntiation, in all points, wherewith it was delivered at first; and of so stupendious a judgment
and conception, that almost naturally he understood
quiddities of philosophy; and as for the abstrusest
and most researched mysteries of other disciplines,
arts, and faculties, the intentional species of them
were as readily obvious to the interiour view and per-
spicacity of his mind, as those of the common visible
colours to the external sight of him that will open
his eyes to look upon them; of which accomplishment and Encyclopedia of knowledge, he gave on a
time so marvelous a testimony at Paris, that the
words of *Admirabilis Scotus*, the Wonderful Scot, in
all the several tongues and idiomes of Europ, were,
(for a great while together), by the most of the echos
resounded to the peircing of the very clouds. To so
great a hight and vast extent of praise did the never
too much to be extolled reputation of the seraphick
wit of that eximious man attaine, for his commanding to be affixed programs on all the gates of the
schooles, halls, and colledges of that famous university, as also on all the chief pillars and posts standing
before the houses of the most renowned men for
literature, resident within the precinct of the walls
and suburbs of that most populous and magnificent
city, inviting them all, (or any whoever else versed in
any kinde of scholastick faculty), to repaire at nine of
the clock in the morning of such a day, moneth, and

yeer, as by computation came to be just six weeks
after the date of the affixes, to the common schoole
of the colledge of Navarre,[1] where, (at the prefixed
time), he should, (God willing), be ready to answer to
what should be propounded to him concerning any
science, liberal art, discipline, or faculty, practical or
theoretick, not excluding the theological nor juris-
prudential habits, though grounded but upon the
testimonies of God and man, and that in any of these
twelve languages,[2] Hebrew, Syriack, Arabick, Greek,
Latin, Spanish, French, Italian, English, Dutch,
Flemish, and Sclavonian, in either verse or prose, at
the discretion of the disputant ; which high enterprise
and hardy undertaking, by way of challenge to the
learndst men in the world, damped the wits of many
able scholars to consider whether it was the attempt
of a fanatick spirit, or lofty designe of a well-poised
judgment ; yet after a few days enquiry concerning
him, when information was got of his incomparable
endowments, all the choicest and most profound
philosophers, mathematicians, naturalists, mediciners,
alchymists, apothecaries, surgeons, doctors of both
civil and canon law, and divines both for controversies and positive doctrine, together with the pri-
mest grammarians, rhetoricians, logicians, and others,
professors of other arts and disciplines at Paris,
plyed their studys in their private cels for the space
of a moneth, exceeding hard, and with huge paines
and labor set all their braines awork how to contrive
the knurriest arguments, and most difficult questions
could be devised, thereby to puzzle him in the resolving of them, meander him in his answers, put

[1] The College of Navarre was founded by Jeanne of Navarre,
consort of Philippe the Fair, in 1305.   Throughout the fourteenth
and fifteenth centuries it was the foremost foundation of the
University of Paris (F. W. S.).

[2] John Hill Burton points out the somewhat curious fact that,
among the hero's linguistic accomplishments, Gaelic, which must
have been talked at his own door, does not appear.

him out of his medium, and drive him to a *non plus ;*
nor did they forget to premonish the ablest there of
forraign nations not to be unprepared to dispute
with him in their own material dialects, and that
sometimes metrically, sometimes otherwayes, *pro
libitu.*[1]   All this while the Admirable Scot, (for so
from thenceforth he was called), minding more his
hawking, hunting, tilting, vaulting, riding of well-
managed horses, tossing of the pike, handling of the
musket, flourishing of colours, dancing, fencing, swim-
ming, jumping, throwing of the bar, playing at tennis,
baloon, or long catch ; and sometimes at the house
games of dice, cards, playing at the chess, billiards,
trou-madam, and other such like chamber sports,
singing, playing on the lute and other musical instruments, masking, balling, reveling ; and, which did most
of all divert, or rather distract him from his speculations and serious employments, being more addicted
to, and plying closer the courting of handsome ladyes,
and a jovial cup in the company of bacchanalian
blades, then [than] the forecasting how to avoid,
shun, and escape the snares, grins [gins ?], and nets
of the hard, obscure, and hidden arguments, ridles,
and demands, to be made, framed, and woven by the
professors, doctors, and others of that thrice-renowned
university.   There arose upon him an aspersion of
too great proness to such like debordings and youth-
ful emancipations, which occasioned one less acquainted with himself then [than] his reputation, to
subjoyn, (some two weeks before the great day
appointed), to that program of his, which was fixed
on the Sorbone gate, these words: 'If you would
meet with this monster of perfection, to make search
for him . . . in the taverne . . . is the readyest way
to finde him.'   By reason of which expression,
(though truly as I think, both scandalous and false),
the eminent sparks of the university, (imagining that

---

[1] In the matter of length this is surely a record sentence.

those papers of provocation had been set up to no
other end, but to scoff and delude them, in making
them waste their spirits upon quirks and quiddities,
more then [than] was fitting), did resent a little of
their former toyle, and slack their studyes, becoming
almost regardless thereof, till the several peals of
bells ringing an hour or two before the time assigned,
gave warning that the party was not to flee the
barriers, nor decline the hardship of academical
assaults; but, on the contrary, so confident in his
former resolution, that he would not shrink to sus-
taine the shock of all their disceptations. This
sudden alarm so awaked them out of their last fortnight's lethargy, that, calling to minde, the best way
they might, the fruits of the foregoing moneth's
labour, they hyed to the fore-named schoole with all
diligence; where, after all of them had, according to
their several degrees and qualities, seated themselves,
and that by reason of the noise occasioned through
the great confluence of people, which so strange a
novelty brought thither out of curiosity, an universal
silence was commanded, the Orator of the University,
in most fluent Latine, addressing his speech to
Crichtoun, extolled him for his literature, and other
good parts, and for that confident opinion he had of
his own sufficiency, in thinking himself able to justle
in matters of learning with the whole university of
Paris. Crichtoun answering him in no less eloquent
terms of Latine, after he had most heartily thanked
him for his elogies, so undeservedly bestowed, and
darted some high encomiums upon the university
and the professors therein; he very ingeniously
[ingenuously] protested that he did not emit his
programs out of any ambition to be esteemed able to
enter in competition with the university, but meerly
to be honoured with the favour of a publick conference with the learned men thereof. In complements
after this manner, *ultro citroque habitis*, tossed to and

15

again, retorted, contrerisposted, backreverted, and
now and then graced with a quip or a clinch for the
better relish of the ear, being unwilling in this kind
of straining curtesie to yeeld to other, they spent a
full half hour and more; for he being the centre to
which the innumerable diameters of the discourses
of that circulary convention did tend, although none
was to answer but he, any of them all, according to
the order of their prescribed series, were permitted
to reply, or commence new motions on any subject,
in what language soever, and howsoever expressed;
to all which, he being bound to tender himself a
respondent, in matter and form suitable to the im-
pugners propounding, he did first so transcendently
acquit himself of that circumstantial kinde of oratory,
that, by well-couched periods, and neatly running
syllables, in all the twelve languages, both in verse
and prose, he expressed to the life his courtship
[courtliness] and civility; and afterwards, when the
Rector of the university, (unwilling to have any more
time bestowed on superficial rhetorick, or to have
that wasted on the fondness of quaint phrases, which
might be better employed in a reciprocacy of dis-
cussing scientifically the nature of substantial things),
gave direction to the professors to fall on, each
according to the dignity or precedency of his faculty,
and that conform to the order given. Some meta-
physical notions were set abroach, then mathematical,
and of those arithmetical, geometrical, astronomical,
musical, optical, cosmographical, trigonometrical,
statical, and so forth through all the other branches
of the prime and mother sciences thereof; the next
bout was through all natural philosophy, according
to Aristotle's method, from the acroamaticks, going
along the speculation of the nature of the heavens,
and that of the generation and corruption of sub-
linary things, even to the consideration of the soul
and its faculties; in sequel hereof, they had a hint

at chymical extractions, and spoke of the principles
of corporeal and mixed bodies, according to the precepts of that art.   After this, they disputed of
medicine, in all its thereapeutick, pharmacopeutick,
and chirurgical parts ; and not leaving natural magick
untouched, they had exquisite disceptations concerning the secrets thereof.   From thence they proceeded
to moral philosophy, where, debating of the true
enumeration of all vertues and vices, they had most
learned ratiocinations about the chief good of the life
of man;   and seeing the [that] œcumenicks and
politicks are parts of that philosophy, they argued
learnedly of all the several sorts of governments,
with their defects and advantages; whereupon per-
pending, that, without an established law, all the
duties of ruling and subjection, to the utter ruin of
humane society, would be as often violated as the
irregularity of passion, seconded with power, should
give way thereto.   The Sorbonist, canonical, and
civilian doctors most judiciously argued with him
about the most prudential maximes, sentences, ordin-
ances, acts, and statutes for ordering all manner of
persones in their consciences, bodyes, fortunes, and
reputation ;   nor was there an end put to those
literate exercitations till the grammarians, rhetoricians, poets, and logicians had assailed him with all
the subtleties and nicest quodlibets their respective
habits could afford.   Now when, to the admiration
of all that were there, the incomparable Crichtoun
had, in all these faculties above written, and in any
of the twelve languages wherein he was spoke to,
whether in verse or prose, held tack to all the dis-
putants, who were accounted the ablest scholars
upon earth in each their own profession; and pub-
lickly evidenced such an universality of knowledge,
and accurate promptness in resolving of doubts, distinguishing of obscurities, expressing the members
of a distinction in adequate terms of art, explaining

those compendious tearms with words of a more
easie apprehension to the prostrating of the sublimest
mysteries to any vulgar capacity, and with all
excogitable variety of learning, (to his own everlasting
fame), entertained, after that kinde, the nimble witted
Parisians from nine o'clock in the morning till six
at night; the Rector now finding it high time to give
some relaxation to these worthy spirits, which, during such a long space, had been so intensively bent
upon the abstrusest speculations, rose up, and saluting
the divine Crichtoun, after he had made an elegant
panegyrick, or encomiastick speech of half an houre's
continuance, tending to nothing else but the extolling
of him for the rare and most singular gifts wherewith
God and nature had endowed him, he descended
from his chaire, and, attended by three or four of
the most especial professors, presented him with a
diamond ring and a purse ful of gold, wishing him to
accept thereof, if not as a recompense proportional
to his merit, yet as a badge of love, and testimony of
the universitie's favour towards him. At the tender
of which ceremony, there was so great a plaudite in
the schoole, such a humming and clapping of hands,
that all the concavities of the colledges there about
did resound with the echo of the noise thereof.

" Notwithstanding the great honor thus purchased
by him for his literatory accomplishments, and that
many excellent spirits, to obteine the like, would be
content to postpose all other employments to the
enjoyment of their studyes, he, nevertheless, the very
next day, (to refresh his braines, as he said, for the
toile of the former day's work), went to the Louvre in
a buff-suit, more like a favourite of Mars then [than]
one of the Muses' minions; where, in presence of
some princes of the court, and great ladies, that
came to behold his gallantry, he carryed away the
ring fifteen times on end, and broke as many lances
on the Saracen.

" When for a quarter of a yeer together he after this manner had disported himself, (what martially, what scholastically), with the best qualified men in any faculty so ever, that so large a city, (which is called the world's abridgement), was able to afford, and now and then solaced these his more serious recreations, (for all was but sport to him), with the alluring imbellishments of the tendrer sexe, whose *inamorato* that he might be, was their ambition; he on a sudden took resolution to leave the Court of France, and return to Italy, where he had been bred for many yeers together; which designe he prosecuting within the space of a moneth, (without troubling himself with long journeys), he arrived at the Court of Mantua, where immediately after his abord, (as hath been told already), he fought the memorable combat whose description is above related. Here it was that the learned and valiant Crichtoun was pleased to cast anchor, and fix his abode; nor could he almost otherwise do, without disobliging the Duke, and the Prince his eldest son; by either whereof he was so dearly beloved, that none of them would permit him by any means to leave their Court, whereof he was the only *privado*, the object of all men's love, and subject of their discourse; the example of the great ones, and wonder of the meaner people; the paramour of the female sexe, and paragon of his own. In the glory of which high estimation, having resided at that Court above two whole yeers, the reputation of gentlemen there was hardly otherwayes valued but by the measure of his acquaintance; nor were the young unmaryed ladies, of all the most eminent places thereabouts, any thing respected of one another, that had not either a lock of his hair, or copy of verses of his composing. Nevertheless it happening on a Shrove-tuesday at night, (at which time it is in Italy very customary for men of great

sobriety, modesty, and civil behaviour all the rest of
the yeer, to give themselves over on that day of
carnavale, as they call it, to all manner of riot,
drunkenness, and incontinency, which that they may
do with the least imputation they can to their credit,
they go maskt and mum'd with vizards on their faces,
and in the disguise of a Zanni or Pantaloon, to
ventilate their fopperies, and sometimes intolerable
enormities, without suspicion of being known), that
this ever renowned Crichtoun, (who, in the afternoon of that day, at the desire of my Lord Duke, the
whole court striving which should exceed each other
in foolery, and devising of the best sports to excite
laughter, neither my Lord, the Dutchess, nor Prince,
being exempted from acting their parts, as well as
they could), upon a theater set up for the purpose,
begun to prank it, à la Venetiana, with such a
flourish of mimick and ethopoetick gestures, that all
the courtiers of both sexes, even those that a little
before were fondest of their own conceits, at the sight
of his so inimitable a garb, from ravishing actors that
they were before, turned them ravished spectators.
O with how great liveliness did he represent the conditions of all manner of men ! how naturally did he
set before the eyes of the beholders the rogueries of
all professions, from the overweening monarch to the
peevish swaine, through all the intermediate degrees
of the superficial courtier or proud warrior, dissembled churchman, doting old man, cozening lawyer,
lying traveler, covetous merchant, rude seaman,
pedantick scholar, the amourous shepheard, envious
artisan, vainglorious master, and tricky servant; he
did with such variety display the several humours of
all these sorts of people, and with a so bewitching
energy, that he seemed to be the original, they the
counterfeit ; and they the resemblance whereof he
was the prototype.   He had all the jeers, squibs,
flouts, buls, quips, taunts, whims, jests, clinches,

gybes, mokes, jerks, with all the several kinds of equivocations, and other sophistical captions, that could properly be adapted to the person by whose representation he intended to inveagle the company into a fit of mirth; and would keep in that miscelany discourse of his, (which was all for the splene, and nothing for the gall), such a climacterical and mercurially digested method, that when the fancy of the hearers was tickled with any rare conceit, and that the jovial blood was moved, he held it going with another new device upon the back of the first, and another, yet another, and another againe, succeeding one another for the promoval of what is a-stirring into a higher agitation; till in the closure of the luxuriant period, the decumanal wave of the oddest whimsy of all, enforced the charmed spirits of the auditory, (for affording room to its apprehension), suddenly to burst forth into a laughter, which commonly lasted just so long as he had leisure to withdraw behind the skreen, shift off, with the help of a page, the suite he had on, apparel himself with another, and return to the stage to act afresh; for by that time their transported, disparpled, and sublimated fancies, by the wonderfully operating engines of his solacious inventions, had from the hight to which the inward scrues, wheeles, and pullies of his wit had elevated them, descended by degrees into their wonted stations, he was ready for the personating of another carriage; whereof to the number of fourteen several kinds, (during the five hours space that at the Duke's desire, the solicitation of the court, and his own recreation, he was pleased to histrionize it), he shewed himself so natural a representative, that any would have thought he had been so many several actors, differing in all things else, save only the stature of the body; with this advantage above the most of other actors, whose tongue, with its oral implements, is the onely instru-

ment of their minds' disclosing, that, besides his
mouth with its appurtenances, he lodged almost a
several oratour in every member of his body; his
head, his eyes, his shoulder, armes, hands, fingers,
thighs, legs, feet, and breast, being able to decipher
any passion whose character he purposed to give.

"First, he did present himself with a crown on his
head, a scepter in his hand, being clothed in a purple
robe furred with ermyne; after that, with a miter on
his head, a crosier in his hand, and accoutred with a
paire of lawn-sleeves; and thereafter, with a helmet
on his head, the visiere up, a commanding stick in
his hand, and arayed in a buff-suit, with a scarf
about his middle. Then, in a rich apparel, after the
newest fashion, did he shew himself, (like another
Sejanus), with a periwig daubed with Cypres powder;
in sequel of that, he came out with a three-corner'd
cap on his head, some parchments in his hand, and
writings hanging at his girdle like Chancery bills;
and next to that, with a furred gown about him, an
ingot of gold in his hand, and a bag full of money by
his side; after all this, he appeares againe clad in a
country-jacket, with a prong in his hand, and a
Monmouth-like-cap on his head; then very shortly
after, with a palmer's coat upon him, a bourdon in
his hand,[1] and some few cockle-shels stuck to his
hat, he look'd as if he had come in pilgrimage from
St Michael; immediately after that, he domineers
it in a bare unlined gown, with a pair of whips in the
one hand, and Corderius in the other; and in suite
thereof, he honderspondered[2] it with a pair of
pannier-like breeches, a mountera-cap on his head,
and a knife in a wooden sheath dagger-ways by his

---

[1] "*A bourdon in his hand*"—"A musical instrument resembling a
bassoon, in use with pilgrims who visit the body of St James at
Compostella" (Sir John Hawkins).

[2] "*Honderspondered*"—*i.e.* floundered. Fr. *hondrespondres* (*Rab.*
iii. 42)—"hundred-pounders," heavy, burly fellows.

side ; about the latter end, he comes forth again with a square in one hand, a rule in the other, and a leather apron before him ; then very quickly after, with a scrip by his side, a sheep-hook in his hand, and a basket full of flowers to make nosegayes for his mistris ; now drawing to a closure, he rants it first *in cuerpo*, and vapouring it with gingling spurs, and his armes a kenbol like a Don Diego he strouts it, and by the loftiness of his gate, plaies the Capitan Spavento ; then in the very twinkling of an eye, you would have seen him againe issue forth with a cloak upon his arm, in a livery garment, thereby representing the serving-man ; and lastly, at one time amongst those other, he came out with a long gray beard, and bucked ruff, crouching on a staff tip't with the head of a barber's cithern,[1] and his gloves hanging by a button at his girdle.

"Those fifteen several personages did he represent with such excellency of garb, and exquisiteness of language, that condignely to perpend the subtlety of the invention, the method of the disposition, the neatness of the elocution, the gracefulness of the action, and wonderful variety in the so dextrous performance of all, you would have taken it for a comedy of five acts, consisting of three scenes, each composed by the best poet in the world, and acted by fifteen of the best players that ever lived, as was most evidently made apparent to all the spectators in the fifth and last hour of his action, (which, according to our western account, was about six a clock at night, and by the calculation of that country, half an hour past three and twenty, at that time of the yeer), for, purposing to leave off with the setting of the sun, with an endeavour nevertheless to make his

---

[1] *"Barber's cithern"*—"The instrument now ignorantly called a guitar. It was formerly part of the furniture of a barber's shop, and was the amusement of waiting customers" (Sir John Hawkins).

conclusion the master-piece of the work, he, to that effect, summoning all his spirits together, which never failed to be ready at the cal of so worthy a commander, did by their assistance, so conglomerate, shuffle, mix, and interlace the gestures, inclinations, actions, and very tones of the speech of those fifteen several sorts of men, whose carriages he did personate into an inestimable *ollapodrida* of immaterial morsels of divers kinds, suitable to the very ambrosian relish of the Heliconian nymphs, that, in the peripetia of this drammatical exercitation, by the inchanted transportation of the eyes and eares of its spectabundal auditorie, one would have sworne that they all had looked with multiplying glasses, and that, (like that angel in the Scripture whose voice was said to be like the voice of a multitude), they heard in him alone the promiscuous speech of fifteen several actors; by the various ravishments of the excellencies whereof, in the frolickness of a jocund straine beyond expectation, the logofascinated spirits of the beholding hearers and auricularie spectators, were so on a sudden seazed upon in their risible faculties of the soul, and all their vital motions so universally affected in this extremitie of agitation, that, to avoid the inevitable charmes of his intoxicating ejaculations, and the accumulative influences of so powerfull a transportation, one of my lady Dutchess' chief maids of honour, by the vehemencie of the shock of those incomprehensible raptures, burst forth into a laughter to the rupture of a veine in her body; and another young lady, by the irresistible violence of the pleasure unawares infused, where the tender receptibilitie of her too tickled fancie was least able to hold out, so unprovidedly was surprised, that, with no less impetuositie of ridibundal passion then [than], (as hath been told), occasioned a fracture in the other young ladie's modestie, she, not being able longer to support the well beloved burthen of so excessive delight, and intransing joys of such mercurial exhilations through the ineffable extasie of an overmastered apprehension, fell back in a swown, without the appearance of any other life into her then [than] what, by the most refined wits of theological speculators, is conceived to be exerced by the purest parts of the separated entelechises of blessed saints in their sublimest conversations with the celestial hierarchies; this accident procured the incoming of an apothecary with restoratives, as the other did that of a surgeon with consolidative medicaments.[1] The Admirable Crichtoun now perceiving that it was drawing somewhat late, and that our occidental rays of Phœbus were upon their turning oriental to the other hemisphere of the terrestrial globe; being withall jealous that the uninterrupted operation of the exuberant diversitie of his jovial-issime entertainment, by a continuate winding up of the humours there present to a higher, yet higher, and still higher pitch, above the supremest Lydian note of the harmonie of voluptuousness, should, in such a case, through the too intensive stretching of the already super-elated strings of their imagination,

---

[1] This incident reminds one of the effect produced upon the lawyers in court when "Pantagruel gave judgment upon the difference of the two lords." Our readers will remember that it is the author of the above description who is the translator of the narrative which tells of that wonderfully satisfactory decision. "As for the counsellors, and other doctors in the law that were there present, they were all so ravished with admiration at the more than humane wisdom of Pantagruel, which they did most clearly perceive to be in him, by his so accurate decision of this so difficult and thornie cause, that their spirits, with the extremity of the rapture, being elevated above the pitch of actuating the organs of the body, they fell into a trance and sudden extasie, wherein they stayed for the space of three long houres; and had been so as yet, in that condition, had not some good people fetched store of vinegar and rose water to bring them again into their former sense and understanding, for the which God be praised everywhere. And so be it." (*Rabelais*, ii. 13.)

with a transcendencie over-reaching Ela, and beyond
the well concerted gam of rational equanimitie, involve the remainder of that illustrious companie into
the sweet labyrinth and mellifluent aufractuosities of
a lacinious delectation, productive of the same incon-
veniences which befel the two afore-named ladies;
whose delicacie of constitution, though sooner overcome, did not argue, but that the same extranean
causes from him proceeding of their pathetick alteration, might by a longer insisting in an efficacious
agencie, and unremitted working of all the consecu-
tively imprinted degrees that the capacity of the
patient is able to containe, prevaile at last, and have
the same predominancie over the dispositions of the
strongest complexioned males of that splendid society,
did, in his own ordinary wearing apparel, with the
countenance of a Prince, and garb befitting the
person of a so well bred gentleman and cavalier,
κατ' ἐξοχήν, full of majestie, and repleat with all excogitable civilitie, (to the amazement of all that beheld
his heroick gesture), present himself to epilogate this
his almost extemporanean comedie, though of five
hours continuance without intermission; and that
with a peroration so neatly uttered, so distinctly
pronounced, and in such elegancie of selected tearmes,
expressed by a diction so periodically contexed with
isocoly of members, that the matter thereof tending
in all humility to beseech the highnesses of the
Duke, Prince, and Dutchess, together with the
remanent lords, ladies, knights, gentlemen, and
others of both sexes of that honourable convention,
to vouchsafe him the favour to excuse his that afternoon's escaped extravagancies, and to lay the blame
of the indigested irregularity of his wits' excursions,
and the abortive issues of his disordered brain, upon
the customarily dispensed with priviledges in those
Cisalpinal regions, to authorize such like impertin-
encies at Carnavalian festivals; and that, although,

according to the most commonly received opinion in that country, after the nature of Load-him, (a game at cards), where he that wins loseth, he who, at that season of the year, playeth the fool most egregiously, is reputed the wisest man; he, nevertheless, not being ambitious of the fame of enjoying good qualities, by vertue of the antiphrasis of the fruition of bad ones, did meerly undergo that emancipatorie task of a so profuse liberty, and to no other end embraced the practising of such roaming and exorbitant diversions but to give an evident, or rather infallible, demonstration of his eternally bound duty to the House of Mantua, and an inviolable testimony of his never to be altered designe, in prosecuting all the occasions possible to be laid hold on that can in any manner of way prove conducible to the advancement of, and contributing to, the readiest means for improving those advantages that may best promove the faculties of making all his choice endeavours, and utmost abilities at all times, effectual to the long-wished-for furtherance of his most cordial and endeared service to the serenissime highnesses of My Lord Duke, Prince, and Dutchess, and of consecrating with all addicted obsequiousness, and submissive devotion, his everlasting obedience to the illustrious shrine of their joynt commands. Then incontinently addressing himself to the Lords, ladies, and others of that rotonda, (which, for his daigning to be its inmate, though but for that day, might be accounted in nothing inferior to the great Colisee of Rome, or Amphitheater of Neems), with a stately carriage, and port suitable to so prime a gallant, he did cast a look on all the corners thereof, so bewitchingly amiable and magically efficacious as if in his eys had bin a muster of ten thousand cupids eagerly striving who should most deeply pierce the hearts of the spectators with their golden darts. And truly so it fell out, (that there not being so much as one

arrow shot in vain), all of them did love him, though
not after the same manner, nor for the same end;
for, as the manna of the Arabian desarts is said to
have had in the mouths of the Egyptian Israelites,
the very same tast of the meat they loved best, so
the Princes that were there did mainly cherish him
for his magnanimity and knowledge; his courtliness
and sweet behaviour being that for which chiefly the
noblemen did most respect him; for his pregnancie
of wit, and chivalrie in vindicating the honour of
ladies, he was honoured by the knights, and the
esquires and other gentlemen courted him for his
affability and good fellowship; the rich did favour
him for his judgment and ingeniosity; and for his
liberality and munificence, he was blessed by the
poor; the old men affected him for his constancie
and wisdome, and the young for his mirth and
gallantry; the scholars were enamoured of him
for his learning and eloquence, and the souldiers for
his integrity and valour; the merchants, for his
upright dealing and honesty, praised and extolled
him, and the artificers for his goodness and
benignity; the chastest lady of that place would
have hugged and imbraced him for his discretion
and ingenuity; whilst for his beauty and comeliness
of person he was, at least in the fervency of their
desires, the paramour of the less continent; he was
dearly beloved of the fair women, because he was
handsome, and of the fairest more dearly, because
he was handsomer: in a word, the affections of the
beholders, (like so many several diameters drawn
from the circumference of their various intents), did
all concenter in the point of his perfection. After
a so considerable insinuation, and gaining of so
much ground upon the hearts of the auditory, (though
in a shorter space then [than] the time of a flash of
lightning), he went on, (as before), in the same thred
of the conclusive part of his discourse, with a resolu-

tion not to cut it, till the overabounding passions
of the company, their exorbitant motions and discom-
posed gestures, through excess of joy and mirth,
should be all of them quieted, calmed, and pacified,
and every man, woman, and maid there, (according
to their humour), reseated in the same integrity they
were at first; which when by the articulatest
elocution of the most significant words, expressive
of the choisest things that fancie could suggest, and,
conforme to the matter's variety, elevating or depress-
ing, flat or sharply accinating it, with that proportion
of tone that was most consonant with the purpose,
he had attained unto, and by his verbal harmony and
melodious utterance, setled all their distempered
pleasures, and brought their disorderly raised spirits
into their former capsuls, he with a tongue tip't with
silver, after the various diapasons of all his other
expressions, and making of a leg for the spruceness
of its courtsie, of greater decorement to him then
[than] cloth of gold and purple, farewel'd the
companie with a complement of one period so
exquisitely delivered, and so well attended by the
gracefulness of his hand and foot, with the quaint
miniardise of the rest of his body, in the performance
of such ceremonies as are usual at a court-like
departing, that from the theater he had gone into a
lobie, from thence along three spacious chambers,
whence descending a back staire, he past through
a low gallerie which led him to that outer gate,
where a coach with six horses did attend him, before
that magnificent convention of both sexes, (to whom
that room, wherein they all were, seemed in his
absence to be as a body without a soul), had the full
leisure to recollect their spirits, (which, by the neatness of his so curious a close, were *quoquoversedly*
scattered with admiration), to advise on the best
expediency how to dispose of themselves for the
future of that [delightful] night."

INDEX

16

"The work is one of high literary ability, is of more than ordinary value for the light it throws on the religious and moral condition of the times it covers, and is specially interesting from the uniqueness of the character of Mr. Mill."—*North British Daily Mail.*

"A curious and interesting picture or old Shetland life."—*Elgin Courant.*

"Mr. Mill's idiosyncrasies furnish an unfailing source of amusement."—*United Presbyterian Magazine.*

"The whole work is excellent, and, we cannot doubt, will be welcomed in a wider area than the northern islands in which Mr. Mill spent his life."—*Banffshire Journal.*

"A very interesting biography, which has already and deservedly attracted a good deal of attention."—*Northern Ensign.*

"We commend the perusal of the volume to all those in any way interested in Scotland and her past."—*Liverpool Daily Post.*

"We can recommend the book as interesting to many more than Shetland readers."—*Life and Work.*

"One can see what a romance Stevenson could have constructed out of Mill's diary, which seems incredibly old-fashioned and primitive."—*Sketch.*

"A most interesting and readable volume, containing many quaint and curious pictures of Shetland life and manners during last century."—*Orkney Herald.*

"Mr. Willcock has done well to provide this record of a man so memorable."—*United Presbyterian Record.*

"There is a great deal that is interesting in this book. . . . Mr. Willcock has done his work well, and we feel indebted to him for making us acquainted with a character which ought not to be forgotten."—*Free Church Monthly.*

"Mr. Mill stands out as quite a remarkable man. Though the volume will have a special interest to the people of the Shetland Isles, it will be read with much interest on the mainland."—*Perthshire Advertiser.*

"A succinct and readable account of Mill's life. . . . Nothing essential has been omitted, and nothing unnecessary has been retained. . . . The volume furnishes interesting reading from beginning to end."—*Shetland News.*

"The book is eminently readable, and will well repay perusal. . . . A vein of quiet humour, mingled with delicate satire, crops up every here and there in its pages."—*Shetland Times.*

To be had from

OLIPHANT, ANDERSON & FERRIER,
ST. MARY STREET, EDINBURGH;
21 PATERNOSTER SQUARE, LONDON, E.C.

OLIPHANT ANDERSON & FERRIER'S "FAMOUS SCOTS" SERIES.

Post 8vo, canvas binding, 1s. 6d.; extra gilt binding, gilt top, uncut, 2s. 6d.

Thomas Carlyle. By HECTOR C. MACPHERSON.
"One of the best books on Carlyle yet written."—*Literary World.*

Allan Ramsay. By OLIPHANT SMEATON.
"Full of sound knowledge and judicious criticism."—*Scotsman.*

Hugh Miller. By W. KEITH LEASK.
"Leaves on us a very vivid impression."—*Daily News.*

John Knox. By A. TAYLOR INNES.
"There is vision in this book as well as knowledge."—*Speaker.*

Robert Burns. By GABRIEL SETOUN.
"A very valuable and opportune addition to a useful series."—*Bookman.*

The Balladists. By JOHN GEDDIE.
"One of the most delightful and eloquent appreciations of the ballad literature of Scotland that has ever seen the light."—*New Age.*

Richard Cameron. By Professor HERKLESS.
"Interesting study of Cameron and his times."—*National Observer.*

Sir James Y. Simpson. By EVE BLANTYRE SIMPSON.
"It is indeed long since we have read such a charmingly-written biography as this little Life of the most typical and 'Famous Scot' that his countrymen have been proud of since the time of Sir Walter. . . . There is not a dull, irrelevant, or superfluous page in all Miss Simpson's booklet, and she has performed the biographer's chief duty—that of selection—with consummate skill and judgment." —*Daily Chronicle.*

Thomas Chalmers. By Professor W. GARDEN BLAIKIE.
"The most notable feature of Professor Blaikie's book—and none could be more commendable—is its perfect balance and proportion. In other words, justice is done equally to the private and to the public life of Chalmers, if possible greater justice than has been done by Mrs. Oliphant."—*Spectator.*

James Boswell. By W. KEITH LEASK.
"One of the finest and most convincing passages that have recently appeared in the field of British Biography."—*Morning Leader.*

Tobias Smollett. By OLIPHANT SMEATON.
"Mr. Smeaton has produced a very readable and vivid biography."—*Academy.*

Fletcher of Saltoun. By G. W. T. OMOND.
"Unmistakably the most interesting and complete story of the life of Fletcher of Saltoun that has yet appeared."—*Leeds Mercury.*

The "Blackwood" Group. By Sir GEORGE DOUGLAS.
"Sir George Douglas, in addition to summarising their biographies, criticises their works with excellent and well-weighed appreciation."—*Literary World.*

Norman Macleod. By JOHN WELLWOOD.
"Its general picturesqueness is effective, while the criticism is eminently liberal and sound."—*Scots Pictorial.*

Sir Walter Scott. By GEORGE SAINTSBURY.
"Mr. Saintsbury's miniature is a gem of its kind.—*Pall Mall Gazette.*

Kirkcaldy of Grange. By LOUIS A. BARBÉ.
"A conscientious and thorough piece of work, showing wide and accurate knowledge."—*Glasgow Herald.*

Robert Fergusson. By A. B. GROSART, D.D., LL.D.
"It is a creditable, useful, and painstaking book, a genuine contribution to Scottish literary history."—*British Weekly.*

James Thomson. By WILLIAM BAYNE.
"The story of Thomson's claim to the disputed authorhip of 'Rule Britannia' is sustained by his countryman with spirit and in our judgment with success."— *Literature.*

OLIPHANT ANDERSON & FERRIER'S "FAMOUS SCOTS" SERIES.

Mungo Park. By T. BANKS MACLACHLAN.
"Not only a charming life-story, if at times a pathetic one, but a vivid chapter in the romance of Africa."—*Leeds Mercury.*

David Hume. By HENRY CALDERWOOD, LL.D.
"Fulfils admirably well the purpose of the writer, which was that of presenting in clear, fair, and concise lines Hume and his philosophy to the mind of his countrymen and of the world."—*Scotsman.*

William Dunbar. By OLIPHANT SMEATON.
"A graphic and informed account not only of the man and his works, but of his immediate environment and of the times in which he lived."—*Bailie.*

Sir William Wallace. By Professor MURISON.
"Mr. Murison is to be heartily congratulated on this little book. After much hard and discriminate labour, he has pieced together by far the best, one might say the only rational and coherent, account of Wallace that exists."—*Speaker.*

Robert Louis Stevenson. By MARGARET M. BLACK.
"Certainly one of the most charming biographies we have ever come across. The writer has style, sympathy, distinction, and understanding. We were loth to put the book aside. Its one fault is that it is too short."—*Outlook.*

Thomas Reid. By Professor CAMPBELL FRASER.
"Supplies what must be allowed to be a distinct want in our literature, in the shape of a brief, popular, and accessible biography of the founder of the so-called Scottish School of Philosophy, written with notable perspicuity and sympathy by one who has made a special study of the problems that engaged the mind of Reid."
—*Scotsman.*

Pollok and Aytoun. By ROSALINE MASSON.
"Miss Masson tells the story of the lives of her two subjects in a bright and readable way. Her criticisms are sound and judicious, and altogether the little volume is a very acceptable addition to the series."—*North British Daily Mail.*

Adam Smith. By HECTOR C. MACPHERSON.
"I have learned much from your sketch of Adam Smith's life and work. It presents the essential facts in a lucid and interesting way."—Mr. HERBERT SPENCER *to the Author.*

Andrew Melville. By WILLIAM MORISON.
"The story is well told, and it takes one through a somewhat obscure period with which it is well to be acquainted. No better guide could be found than Mr. Morison."—*Spectator.*

James Frederick Ferrier. By E. S. HALDANE.
"Ferrier the man, and even Ferrier the professor, Miss Haldane brings near to us, an attractive and interesting figure."—*Scotsman.*
"This biography of him will be highly esteemed because of the grace and v. with which Miss Haldane has done her work. To the 'Famous Scots' series of volumes there have been many excellent contributions, but not one of them is more interesting than this latest addition."—*Dundee Courier.*

King Robert the Bruce. By Professor MURISON.
"Professor Murison has given us a book for which not only Scots, but every man who can appreciate a record of great days worthily told, will be grateful."—*Morning Leader.*
"The story of Bruce is brilliantly told in clear and flexible language, which draws the reader on with the interest of a novel. Professor Murison is a most impartial and thoroughly reliable critic, and may be followed with confidence by all who desire a truthful and unprejudiced picture of this greatest of the Scots."—*Aberdeen Journal.*

James Hogg. By Sir GEORGE DOUGLAS. With Sketches of Tannahill, Motherwell, and Thom.

OLIPHANT   ANDERSON   &   FERRIER,
30 ST. MARY STREET, EDINBURGH ;
21 PATERNOSTER SQUARE, LONDON, E.C.